## *MEET THE FIRE-BLOODED CREW OF OUTPOST NINE...*

**MATT KINCAID** . . . West Point, class of '69. A Connecticut Yankee turned Indian fighter. He's Regular Army, frontier tough—and Easy Company's second-in-command.

**WARNER CONWAY** . . . Captain of the Post. He's a virile Virginian, a Civil War hero, a born leader . . . and putty in his sexy wife's hands.

**FLORA CONWAY** . . . The Captain's Lady. She's an Army wife through and through . . . and a stunning beauty with a soft woman's ways.

**SERGEANT BEN COHEN** . . . The tough, brawny top kick. He'd taken many a wise-cracking recruit to "fist city" behind the barracks, but to those ready to soldier, he was as fair as they came.

**WINDY MANDALIAN** . . . Easy's buckskin-clad chief scout. Doesn't say much. But you couldn't have a better man beside you in a firefight with hostiles.

**MALONE** . . . A born soldier, drinker, brawler. With his Irish brogue and fiery pride, he loved nothing more than a good fight.

**PHOEBE MILLS**. . . A blonde beauty, heading for California. Her brush with frontier violence—and Matt Kincaid—would never be forgotten.

## EASY COMPANY

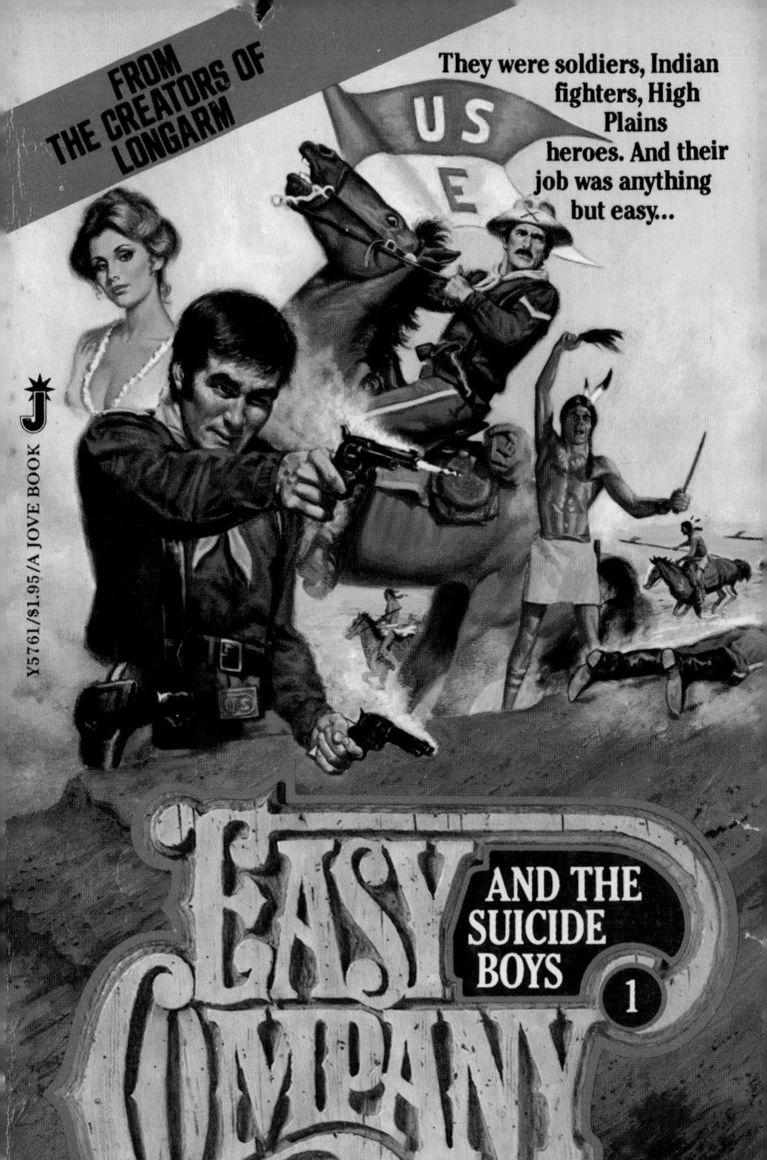


JOHN WESLEY HOWARD

# EASY COMPANY AND THE SUICIDE BOYS

JOHN WESLEY HOWARD

A JOVE BOOK

First Jove edition published April 1981

First printing

Printed in the United States of America

Jove books are published by Jove Publications, Inc.,
200 Madison Avenue, New York, NY 10016

*Also in the Easy Company series*
*from Jove*

EASY COMPANY AND THE MEDICINE GUN
EASY COMPANY AND THE GREEN ARROWS

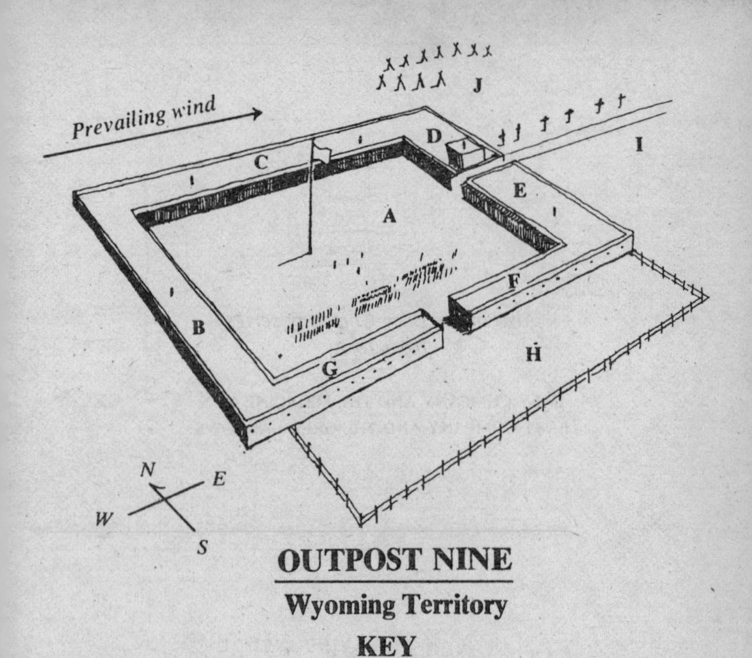


## OUTPOST NINE

### Wyoming Territory

### KEY

**A.** Parade and flagstaff

**B.** Officers' quarters ("officers' country")

**C.** Enlisted men's quarters: barracks, day room, and mess

**D.** Kitchen, quartermaster supplies, ordnance shop, guardhouse

**E.** Suttler's store and other shops, tack room, and smithy

**F.** Stables

**G.** Quarters for dependents and guests; communal kitchen

**H.** Paddock

**I.** Road and telegraph line to regimental headquarters

**J.** Indian camp occupied by transient "friendlies"

## OUTPOST NUMBER NINE
*(DETAIL)*

Outpost Number Nine is a typical High Plains military outpost of the days following the Battle of the Little Big Horn, and is the home of Easy Company. It is not a "fort"; an official fort is the headquarters of a regiment. However, it resembles a fort in its construction.

The birdseye view shows the general layout and orientation of Outpost Number Nine; features are explained in the Key.

The detail shows a cross-section through the outpost's double walls, which ingeniously combine the functions of fortification and shelter.

The walls are constructed of sod, dug from the prairie on which Outpost Number Nine stands, and are sturdy enough to withstand an assault by anything less than artillery. The roof is of log beams covered by planking, tarpaper, and a top layer of sod. It also provides a parapet from which the outpost's defenders can fire down on an attacking force.

# one

The summer sun rose early on the High Plains of the Wyoming Territory, and a distant bugle was sounding reveille as the Cheyenne slithered up the slope on their bellies in the summer-brown but dew-wet grass. There were nine of them, stripped for action to breechclouts and paint, despite the morning chill. The strawflowers braided in their hair matched the indigo stripes on their faces as they topped the rise to peer over the ridge, their features desperately calm, hearts pounding against the prairie sod. They were far less frightened by the U.S. Army outpost over on the next rise than they were by their own audacity. The flowers in their hair were lawful camouflage, but they were "suicide boys," as their own people called them—young, untested, would-be warriors, out to prove their bravery—and they had painted themselves without consulting the older men of the Dog Soldier Society. Medicine Wolf had said he didn't think anyone should count coup on the Americans until The People Who Cut Fingers found out where the other bands had scattered after the Custer Fight at the Greasy Grass. The young men scouting the outpost from this rise knew it was possible that they were doing a bad thing.

Twisted Rifle rose on his elbows behind a clump of soapweed and stared disdainfully across the shallow draw at the limp flag above the sod ramparts of Outpost Number Nine. Unlike his comrades, Twisted Rifle had painted half of his face black. The older men had not yet invited him to join the Contrary Society, but Twisted Rifle was an independent thinker, even for a Cheyenne.

A moon-faced youth at Twisted Rifle's side said, "The American fort is bigger than you told us it would be. Those sod walls are thick. The Americans built cleverly. It is one big, hollow square. They made their houses and ramparts as one. The Americans can run freely along the level rooftops, save for that lookout tower by the far gate. They have a singing wire, too. Do you see those poles running over the horizon to the east?"

The Indian on the other side of Twisted Rifle said, "Hear me. I don't think this would be a good place to fight. Lame Calf is right about the strong walls. They have been clever about clearing away all cover within rifle range, too. Long before we could wear them down, they would get help over the Singing Wire and—"

"Red Lance speaks like an ignorant person," cut in Twisted Rifle, adding, "Long before I led an attack, I would make certain the Singing Wire was cut. But I am not a fool. I said nothing about attacking the Americans behind those walls. They have horses, many horses, grazing on the far side, to the south. Look over there, those black dots against the sunrise, two rifle shots from the fort's northeast corner."

Red Lance squinted into the brightening horizon. "I see maybe fifteen tipis circled over that way. What of it? None of our band would be camped so close to an American outpost."

Twisted Rifle's voice dripped venom as he said, "They are evil people. Indians and half-bloods who trade and shelter near the blue sleeves of the American chief in Wah-shah-tung."

The normally amiable young Lame Calf frowned and Red Lance bared his teeth as he hissed, "Does my brother mean they are Pawnee or Crow?"

"Worse," said Twisted Rifle. "They used to be People Who Cut Fingers. That is the band of Gray Elk. They have made peace with Wah-shah-tung. They live near the Americans because they know all Real People hate them now."

Lame Calf sucked in his breath and said, "Ai! I have heard the old men speak of Gray Elk in the Shining Times! He was once a Crooked Lancer. They say he counted coup on the Utes. They say he once stole a woman from the Pawnee. In his youth he stole many ponies from the Crow, and he lifted Crow hair more than once, too!"

Twisted Rifle sighed deeply. "Once was a long time ago. Once we all ate fat cow and the young women smiled on us because we were brave and beautiful men. Today the old men have become women. Sitting Bull hides in the land of the Great White Mother in Canada. Gray Elk sells his friendship to the Americans for flour and salt. Even our own old leaders like Medicine Wolf cower in their tipis making talk, and no more than talk, as the Americans keep crowding us. Hear me! It is up to us, the beautiful young men, to show the Americans we still have the hearts of Those Who Cut Fingers!"

"Medicine Wolf is the brother of my mother," Red Lance said, frowning. "I don't think I like it when people say bad things about him. He didn't say we had to make friends with the Americans. He only said we should wait and see what the other people are going to do this summer. Medicine Wolf lifted hair at the Custer Fight. I don't think it's right to call him a coward."

The peacemaking Lame Calf said, "We know your uncle is a good person, Red Lance. Twisted Rifle was going to tell us how we could count coup on those Americans across the draw. Is this not so, Twisted Rifle?"

"Yes," replied Twisted Rifle. "We don't have enough young men, yet, to really hurt those people over there. First we will have to show everyone how easy it is to make them look foolish. We will count a few coups in fun. I intend to make a man of each of you. Then we will be able to get others to follow you. Hear me. Each of you will be war chiefs if you do as I say."

Lame Calf said, "I would like to be a war chief. What will you be in the new Shining Times to come, Twisted Rifle?"

"I will be a *big* chief, of course," Twisted Rifle said.

None of the others laughed.

They knew he meant it.

Twisted Rifle was said to have good medicine, and nobody had ever caught him in a lie.

First Lieutenant Matt Kincaid had pulled OD that morning. He walked the perimeter of Outpost Nine atop the sod roofs of the quarters built into the outpost's sod walls. The parade stood empty in the slanting sunlight, although Easy Company was up and getting ready for another day of frontier routine. He was walking over the married enlisted men's quarters at the moment, and he noticed that someone was cooking corned beef for breakfast as he passed one of the stovepipes, rising waist-high above the sod. Corned beef was a cheap as well as an unusual breakfast, but the fortunate noncom who could afford to keep a wife out here on his base pay and fogies was probably enjoying breakfast more than were the privates in the mess hall catty-corner across the parade.

Matt came to the southwest corner of the post, and the guard on duty there snapped to attention and presented arms. Matt thought hard and said, "As you were, Harper. What's your first general order?"

The private licked his lips and stammered, "Sir! My first general order is to walk my post in a military manner, keeping always on the alert and . . ."

"That's enough. Carry on, soldier."

Matt knew the recruit was feeling greatly relieved as he continued his rounds. He felt relieved, too. It was a bitch to remember every man's name, and it was a good thing Harper was a recruit. An older hand would have caught Matt's mistake in not returning the rifle salute while desperately trying to remember a new man's effing name. Matt shook his head to clear it as he told himself to wake up, for God's sake. They'd be holding morning report in a few minutes, and he shuddered to think of making a mistake in front of the first sergeant.

Matt moved up the west wall, noting how the slanting light exposed thin spots in the sod. He'd have to order a sod-cutting detail once he finished his tour as officer of the day. House-keeping in sod quarters was a bitch even when the roof didn't leak.

Walking with his eyes down, Matt didn't spot the next man atop the ramparts right away, but the man spotted him and stiffened awkwardly to a parody of attention. Lieutenant Kincaid was said to be a nice gent, for an officer, but the second in command at Outpost Nine was West Point and looked it. Matt Kincaid was a tall, clean-cut New Englander with wide-set gray eyes that smiled a lot, but could knock a fuck-up clean off his horse. The nervous private waited as Matt took a few more steps, looked up, and stopped with a quizzical frown.

He said, "Private Malone, I hope you have some reason for standing there with a rifle on each shoulder and your pack on backwards. I don't remember you at guard mount, either."

Malone said nervously, "Please, sor, it's the first sergeant's orders and I know it's a fool I look. I've been trying to figure out how to present arms with two Springfields in me hands, but for the life of me . . ."

"You do have a problem, don't you, soldier? Forget the salute. I don't see how it could be done, either. How did you get on Sergeant Cohen's bad side this time, Malone?"

Malone said, "Och, it was only the honor of the outfit I was after defending, Lieutenant, sor."

"I see. You were brawling with the feather merchants in town again, eh? Goddamnit, Malone, the last time I saved you from a court-martial, you promised to behave yourself off post. How in the hell can a man your size get fighting drunk on three-point-two beer?"

"Jasus, Mary and Joseph, I was cold sober this time, sor," Malone protested righteously. "I swear I was minding me own business in the Drover's Rest when this damned auld buffalo skinner looked me right in the eye and called me a cavalry trooper."

"What happened then?"

"Well, sor, I was patiently explaining the difference between mounted infantry and them sissy yellow legs, when a couple of other feather merchants took exception to the way I was gintly tapping him with me fist for emphasis, and then the damned auld regimental MPs came in, and, though I know you'll think I made it up, the MPs was after *helping* as the whole crowd lit into me!"

Matt rolled his eyes heavenward and sighed, "Right. So after the MPs brought you in and turned you over to Sergeant Cohen—"

"Och, what do you take me for, sor, a quartermaster corpsman? Sure and no two MPs born of mortal woman could take a Malone, drunk or sober. I just left peaceful, when I saw I wasn't among friends in that dreadful place. Unfortunately, me blue neckerchief became misplaced in the free-for-all, and Regiment wired the first sergeant about some glass that seems to have gotten broken as I was making me departure."

"Oh, damn, that means we'll probably have to pay for the damages from the company slush fund. I'd take it out of your pay, if you weren't still paying off that last fine I managed to get you off with."

Malone shook his head and said, "If you please, sor, it won't be necessary. It's me understanding that Sergeant Cohen was after informing Regiment he had no idea *who* sort of shoved that cowboy through that window. I heard him tell Four Eyes to put that on the wire just before he called me a worthless son of a bitch and put me up here on company punishment."

It wasn't easy, but Matt managed not to laugh as he said, "All right. As long as the first sergeant has a handle on it, carry on. While you're up here walking double dutch, you may as well keep your eyes open. We have some kids scouting us from that rise to the west."

"Och, I have them spotted, sor. I make it eight or nine of 'em, crawlin' on their bellies like reptiles over there. They'll have another holding their ponies for them on the far slope, and—"

"I said carry on, Malone. This is my second tour out here. If you see 'em, you see 'em. I don't need a lecture on Mr. Lo."

Matt walked on, secretly pleased. Malone was a truly terrible garrison soldier, but a born fighter with a good pair of eyes. The first sergeant had picked the perfect company punishment for him. Malone couldn't see very far, digging the usual pit latrine, and as awkward as he must feel with a rifle on each shoulder, everyone knew that in a pinch Malone could fire right- or left-handed, sharp.

Matt was walking over officer's country, now. The voice of Miss Flora, the CO's wife, lilted up a stovepipe as Matt passed it. He didn't stop to eavesdrop. Flora Conway might not have really been the most beautiful white woman west of the Big Muddy, but there wasn't a man in Easy Company who wouldn't punch you in the nose if you suggested there was a worthy rival to the captain's lady. As a bachelor officer, Matt was a little uncomfortable as he walked above their bedroom, trying not to picture Miss Flora in a nightgown with her long raven's-wing hair unpinned.

Actually, Flora Conway sat stark naked on her bed as she watched her husband, Warner Conway, Captain, Mounted Infantry, overage in grade, finish dressing in front of the pier glass on the sod wall. Conway was a handsome man in his mid-forties, and his ramrod figure was still slim in the slightly faded blues he was buttoning methodically. His wife smiled fondly and said, "Heavens, you look stern this morning, darling. Please don't scold that poor young soldier in the mirror. I'm rather fond of him."

Conway met his wife's eyes in the mirror, and his stern visage mellowed. He said, "I'm rather fond of that shameless hussy I see peeking at me, too. But that fellow in the mirror has a good chewing-out coming to him. He keeps breaking promises to a lady. But honestly, Flora, if they pass me up on the next promotion list, I swear I'll tell them what they can do with these railroad tracks."

Flora rose and came over to him. Despite the fact that they'd just made love, his breath still caught at the sight of her ivory curves in the dim light. She leaned against his back and put her arms around his waist, resting a cheek against his blue-wool-clad shoulder blade as she soothed, "Stop it, you adorable bear. We both know the army is your life. It's not the War Department's fault that that silly old President Hayes won't give them any money."

Conway turned around and took her in his arms, suddenly wanting her again as her nude flesh pressed against his forage dress. But the men were scraping their mess kits just across the way, and the bugle was about to sound assembly. He said, "Jesus, Flora, this is no life for a man and wife who met at a Baltimore ball one night when floors were waxed and walls were papered with satin and—"

"Hush, dear heart," she cut in, adding, "I won't have you carry on so about unimportant trimmings. We have each other, and that's all that matters. Do you really think I'd trade you for a cut-glass chandelier? I knew you were a soldier when I met you, and a very handsome soldier, too, I might add."

He said, "Yeah. Everybody was a soldier that year. When we married, I was a lieutenant colonel and the War was almost over and . . . Jesus, I fed you a line, didn't I?"

Flora stood on her bare tiptoes to kiss him before she shook her head, tossing her black curls, and said, "Pooh, you old silly. I never married you because you were a short colonel. Stop feeling so sorry for yourself. I'm not complaining about this new post. I think it's rather fun. The carpets from home cover most of the rammed-earth floors, and once I hem those new drapes for the windows . . ."

"Flora, for God's sake, you were raised in a gracious Tidewater mansion, and look what I've brought you to, this time. It's worse than Fort Leavenworth. The whole damned place is made out of mud and grass. I've seen Indian pueblos more fit for a white woman to set up housekeeping."

"You just run along and let me worry about housekeeping. It's my house and I love it. Wasn't that the assembly call, just now?"

He said, "It was. I've got to get over to my office. We're expecting visitors."

"Visitors?" she cut in, brightly.

He said, "Yes, the IG's sending some big mugwump to inspect us. I can't get those new repeating rifles and half my men need new boots, but somehow they can always manage an infernal inspection."

The hope in Flora's eyes faded, but she turned her head so her husband couldn't see it as she said cheerily, "You'd better run along and do something inspectish, then. I have to get dressed. This depraved young man I'm living with keeps me in a state of shocking nudity, and I wouldn't want the neighbors to find out."

Conway laughed, kissed his wife, and left.

Flora walked over to the pier glass and stared soberly at her naked reflection in the cruel light that filtered through the bottle-glass windows. She saw a woman, still attractive but no longer young, and even if her breasts were still firmer than those of most others her age, and her torso was still unflawed by stretch marks, Time had tempered its kindness by refusing to give her husband the son she knew he wanted.

Dear Warner never complained, and he certainly treated her as lovingly as ever, but—

"That's enough of that," she told herself as she turned away to see just where she should begin another attempt at putting her new home in order. Like many a frontier wife before her, Flora had the shocking but pragmatic habit of sweeping and dusting in the nude. The dust raised in a soddy was awesome, and it was far easier to wash one's hide than one's sparse wardrobe.

Flora took a broom and went to work as, outside, she heard that nice young Lieutenant Kincaid shouting, "First Sergeant, take the report!"

Flora swept as the men outside went through their own seemingly pointless routine. One by one, each platoon leader bellowed something that sounded to Flora like the chant of a tobacco auctioneer. She'd been Army long enough to know that what sounded like "Bowowowfer" really meant, "First platoon all present and accounted for."

In the years she'd followed her man from post to post, she'd never grasped just what the point of it all was. What did those men get out of all that stamping about in boots and yelling at one another as if they were about to have a fight?

She swept a stripe of rammed-earth floor, and while a cloud rose to film her shins with mustard-colored dust, the floor looked just as dirty as ever. Which was reasonable enough, when you thought about it. The dust got all over everything. Her mock-Persian nine-by-twelve rug looked as though it had been buried and dug up again by ghouls. She thought about letting the floor go and just dusting. As she stared hopelessly around for a place to begin, a dry straw fell from the wall and fluttered down to tickle her bare instep. She bit her lips to keep them from trembling, and after a couple of deep breaths, she knew she wasn't going to scream, after all.

Outside, boots were tramping up and down, as if there weren't already enough dust in this goddamned little mud-pie outpost. Flora put the broom back in the corner and said, "Oh, hell, I may as well get dressed."

American Tears hadn't ridden his favorite pony after the naughty boys from Medicine Wolf's band. It would not have been prudent to ride a Seventh Cavalry bay with a U.S. Army Remount Service brand this close to an American outpost, and though American Tears had left a full war bonnet of coup feathers hanging in his tipi, American Tears was a prudent man.

The seasoned Crooked Lancer dismounted in a draw a mile from Outpost Nine, tethered his buckskin mare to a buffalo skull half-buried in the sod, and took out his Indian Agency pass to make certain he'd brought the right one.

The greasy, many-times-folded paper read:

Office Arapaho and North Cheyenne Agency
I.T. August 19, 1876

The bearer, Lone Antelope, is a North Cheyenne friendly who has been registered and assigned Ration Number 19130187 B.I.A. He is not to be molested by any U.S. Citizen or Soldier unless engaged in acts of hostility or outside Wyoming Territory without special permission. He is recognized as a peaceful man with influence among the North Cheyenne, and should be accorded courtesies due a chieftain.

L. J. Arnold
United States Indian Agent

American Tears refolded the pass and put it in the pocket of the blue cotton shirt he wore. He patted his breast and smiled thinly. He had not scalped the coward who'd been issued the pass because he'd crawled to the Americans after the Good Fight at Greasy Grass and the terrible autumn of vengeance that followed. One does not count coup on a member of one's maternal clan. American Tears knew all Those Who Cut Fingers looked alike to the Blue Sleeves, and his late cousin had resembled him slightly, although Lone Antelope had not been as beautiful as American Tears.

American Tears knew he presented a vision of proud beauty as he left his pony, to move in the rest of the way on foot. He was tall for a Cheyenne, but he had Lakota blood on his father's side, for Those Who Cut Fingers had been allied with the tall Lakota since the coming of the hated Americans to the High Plains.

He wore no paint today. He was dressed in the hand-me-down army shirt and pants of the B.I.A., with a folded red blanket kilted around his hips and a Remington repeater cradled in his left arm. But his feet were clad in beaded moccasins of white deerskin, and his pomaded hair was roached with indigo quills and a fox tail. He was traveling incognito, but that was no reason to look like a poor person.

The young men scouting atop the ridge saw American Tears as he strode grandly up the slope toward them. Twisted Rifle moved back to cover and rose to meet him, saying, "Heya! Be careful, Uncle. The Americans are just over the rise."

American Tears stared down at the youth as if he'd just noticed a fly in his food and said, "I know this, puppy. It is called Outpost Number Nine. The men there are from Easy Company, U.S. Mounted Rifles. Their chief is named Conway, and he fought well against the Southern bands in the Buffalo War three summers ago. His subchief is Kincaid, who fought well and counted coup on the Staked Plains when they sent him there. There are at least two hundred guns in that stronghold. What do you children think you are doing? Medicine

Wolf sent me to get you. Your mothers are worried about you."

Twisted Rifle tried to look older as the other young men moved down to join them. He struck himself on the chest and said, "Hear me, Uncle. I am too old to be called a child. I know I have never hung from the Sun Dance pole. I know I have never lifted hair. But that is not my fault. You older men obey the agent from Wah-shah-tung and refuse to lead us, so—"

American Tears slapped Twisted Rifle's face, stared down at the black paint on his palm as if he'd just noticed it, and said, "The name of the place is *Washington*. If you're going to talk about the Americans, learn the words they use. What is this shit on my hand? If I didn't know better, I'd think my sister's baby had painted himself as a Contrary. When did the Contrary Society start inducing little boys with the smooth chests of girls too young to fuck?"

Twisted Rifle's face turned red where it wasn't covered by smeared paint. He knew he'd die on the spot if he raised a hand to a Crooked Lancer, so he threw his gun down and stamped on it, shouting, "You struck me! That was cruel! Everyone knows the Americans beat their children, but even if my uncle is angry, we are Those Who Cut Fingers. We do not even beat our women, unless they have done something truly dreadful!"

American Tears shrugged and said, "Some people say I am bad-tempered for a Cut Finger. But if I had been a member of the Contrary Society, my naughty nephew would be dead right now. I want you boys to wipe that silly paint off. Real People would laugh at you. Those Americans on the other side of the rise might shoot you if they noticed it and took you for men."

Twisted Rifle grunted disgustedly. "The fools don't know we are scouting them. We thought maybe after dark we might slip in and cut out a few ponies or—"

American Tears grabbed Twisted Rifle's arm in a viselike grip and dragged him along as he strode boldly up the slope, growling, "By Matou, my sister must have stepped on your head when you were a suckling. Come with me. It is time someone took a hand in your education."

As they topped the rise together, Twisted Rifle gasped, "They can *see* us, Uncle! Why are we standing here against the skyline like this?"

American Tears raised his Remington and waved across the draw to a soldier walking the walls of Outpost Nine. The soldier hesitated and then waved back. American Tears said, "They already know we are here, painted puppy. Look over there to the south. Tell me what you see, mighty horse thief."

Twisted Rifle squinted at a rise to the south for a time before he shrugged and said, "I see an old dog coyote, watching the army horses in the paddock over on that side of the fort, my uncle."

"You do, eh? When did God's Dog start stalking full-grown horses? What is a coyote doing in broad daylight, near a place where men with Springfields even shoot rabbits? Use your head, child! That's no coyote. It's one of those damned Delaware scouts the army has working for them. I know the chief scout working for Conway. He is called Windy Mandalian by the Blue Sleeves. He is good. One day one of us is going to lift the other one's hair."

Twisted Rifle looked sullen as he asked, "If they are so good, why have they not attacked us?"

"Oh, Great Matou, give me strength!" sighed American Tears. Then he said, "They haven't attacked because nobody has started a war this summer. Can't you see they have other Indians camped nearby for water and protection? They probably think you are children from that friendly band, playing at war games. They are not far wrong. Would *you* be worried if you commanded that company over there?"

"I still think we could steal some horses, after dark."

"The horses are only pastured outside the walls, under guard, during the daylight hours. Before the sun goes down, they will herd them inside, painted puppy. Come. Let us be on our way before some nosy Delaware moves in to ask questions."

American Tears waved to the "coyote" on the far rise and led the abashed Twisted Rifle down to his subdued young comrades. Red Lance asked, "What do you think, American Tears? Are you going to lead us into battle against this Easy Company?"

American Tears said, "Don't be silly. Medicine Wolf and the other old men say they are not ready for another fight, just yet."

"Medicine Wolf is getting *too* old, if you ask me," Twisted

Rifle said. "I think we should hit the Americans now, before they've fully recovered from the Custer Fight."

American Tears said, "Listen, boys, it's not that simple. It is true we bloodied them at the Greasy Grass last summer. But Washington sent others to replace the five troops we wiped out. The Seventh Cavalry is back to full strength and burning for revenge. Three-quarters of our allies are hiding out in Canada, and even if they were not, there are more Blue Sleeves out here now than there were when we beat Custer. You can see they just sent out that infantry company and—"

"Infantry fight on foot, like Paiute," cut in Lame Calf. "I am not afraid of any man on foot. My pony, Dancing Fox, can catch or outrun any man on foot."

American Tears sighed patiently. "A little knowledge is a dangerous toy for a growing pup. Nobody *walks* on the High Plains. Easy Company is what they call *mounted* infantry. They fight like dragoons. Weren't you just talking about stealing their damned horses?"

"Yes," Red Lance replied. "We were wondering about that. Why do those soldiers call themselves infantry if they ride horses like everyone else?"

"I don't know," American Tears admitted. "The army talks funny. I guess they needed more cavalry out here, so they took an infantry company and put them on horseback. They carry infantry rifles with them. That might be it."

Twisted Rifle said, "If I were Wah-shah-tung—I mean, Washing-tong—I would be worried about having inexperienced fighters out here. My uncle says we are young and inexperienced. But how could those soldiers be any better? If I were Medicine Wolf, I would lead the people against them *now*, before they have time to learn about the way we fight out here."

American Tears shrugged. "Medicine Wolf is the one everyone listens to."

"He is old and has no heart for fighting," Twisted Rifle insisted. "The people would listen if *you* told them it would be a good fight against green troops, my uncle."

American Tears started to shake his head. Then he frowned and said, "I don't think so. I am very beautiful and have counted many coups, but I have never been a leader."

"Hear me. *We* would follow you, American Tears."

The Crooked Lancer stared around at the eager young faces as he thought about that. Lame Calf said, "We know we have a lot to learn. But you are wise. I think you are wiser than Medicine Wolf, and we know you are braver."

"Listen, boys," said American Tears, "I know how you feel and I like you, even though I think you're silly. I was young like you, one time, and my heart still soars every time I remember my first good fight."

Twisted Rifle said earnestly, "We could still have a good fight, my uncle. You say you know these new men. You say you know how they think and fight."

"I do. I have told Medicine Wolf I think I could make them look foolish if he'd let me put on my paint, but—"

"Put on your paint, American Tears! Lead us against the Blue Sleeves, so that the maidens will smile at us when we dance our scalps as real men."

"I don't know, boys. You're all just children and there aren't enough of you to hit anything really big."

"Then lead us against something small," pleaded Twisted Rifle.

Red Lance said, "Hear me. There are other young men like us. Many. They would not follow Twisted Rifle because he has no reputation yet. They would gladly follow *you*. I alone could gather six or eight cousins."

"Me too!" said Lame Calf, and a quiet boy named Broken Pipe spoke for the first time. "My two older brothers laughed at me when I said I was going on a raid. If I told them *you* were leading, they would follow."

American Tears was stone-faced as they pleaded with him, but his heart pounded as he studied the golden opportunity Manitou seemed to be offering.

It was a dangerous idea to consider, but Medicine Wolf *was* getting soft and he, American Tears, was a bold as well as a beautiful person.

The Dog Soldier Society would punish him if the elders told them to. But what could the elders say if he did great deeds and counted many coups for the band?

The Americans would hang him as a renegade if they caught him breaking the treaty he'd made his mark on when the band had surrendered to draw rations and have hunting grounds assigned to them by the Great White Father. But how could any Blue Sleeve tell one Real Person from another, and how could they hope to catch anyone as cunning and clever as he?

As he strode grandly away to get his pony, Twisted Rifle fell in at his side to ask, "What are we going to do, my uncle?"

American Tears took off his shirt, exposing his muscular torso and Sun Dance scars to the sky and spirits. Then he handed the shirt to the boy and said, "Carry this and walk behind me. I am seeking a vision."

# two

The ambulance from regimental HQ was a tiny dot on a vast expanse of tawny, rolling prairie as it moved along under a cloudless cobalt sky, in a dust cloud of its own making. A heavyset rider in the dress blues of a field-grade officer rode ahead of the passenger vehicle. Lieutenant Colonel Madison T. Bradshaw had never inspected Outpost Nine before, but the trail and telegraph line he was following could hardly lead anywhere else, and only fools and artillerymen rode behind wheeled vehicles to catch the dust.

Behind him, in the ambulance, Wilma Dorfler clung desperately to the brass handrail of her seat beside the driver, who was a laconic, obvious maniac who paid no attention at all to the bumps in the rutted trail. Wilma's face was pale and dusty under her sunbonnet, but she didn't think she was going to throw up again. The ambulance bounced on steel springs and was much less sickening to ride in than that awful stagecoach from Laramie to the main fort. Wilma was a vapidly pretty girl of nineteen, and though the trip to join her husband out here had exhausted her, she'd been flattered and pleased by the courtesy shown her, once she'd made her way to her husband's army comrades. She'd never been called "ma'am," back on the farm. She supposed it was because of her gallant young husband's rank. Jimmy was a corporal, whatever that meant. He'd written that he was a squad leader in Easy Company, and a squad sounded like a whole lot of men. He'd written that he'd been granted quarters on the post by his chum, the commanding officer. Wilma had some seeds in her carpetbags for the nice garden she was planning for the dooryard of her first new home.

Behind the army bride and the driver, three enlisted replacements were crowded into the less comfortable rear of the ambulance with their gear, duffel bags, and supplies for the outpost ahead. The more important mail from back East rode up front, under the driver's watchful eye. Easy Company would be annoyed if he lost a green recruit. Corporal Dorfler would doubtless be most upset if he lost his wife. But they'd kill him if he lost the mail from home.

As the little party crossed a shallow draw, a line of riders topped the rise to the west. Colonel Bradshaw spurred his mount forward to meet them as he recognized army blue, but he frowned thoughtfully as he only counted eleven heads. He was used to being met by at least a full platoon, with its pennant dipping in salute. Had this Captain Conway actually sent out a mere corporal's squad and some junior officer to escort him in? He knew he was only a short colonel, but this was ridiculous. Bradshaw made a mental note that Conway was obviously sulking about being passed up for promotion again. If this was Conway's idea of how to get his point across to the brass, it was no wonder he was overage in grade!

Bradshaw reined in imperiously as Matt Kincaid rode forward to meet him. Matt saluted and said, "Captain Conway's compliments, sir. I've been detailed to escort you and the ambulance in."

Bradshaw returned the salute with an annoyed look. "I prefer to ride the rest of the way at gallop, mister. I assume that trooper driving the ambulance knows the way, doesn't he?"

Matt's voice was pleasant but firm as he replied, "I'm sure he does, sir, but this is Indian country and my orders are to make sure you *all* arrive safe and sound."

"Are you being impertinent, mister?"

"No, sir, I'm being careful, and if the colonel will allow me to make another distinction, I'm Easy Company's *first* lieutenant and adjutant. I'm not a mister, and Lance Corporal Burnes over there is not a trooper. He's a mounted infantryman."

Colonel Bradshaw's eyes grew thoughtful as he sized the younger man up. Then he said, "I am aware of the rivalry between you blue legs and the Seventh Cav, ah, Lieutenant.

The Inspector General's Office doesn't give a hill of beans, and for your sake I hope you've prepared for my full inspection."

"We have, sir. Outpost Nine is less than seven miles away and ready when you are."

"You rode seven miles off post with a single squad, and you tell me you're concerned about Indians?"

Matt shook his head and said, "I rode out with the Third Platoon, sir. First squad is flanking us over the horizon to the north. Third squad is scouting over there to the south. The men with me are the second squad."

Mollified, Bradshaw nodded and said, "Ah, then the regular platoon leader and his colors will be joining us when the first squad secures things to the north and rides in to join us, eh?"

Matt lowered his voice so the enlisted men wouldn't hear as he said, "No, sir. I ordered them to ghost our flanks all the way back to the post and come in after we gained the gate. Mr. Lo likes to hit you just as you bunch up for mutual congratulations. Mr. Taylor of third platoon will greet you properly at the post after he and his men finish their patrols and see to their mounts. I'm sorry about the color salute we failed to give you."

"No matter, since it's with the regular platoon leader. Shall we move on?"

Matt swung in his saddle and shouted, "Corporal Kildare, form diamond of pairs and prepare to move out on my command."

He was glad the stuffed shirt hadn't delved further into that nitpicking about the colors. Army regulations called for a blue and white pennant to be shown by each platoon, but Easy Company was an Indian-fighting outfit, and it made more sense for the soldier riding dress position in the column to have a gun instead of a nine-foot flagstaff in his free hand. Easy Company knew who they were; Mr. Lo knew who they were. What was the point of showing your colors in the middle of the North American continent? Were the Cheyenne going to mistake them for the Prussian Army?

Colonel Bradshaw sat his mount in quiet confusion as dusty riders in blue seemed to chase one another around. He didn't ask what they were doing. Although he was a desk soldier, Bradshaw vaguely remembered from his cadet days what a mounted diamond was.

Matt took advantage of the momentary delay to excuse himself and trot over to the ambulance. He took off his hat to the calico-clad girl next to the driver and said, "Your servant, ma'am. I take it you must be Mrs. Dorfler?"

"I am, sir. My husband is a corporal. Do you work for him, uh . . ."

"Kincaid, ma'am. Lieutenant Kincaid. I'm afraid your husband sort of works for me, but he's a fine soldier and you've every right to be proud of him."

"Oh, I am, but I'm sort of confused."

"I noticed, ma'am. But we'll be there in a jiffy and I fear I have to excuse myself for the moment. Is there anything I can do for you right now? You look a little pale."

"Oh, I'll be right as rain as soon as I see my Jimmy, sir. But could I ask a question?"

"Ma'am?"

"I keep hearing you men talking about this Mr. Lo. Who on earth is Mr. Lo?"

"The Indian, ma'am. It's sort of a private joke the army has."

"Oh? I don't get it."

"Folks back East keep saying, 'Lo, the poor Indian.'"

She still didn't get it. One of the privates in back of her said, "I got a question, Looie."

Matt Kincaid's gray eyes glazed over with ice. The driver muttered, "Jesus." Then, realizing his gaffe, he touched his hatbrim to the young woman. "Sorry, ma'am."

Matt ignored the driver as he gazed coldly at the red-headed youth sprawled on the duffel. "What's your name, soldier?"

"My friends call me Red," the youngster replied.

Matt took a deep breath, let it half out so he could modulate his tone, and said, "Red's not good enough, and we're going to get along a lot better if you remember that you call a first lieutenant 'lieutenant' and a second lieutenant 'mister' in this man's army. If that's too complicated, you can call me 'sir,' and I'm not about to call you Red. I asked you a question, soldier."

Red looked uneasy and said, "Uh, I'm Private Bishop, Robert A., uh—sir."

"That's better. We're going to overlook this. You aren't officially a part of Easy Company until you've checked in and been fed and assigned. Carry on, driver. Your servant, ma'am."

Matt wheeled his mount, putting his hat back on, and trotted up to fall in on Colonel Bradshaw's left. He raised his free hand and the party moved out, widely spaced, with two men on point, two out on either flank, and the squad leader, his assistant, and the last two privates bringing up the rear.

Red said, "Gee, he sure has a short fuse."

The driver snorted and replied, "Lieutenant Kincaid's sort of easygoing, for Easy Company. Wait till you meet the first sergeant. He's so mean he sours the milk in a cow, just riding past."

Wilma Dorfler frowned in confusion. These men were all so polite to her and other women, but they growled at one another all the time.

Red said, "Heck, I only wanted to ask him a question."

The driver said, "You don't ask an officer a question, direct, in this man's army, boy. If you've got something important to ask the adjutant, you ask your squad leader if you can speak to the platoon leader. If the corporal says you can, you ask your platoon leader if you can speak to the first sergeant. If you make it to the orderly room, you tell the top kick what you want to ask the adjutant. Then he'll either send you in to see the lieutenant or put you on KP, depending."

"Depending on what, durn it?"

"Depending on if it's a sensible question or not, of course. Easy Company is a fighting outfit, not a debating society."

A pudgy boy sitting next to Red asked, "What did you want to ask that officer, Red?"

Red said, "How to get me a transfer. I never signed up for no durned infantry outfit. The recruiting office said they was gonna make a dragoon out of me. I don't aim to be no sissy blue leg. I joined up to *ride*!"

The driver said wearily, "Son, I can see you are in mortal danger. So I'll tell you friendly that you are purely looking for a trip to Fist City with all that wind coming out of your big old empty head." He clucked his team to a faster pace as he saw they were falling back. Then he added, "Mounted infantry *is* dragoons, when they ain't light cavalry. Dragoons is mounted riflemen."

"Then what in thunder is the cavalry?"

"Out here? Durned if I know. Everybody fights about the same. You ride to where something important is going on, then you dismount and move in on your belly. That saber-waving stuff with colors flying and bugles blowing don't work so good agin Mr. Lo. Don't worry about the color of your pants stripes, Red. You'll get all the riding the Good Lord ever meant any poor cuss to do, on thirteen dollars and all the beans you can eat. When we reach the post, stuff a sock in that mouth and listen sharp. In a month you'll either be buried or you'll whup any man what calls you cavalry."

It was getting hot. Colonel Bradshaw was regretting his choke collar as they topped yet another rise rolling across the Sea of Grass, but appearance counted for more than comfort to the IG Department.

Bradshaw was not an unreasonable man. He knew men in the field were allowed a certain lack of polish, and he assumed the forage dress of the men around him were the oldest uniforms they had. This dust certainly hadn't done a thing for the shine on his own boots, but the tall young officer on his left still seemed too casual as he pointed ahead and said, "That's the post, sir. As you can see, we have it on a dominant rise."

Bradshaw didn't comment that the low sprawl ahead looked more like a giant buffalo chip than a proper army post. He knew the Corps of Engineers had built in a hurry after the Custer disaster had sent Congress into a nervous flap. There was little to see from here, other than the blank sod walls on either side of the east-facing gate and lookout tower. The Stars and Stripes hung limply against a tall pole of whitewashed pine. The only slight surprise, to Bradshaw, was a cluster of conical tents off to his right. He asked, "Are those Indian wigwams, Lieutenant?"

Matt said, "Begging the colonel's pardon, they're tipis. We've a floating population of friendlies over there, just outside our deadline. Right now, we're sheltering Gray Elk's band. They're Cheyenne. A couple of the tipis are Arapaho, and some white squaw men are camped there, too."

Bradshaw said, "I don't understand. It's not the army's job to run a reservation. Why do you let them squat there?"

"There's not much we can do about it, sir. It's federally owned open range, and they told us not to shoot at friendlies. The water table is pretty deep here, and the squaws beg water from our kitchen. Gray Elk's supposed to camp near the Indian Agency, technically, but he says he feels safer near us. The agency folks have their own hair to worry about, and some of the more truculent Cheyenne have threatened to wipe him and his people out, when and if they get the chance."

Bradshaw said, "Your job is not playing nursemaid to Indians. As I understand it, this outpost is guarding one of the vital approaches to the South Pass. You realize, of course, that the transcontinental rails and telegraph lines go through the bottleneck of the South Pass?"

"Yessir. They explained that to us when they sent us out here this spring. They told us to keep an eye on the Indians, too. Gray Elk is camped where we can keep an eye on him. Our scouts drop by of an evening to smoke and powwow with those friendlies, too. Indians gossip some. Gray Elk's people have given us some good tips in the past, and Captain Conway allows it's worth a few buckets of water and a little leftover chow from time to time."

Bradshaw shrugged and said, "I suppose I can write it off as military intelligence, but it's still a bit sloppy. While we're on the subject, I notice your men are armed with pistols as well as their regulation Springfields, Lieutenant."

Matt said, "Yessir. The glamour boys with yellow legs have been issued the new Colt '74s. We managed to wangle some Schofield .45s. They're not bad guns. It's sort of comforting to have a sixgun on your hip when they send you out to fight with single-shot rifles."

"The Springfield Trapdoor .45 is a fine rifle," Bradshaw sniffed.

"Yessir. But some of the Indians have Remington repeaters. I'm sure the colonel will find we didn't steal our pistols. We had to argue with Ordnance a bit, but—"

"I'll take your word for that," Bradshaw cut in. "I also notice some of your men have *two* pistols, and they've cut the flaps off the regulation holsters. How do you account for that?"

"Well, sir, soldiers out here tend to be ingenious, if they live through their first couple of fights. We issue one pistol to a rider. They somehow don't seem to feel one gun is better than two when you're in need of maybe three or four. Men transfer out. Men get killed. A gun here and a gun there tends to get lost in the paperwork."

Bradshaw said, "At least you're honest. You realize, of

course, that cutting the flaps off a regulation holster constitutes destruction of government property?"

"I do, sir. When we stand inspection for you, I'm sure you'll find us with all our buttons buttoned and all our flaps in place. Meanwhile, if we'd been jumped out here, you'd have been surprised how fast my men can draw from those less formal holsters. More to the point, you'd have had a better chance of living."

Bradshaw smiled in spite of himself. He nodded and said, "I see I'm going to get the usual surface neatness, with all the dust swept under the rug until I've completed my inspection, eh?"

"Isn't that the way it always is, sir?"

"Yes, damn it. You've leveled with me and I like you, uh, Matt. Can I level with you?"

"Sir?"

"I know what you field commanders think of us pencil-pushers, but the IG has his reasons for existing, too. I'm going to tell you frankly that the War Department is worried. The new administration has vetoed the Senate's expanded military budget. We got a big black eye out here when Custer screwed up, and—"

"Begging the colonel's pardon," Matt interrupted firmly. "Colonel Custer did not screw up. I knew him. I didn't *like* him. Custer was not an easy man to like. But he was not in command at Little Big Horn. General Terry sent him ahead of the main column, against the advice of everyone who'd ever really fought out here. The Seventh was under-strength and underarmed and—"

"I stand corrected, Matt," Bradshaw admitted. "That's ancient history. My point is that I wasn't sent all the way out here to count brass buttons. War wants IG to report on the combat-readiness of the few units we have out here. I don't want you men to hand me the usual spit-and-polish nonsense. We have to go through the motions of an IG inspection. I'll listen to the men's gripes and make sure your mess sergeant isn't getting rich selling rations and all that, but my main task will be to report on true conditions out here, warts and all. We don't really give a damn if your flagstaff needs another coat of whitewash or if someone's missing a tent peg. I intend to report on how able I feel you are to keep a lid on Mr. Lo this summer. Do you understand?"

Matt nodded smartly. "Yessir."

He understood. He'd have to warn the captain and first sergeant that *this* son of a bitch was *dangerous*! He'd met IG men like Bradshaw before—fucking glad-handers who acted like politicians running for office. Any soldier worth his salt could cover up when the usual pompous ass strutted around running a white glove over the furniture. But Bradshaw was one of the sly inspectors who got you in a confiding mood, then gigged the hell out of you in his report. Matt made a mental note to send Mr. Taylor out on patrol until this bastard left. Taylor was inclined to be friendly and outspoken in the officer's mess. The others were old hands who knew that it was war to the death between honest soldiers and the shit-for-brains Inspector General.

The IG Department had its reasons to exist, all right. It existed for the sole purpose of getting everyone else in the army in trouble.

The man behind the orderly-room desk looked something like a smooth-shaven grizzly bear in army blue as the three recruits lined up on the stripe that was painted on the floor a full pace in front of the desk. The burly noncom seated behind the desk wore only three stripes, so he said, "All right. You men listen and listen sharp. I am Acting First Sergeant Ben Cohen and I welcome you to Easy Company because that's where the War Department sent you in its infinite wisdom. You will find me firm but fair, and when I holler froggie I will expect you to jump. I am sending the three of you over to the mess hall to grub up. When you've eaten, you will come back here and I'll assign you to your squads and bunks. I will also have your names at the head of the detail lists, so make sure you read the bulletin board and don't plan on going anyplace important for the next few nights. That's all for now. Any questions?"

Red said, "Yeah, Sarge. Who do we see to get a pass?"

Cohen said, "Me. But you don't get a pass to town until I see if I want to give you one. You guys soldier for me and I'll treat you fair. If you turn out to be fuck-ups, you won't see a pass to town in the foreseeable future."

"Hey, Sarge, the rules say we get to have off-duty time."

Cohen said flatly, "That fat-ass remark just cost you another day on KP, Bishop. Do you want to try for extra guard duty?"

"Boy, some fellows sure get brave and ornery with a few stripes on their durned old sleeves."

Sergeant Cohen rose—and continued to rise, until he stood

well over six feet, towering above his desk as he unbuttoned his blouse with ominous calm. Red said, "Hey, I was just funning, Sarge."

Cohen removed his forage blouse, folded it, and put it on the desk as he said, "I am not wearing any stripes. Would you like to join me in the tack room and repeat that last remark, soldier?"

"No, *sir*! I said I was just funning!"

"I figured you might be, and you're still pulling extra guard. Do any of you others want to settle who's the first soldier around here?"

Nobody answered.

Sergeant Cohen nodded and said, "Right. Nobody has to 'sir' me. I'm a noncom, not an effing officer. If nobody here wants to fight, what in the hell are you waiting for, a kiss goodbye? I told the three of you to report to the mess hall. *Move*, goddamn your eyes!"

The three recruits stumbled over each other, beating a hasty retreat. The fat one called Pud saluted on his way out. Sergeant Cohen ignored it as he put his blouse back on and sat down. Pud meant well. The one called Red was a guardhouse lawyer. The third man, Wilson, was still a question mark.

Cohen turned in his swivel chair and spoke toward the dim corner of the office. "Put Red Bishop down for KP, guard mount, and stable detail. I think Pud will be no trouble, so just give him KP to show our soft side. Where's that fucking IG who rode in with the lieutenant just now?"

Four Eyes, the company clerk, looked up from his mouse-hole desk in the corner and said, "I seen them heading for the officer's mess with the captain, Sarge. Hey, did you know that colonel has the same last name as me? I didn't know there were any other Bradshaws in this man's army."

"There still ain't," Cohen replied, smiling. "He's a headquarters john and you'll never be a soldier till you learn to fire your rifle right. The CO says we have to fire for record again this week, and he told me to make sure everybody qualified this time. If you fuck up on the rifle range again, you'd better pray that Colonel Bradshaw is a relative as well as a namesake. I'm getting tired of explaining your unusual shooting, Four Eyes."

The small, wispy man in the corner took off his thick glasses and wiped them nervously as he murmured, "I just need time,

Sarge. I hit the target a couple of times the last time we went out, didn't I?"

Cohen snorted and turned away. Privately, he was worried about his half-blind clerk, but he knew some of the kid's trouble was that folks in the past had made allowances for him. What Four Eyes was doing in the army was a question Ben Cohen had never answered to his own satisfaction. Four Eyes wrote a fine Spenserian hand and he was a good clerk. Cohen knew he could make more as a civilian, even clerking in a dress shop. The one night they'd talked about it over beer, Four Eyes had blubbered a lot of bullshit about a brother killed in the War and the honor of his family, until he'd been told to stuff a sock in it. Cohen didn't like to listen to such tales. He knew half of the men in the outfit were misfits. He knew *he* was in the army because he'd learned, in the War, that he seemed to be a born soldier for some reason, and there wasn't another job he could think of that he wanted more. But, damn it, he was getting sick and tired of holding down a first sergeant's desk on a buck sergeant's pay, and one of these days . . .

There was a knock on the door and Cohen yelled, "It's open."

Corporal James Dorfler entered, stopped at the toe line, and said, "Sarge, my wife just came in on that ambulance with the others."

Cohen said, "I know. I saw her. She's a pretty lady and you're a lucky man, Dorfler. What can I do for you? You've already gotten quarters and rations for her out of us."

"Uh, Sarge, I just read the board. You have me on guard duty tonight."

"I do. It's your turn. What about it?"

Dorfler frowned and said, "What *about* it? Damn it, I haven't seen Wilma since our honeymoon and she just got here and, hell, I can't pull Corporal of the Guard *tonight*!"

"Sure you can. You just walk up and down between the posts, like anybody else. You know I never change the details once they're assigned, Dorfler. It's not fair to the man who'd have to pull duty in your place."

"Oh, I talked to Corporal Bancroft. He says he's willing to fill in for me, seeing as my wife just got here."

Cohen shook his head and said, "Bancroft doesn't assign duty on this post. I do. I didn't put you on tonight because I'm an ogre; I put you on because it's your turn. My wife is over in your quarters, right now, making your bride welcome to the post. If I know the captain's lady, she'll probably get invited to tea."

"Damn it, Sarge!"

"Damn me no damns, old son. I'm a married man and I can understand your problem. But you've got to understand mine. I run a mounted infantry company, not a honeymoon hotel. Once I start changing the duty roster around to suit everybody on the post, we'll have no company at all. My heart feels for you, but I just can't reach you."

"In other words, there's no way in hell for me to spend the night with my new bride? Permission to speak to the adjutant, Sergeant?"

"Permission denied. You're right. There's no way in hell. Lieutenant Kincaid would back me, but I see no reason to pester him about the hot weather we've been having, either."

Dorfler's face was red with anger as he said, "I had you wrong, Sarge. I used to think you were a square fellow, but . . ."

"Stop right there, Dorfler. You can't afford a wife *at all* out here on a private's pay. I was going to suggest a three-day pass after you got off duty in the morning, but since we ain't friends no more, you just get your ass out of here and make damned sure I see you at guard mount this evening."

Dorfler started to say something, but he didn't. He knew Cohen could and would give him CQ to cost him *two* nights away from Wilma, if he wanted to. It sure was a chicken outfit for a newlywed to serve in.

Wilma Dorfler sat on her stringbed, trying not to cry, as she stared around her quarters in dismay. The stout woman seated across from her was saying something and Wilma said, "I'm sorry, ma'am, I wasn't listening." Maggie Cohen said, "Just call me Maggie, dearie. I was saying we've been invited over to officer's country by herself, Miss Flora. You'll find herself a darling woman, and not jumped-up like so many officers' wives."

Wilma blurted, "I can't go visit anyone like this! I haven't had a bath and my clothes are all dusty and—"

"Och, I told you we'd arrange a bath for you after grub. The KPs will be after filling a tub for you once they finish cleaning up and all. But we mustn't keep herself waiting. She's used to dust, I'd be thinking, and she sent me over to fetch you. So on your feet, me girl. Miss Flora always greets the new wives when they arrive."

The stout Maggie got to her feet, hands on hips, and Wilma felt that she'd better do as she was told. Maggie Cohen's Black Irish face was pretty, despite an extra chin, but like her husband, the first sergeant, she was used to giving orders, and it showed.

Wilma rose and followed her, saying, "My hair is a mess and I don't see how on earth I'll ever make a home out of this awful place and Jimmy says he has guard duty tonight and—"

"Whisht, there's no use frushing about what can't be helped, girl. The captain's quarters are this way. Stay under the overhang and the noonday sun might not fry our brains after all."

As they started walking, Wilma asked, "Do you think it's fair for my Jimmy to pull guard duty on our first night out here together, ma'am?"

"I don't, and himself will be after sleeping on the couch alone this night for being such a brute. But it can't be helped and I said you was to call me Maggie. It's all right to call herself, the captain's lady, 'ma'am.' I'd better warn you that herself is a dear familiar person and some women have gotten in trouble by forgetting their place. You see, herself isn't one for pulling rank. But if you're to make a good army wife, you must never forget the delicacy of your position."

"Oh, does a captain's wife get to boss a corporal's wife?"

"Yes and no. We're neither fish nor fowl, to the army. If they had their way, the darling boys would serve out here as celibate as monks. The War Department calls us an 'accommodation.' That's a fancy way of saying it's all right for us to be here if we don't make trouble. If push comes to shove, it's up to the CO whether a married man has his wife out here or not, and herself sleeps with the CO, if you take me meaning."

"In other words, if Miss Flora tells me to do something, I'd better do it."

"Well, you'll find she's not at all bossy, but for God's sake, don't ever try to boss *her*! Miss Flora makes what she calls suggestions and the rest of us agree they're grand ideas."

Maggie stopped at a door that looked much the same as all the others set in the sod walls under the split-wood awning around the inner side of the post. The door opened and a pleasant voice said, "Oh, there you are, Maggie, dear. And you must be our new arrival, dear heart. Won't you both come in?"

As she stepped inside, Wilma saw that somehow the sod walls and dirt floors of the captain's lady managed to look almost neat, and the woman smiling at her was about her mother's age, but ever so much prettier. Flora Conway took Wilma's hand and said, "Come, dear, let's sit over here and get acquainted."

And then something broke inside Wilma and she was sobbing in Flora's arms, with her face buried against the older woman's lace bodice. Flora looked in dismay at Maggie and said, "Oh, dear."

Maggie sighed and said, "It's company business, ma'am. You know how unreasonable the men are after acting at times, but I've explained there's nothing we can do about it."

Flora patted Wilma's trembling shoulder and soothed, "There, there, let's all sit down and dry our tears, dear heart. We'll have some tea and you can tell me all about it."

Maggie looked uncomfortable as she said, "Ma'am, it's not a matter for yourself to concern herself with."

But Flora said, "We'll see, girls. We'll just sit down over here and you can both tell me all about it."

# three

Warner Conway stared stubbornly down at his plate as he ate supper in his quarters that evening. He said, "I'm sorry, Flora, but there's nothing I can do about our newlyweds. The flag is down, the guard is mounted, and Sergeant Cohen's word is law."

Flora looked sincerely puzzled as she stared at her husband across the candlelit table and murmured, "I thought *you* were the commanding officer here, darling. They're both so young, and I thought—"

"Damn it, Flora, I know what you thought. Had you known last week that young Dorfler was slated for guard duty, I might have been able to mention it to the sergeant. But we didn't know the exact day the poor girl would arrive and, to be fair, neither did Ben Cohen. The duty roster was posted three days ago and—"

"Pooh," his wife interrupted. "That silly duty roster is just a scrap of paper. You know very well that Sergeant Cohen would make up a new one if you ordered him to."

"You're right, but I won't, Flora. A good CO doesn't interfere with his top kick. He backs him. What would it look like if we changed the orders every time they inconvenienced someone?"

"Like you were human, dear? I'm sure everyone would understand if you saw fit to let those poor children spend their first night out here together."

Conway nodded and said, "I know. A couple of other noncoms have already volunteered to take Dorfler's place tonight."

"Then what on earth is the problem, dear?"

"The problem is that we can't and don't play favorites. Sure, we could give Dorfler a break and the men would understand. But suppose someday I have to put some other man out on point and he takes a Cheyenne arrow in the gut? Will he understand that he was out on point because it was his turn, or will he wonder, as he's dying, if he could have gotten out of it by having a good excuse?"

Flora grimaced and said, "I'll just never understand the way you men think. I fail to see any connection between that poor, frightened bride having to spend the night alone in strange quarters and some mythical Indian doing something dreadful to someone else. I thought you said the Indians were lying low right now."

"Nobody knows what the Indians are doing," he said. "Not even the Indians. I don't want to talk about the Dorflers, Flora. I have to go back on duty in a few minutes and it looks like a busy night. I didn't know that damned IG inspector would arrive the night I was pulling OD, either. I've got to wear two hats tonight and—"

"Warner," Flora cut in, "you're really being very silly this evening, aren't you? I don't see why the commanding officer has to take his turn at OD with the junior officers, anyway! I thought rank had its privileges."

"It does," he replied. "It has it's responsibilities, too. I know I don't have to pull OD, but when you only have three officers in an outfit, everyone has to take his turn. None of us *enjoy* OD twice a week, but the ARs call for it, so we'll say no more about it."

He started to rise and Flora asked, "Don't you want dessert, dear?"

He said, "Save it for me. It's time for me to make my rounds."

"Oh, pooh, everyone knows where you are if you're really needed."

"I know. The men walking their posts right now are probably a bit wistful about it, too. The sergeant of the guard and I get to goldbrick a bit. But I like to set an example."

She followed him to the door as he adjusted the OD brassard on his sleeve. It seemed so silly that the commanding officer had to wear a sign on his uniform to let everyone know he was in charge, but that was the army for you. She said, "I promised poor little Wilma I'd do what I could about her problem, dear."

He smiled at her. "You did what you could. Do I get a kiss, or are you as mad at me as Maggie is at poor Ben Cohen?"

Flora smiled and pecked him on the cheek as she said, "I'm terribly cross, but I'm just a weak-willed thing. Do you think you could sneak back to tuck me properly in bed, later?"

He said, "You know I can't, honey. We have to set an example and they always know where I am."

She sighed and said, "I know. There are probably British spies all around, too. We're only a few hundred miles from the border. Do you suppose the Mexicans are watching our bedroom window, too?"

He patted her fondly and said, "You'll pay for that tomorrow night, me proud beauty. I've really got to go, honey."

The captain left his quarters in restored humor. Flora was all right. She'd let her mothering instincts get in the way of her good judgment again, but at least this time she wasn't really mad at him.

He came to a ladder and moved up to the flat roof to avoid passing the officer's mess. Matt Kincaid was entertaining that damned IG man, and he didn't want to answer any more dumb questions about battered hats and threadbare uniforms. What in the hell was he supposed to do if the goddamned quartermaster couldn't seem to remember where they were? He'd sent requisitions for the damned supplies; apparently, QM had a special wastebasket for filing requests from line outfits.

He wasn't too happy with Ordnance, either. He'd gladly give up new boots and even beans for a few reserve cases of ammo. Sometimes he wondered why the Indian agency found it so much easier to get cartridges for their wards to "hunt" with. Maybe with half the buffalo shot off, Washington didn't want their Mr. Lo to lack for targets.

As Conway popped up on the perimeter walk, a startled private snapped to attention and presented arms. Conway said, "Great. I could have been a Cheyenne. Why didn't you challenge me, soldier? Cat got your tongue?"

"No excuse, sir. I thought it was you, though."

"Thinking isn't good enough. What's your seventh general order?"

"Sir, my seventh general order is to talk to no one except in the line of duty."

"Right. Where's the corporal of the guard?"

"He was here just a minute ago, sir. I reckon he's in the guardhouse with the others, right now."

Conway said, "Carry on," and started walking toward the gate and lookout tower. He didn't really have anything to say to Dorfler, anyway. It was shitty to walk your post in a military manner with a pretty wife sleeping just under you, but he was in the same boat, too, so what the hell.

Conway saw the next corner guard and was expecting to be challenged, when a more distant voice rang out, "Corporal of the guard, Post Number One!" and Conway started running toward the gate and tower.

As he got there, the man on duty recognized him and said, "Rider coming in, sir. Looks like he's got somebody after him!"

Conway glanced out across the moonlit prairie and muttered, "Looks more like two." Then he shouted down, "Open the sally port and look alive. Looks like scouts coming in, but cover 'em anyway!"

He ran to the nearest ladder and slid down it as the smaller square doorway set in the main gate opened and two men boiled through on horseback, leaning low on the necks of their mounts. Chief Scout Windy Mandalian slid his pony to a halt as the man with him rode a quarter of the way across the parade before falling off his horse. Windy yelled, "That boy has a bullet in him!" and followed the captain as Conway ran to the fallen man.

Rectangles of light winked on as doors opened all around. Conway dropped to one knee and rolled the man over. He was one of Mandalian's Delawares, and he was hurt bad. The captain shouted, "Litter bearers on the double!" He knew the cry would assure that the mess crew had water boiled and ready by the time the wounded man needed it. He glanced up at Windy and said, "Report."

The civilian scout shifted in his greasy buckskins and said, "Well, to give the long and the short of it, Cap, we got jumped. I lost old Crying Boy out there someplace, so they likely have his hair."

"I can see you only came in with one man. Who jumped you?"

"Injuns. I'd tell you the tribe if I knew it. We didn't hang about to jaw with 'em. But if you want an educated guess, I'll be surprised as hell if they turn out to be anything but Cheyenne. One of 'em gave a war cry. It was a Lakota Confederacy cry, but he had an Algonquin accent."

Matt Kincaid and Colonel Bradshaw ran over, followed by two mess attendants with a stretcher, and half of the post bringing up the rear. Conway looked up and said, "Mr. Lo is restless tonight." Then he spotted the sergeant of the guard in the crowd and snapped, "Take the supernumeraries and get up on the walls, damn it."

Abashed, the sergeant ran for the guardhouse to get the guards on duty there as extra men in emergencies. Matt said, "We still might catch them, with your permission, sir."

Conway looked up at Mandalian. The scout said, "I wouldn't. By now they're long gone, if they ain't set up a moonlight ambush, hoping you boys are a mite green. We can't cut sign in the light out there."

"Taylor's out on patrol!" Kincaid said anxiously.

The captain felt a lot older as he said, "We'll wait until daybreak. Did you hear any other fire, Windy?"

The scout said, "Nope. Mr. Taylor's good, considering. If he was close enough to hear them smoking *us* up, he's alerted by now. If he's far off, it don't matter. I'd say we'd best stay put and study it by sunlight."

Corporal Dorfler ran up, buttoning his shirt and obviously in a state of confusion. Matt turned on him, eyes blazing, as the mess men rolled the wounded Indian onto the litter. Dorfler licked his lips and said, "No excuse, sir. I was over in the latrine when I heard someone shouting for me and—"

"I know where you were, *Private* Dorfler," snapped the tall, grim-faced officer. Then he said, "My regards to your missus when you report back to her. Consider yourself under arrest in quarters till I have time to deal with you."

"But, sir, I never really deserted my post."

"I said I knew where you were and what you were doing and you're still under arrest, goddamnit! Go to your quarters and comfort your wife. If we find you guilty at your court-martial, she'll be a widow by this time tomorrow."

Matt Kincaid halted his morning patrol on a rise and dismounted to walk over to Windy Mandalian and the object the scout had found in the grass. Matt had spotted the carrion crows the scout had flushed, and he knew the scent of death might spook some of the newer mounts.

Windy was hunkered down on his buckskinned haunches as Matt joined him by the body. The Delaware, Crying Boy, lay spread-eagled on his back, screaming silently up at them. He'd been scalped, of course, and the fingers of his right hand were missing. He'd been stripped, gutted, and castrated. The crows had probably taken his eyes. Windy shifted the cud in his mouth and said laconically, "Looks like they took him alive."

Matt nodded and asked, "Cheyenne?"

"Cheyenne take fingers like that, but fair is fair. Bad habits tend to spread. I'd feel better about laying the blame iffen there was a blue-striped arrow with raven feathers laying about, Matt." Mandalian spat and added, "It sure was easier afore the Indian agency issued all them rifles. The bullets they put in this poor cuss don't bear no tribal markings. He was scalped Cheyenne, too, though. I'm going to be sort of surprised iffen they turn out to be Apache. But that's as close as I care to cut her."

Matt nodded and asked, "Do you think Gray Elk can tell us anything about this, Windy?"

"Don't know. Ain't asked him yet. I'll be surprised if he does, though. I spent night afore last in Tipi Town with Gray Elk's best-lookin' granddaughter, and you know how women talk. Gray Elk seems to know he's whipped, but he don't lead but one band. What makes you suspicion him, Matt?"

"Remember those bucks scouting us from the rise to the west, yesterday afternoon?"

Mandalian rose to his feet with a shrug as he said, "They was just kids. Crying Boy, here, had an eye on 'em. He told me an older Injun come out to fetch 'em home for supper. I'll ask Gray Elk about that, too, but what we run into out here last night wasn't kid stuff."

Matt grimaced and said, "I don't see any trail for us in this grass, Windy. I guess you mean to tell me I'm blind, and point out which way they rode after cutting your scout up?"

Windy said, "Nope. You track tolerable, for an officer. I wouldn't want this to get around, but I can't read sign in prairie sod after the dew has sprung the grass stems back up, neither.

I see a horse turd over yonder, but that don't tell me which way the rascals rode. Unshod Injun mounts don't tear the sod worth mention. Afore we go tear-assing all over Robin Hood's barn, I'd best have a powwow with the friendlies and get me a line on who's mad at us this summer."

Matt nodded, turned, and called out, "Corporal Kildare, detail two men to get this body back to the post. Use the canvas groundcloth lashed to my saddle. He's pretty messy."

Mandalian said, "Hell, I knowed enough to bring a tarp. I'll fetch it and bundle Crying Boy."

Matt called out, "As you were, Kildare!" The corporal holding the reins of Matt's mount nodded. Windy walked toward his own nearby pony, looking tired and older. Matt knew the grizzled scout had ridden with Crying Boy for a while, but men were not allowed to cry. With one of his Delawares dead and the other badly wounded, Windy was scouting alone at a bad time.

One of the mounted men said something to the corporal, and Kildare called out, "Riders coming from the north, sir."

Afoot on lower ground, Matt, of course, could see nothing. He legged it up to the others and swung himself into the saddle as Kildare added, "It looks like Mr. Taylor's platoon, sir."

Matt steadied his bay gelding and studied the distant dots as he nodded and observed, "I'd say you were right. They have company. Looks like they encountered a wagon party."

Matt raised his gauntlet and the distant patrol leader, who'd obviously spotted them, waved back. Matt said, "Stay here. I don't want those pilgrims to see what we found here until Windy wraps it up."

Matt spurred his mount forward to head off the incoming party. Second Lieutenant Taylor was wise enough to notice this and halt his own people on a rise.

As Matt joined Taylor's patrol, he noticed the civilians from the wagon party riding among the soldiers. He didn't want to chew a junior officer out in front of feather merchants. He made a quick head count and saw that Taylor had men out on the flanks and to the rear, over the horizon. The shavetail was too friendly for this man's army, but he knew his job.

Taylor rode forward to get out of earshot as they greeted one another. Matt said, "We lost a Delaware yonder. Ugly. Report."

Taylor said, "We haven't seen any Indians, sir. We were headed back at dawn when we came across this wagon party. They're headed for South Pass."

Matt consulted the mental map he carried of the surrounding Sea of Grass and mused, "They're pretty far off the usual wagon trace to the pass, aren't they?"

"Yessir. I told them they were lost. That gent over there in the white buckskins is their hired guide. He claims to be an old hand. I'd say he was the blind leading the blind, if I wasn't so polite."

As if he'd heard, an imposing figure in rather dramatic costume rode toward them, trailed by a more sensibly dressed male rider and a woman in a linen duster, riding sidesaddle. Matt removed his hat as Taylor introduced them. The worried-looking man in faded denim was the nominal leader of the small immigrant party. His name was Penderson. The woman, rather attractive under her shapeless duster and veiled straw boating hat, was a Miss Phoebe Mills. The flamboyant man in the white buckskins claimed to be one Colonel Billy Hawkins, their hired trail guide. The party was headed for California, which seemed fair enough. Hawkins said he'd been leading them to a shortcut he knew over the mountains to the west, which seemed as silly as his shirt.

Matt said, "We'll put you folks on the wagon trace to the South Pass as soon as we know it's safe. At the moment, as you can see, we're looking for a party of hostiles. You'll shelter with us at Outpost Nine until we have a handle on the situation."

Colonel Billy Hawkins said, "I'm sure there's no need of that, Captain. I've always gotten on well with my blood brothers, the Kiowa."

Matt smiled thinly as he replied, "I'm sure you have, sir. But the Kiowa are well south of here, and some Cheyenne just lifted hair. By the way, I'm not a captain, I'm a first lieutenant."

Penderson looked worried and asked, "How far are we from your fort, Lieutenant? We're way behind schedule as it is."

"I can see how that might happen," Matt observed with just the slightest trace of sarcasm. "Our outpost isn't far. You and your people will be safe there, and as soon as we know the trail is clear, we'll put you back on it."

"I thank you for your concern, young sir," Colonel Billy Hawkins said, "but I assure you these folks are safe enough with me. I have a way with Indians."

"That may well be," Matt replied evenly. "But we're wasting time if we mean to get back in time for supper. I'd like to put this more delicately, folks. But I'm not *asking* you to ride in with us; I'm *telling* you. Let's move it out, Mr. Taylor."

Taylor raised his gauntlet to move his patrol forward, and the wagons more or less joined in. But Colonel Billy Hawkins said, "See here, I find this a bit high-handed, young sir. I'm not used to taking orders from the army!"

Matt said, "You'd better *get* used to it, then. I thought an old trail hand like you would know the facts of life out here, uh, *Colonel*. You're on federal land, patrolled by the U.S. Army. *Everybody* takes orders from us, except maybe a few Indians. Swing a little wide, Taylor. The mounts and wagon teams might spook if we go too near the place where Crying Boy was killed."

Matt rode his mount forward, turning his back on the others. Another horse fell in at his right side, so he knew before he looked that it wasn't his junior, Taylor. He saw that it was Miss Mills, so he didn't tell her to drop back. He was only annoyed with the ridiculous *poseur* who'd somehow convinced these folks, and maybe himself, that he knew what he was doing.

It wasn't Matt's job to unmask the so-called colonel, as long as he behaved. The army had enough on its plate without trying to convince half the people who came out here that they should have stayed on the safe side of the Big Muddy.

The girl's voice was modulated and refined as she asked, "Are you seriously suggesting there may be Indian trouble this summer, Lieutenant? We were told it's all over. The papers say Sitting Bull is in Canada and that most of the chiefs have signed new peace treaties."

"Some Indians don't read the papers, ma'am," Matt told her. "You're right about most of the bands behaving themselves lately. There's one bunch around here that isn't. But don't worry. You'll be safe with us."

Phoebe sniffed and said, "Perhaps. Frankly, it's my opinion there'd be less Indian trouble if you soldiers would just leave them be. Colonel Hawkins says his Kiowa friends never wanted to fight any whites, but that the War Department doesn't understand Indians—"

"Ma'am," Matt said wearily, "if you'll look over there at that bundle they just loaded on that bay, you'll see it's a corpse. We just found one of our Indian scouts shot full of bullets and mutilated. I doubt he was killed by your guide's Kiowa drinking buddies, if he has any. I'm not up to arguing the rights and wrongs of Uncle Sam's Indian policy. I'm not sure he has one. The point, right now, is that at least one band of hostiles is out for hair. It won't matter whose fault it is if they catch you folks alone on the trail. I'm sorry you don't like soldiers, but you're going to spend the next few days with us anyway."

She said bitterly, "I can see we have no more choice than the poor Indians. Does it make you feel good, bossing people around like that?"

"No, ma'am. I boss people because it's my job to be a boss. Is Mr. Penderson your man or whatever?"

"Heavens, no! I'm joining my fiancé in California, if I ever get there. What made you ask a thing like that?"

"Oh, I didn't mean anything by it. Just trying to sort things out. I mean to have a few words with your leader, as soon as I get the chance."

Phoebe nodded as they rode within hailing distance of the other party. Everyone was riding south, well spaced out. "Colonel Billy said he didn't get along with soldiers," she said.

"I noticed. Funny how a colonel can't tell a lieutenant from a captain. That fringed shirt he's wearing isn't Kiowa, either. I guess he has blood brothers among the Chippewa, too. It's lucky you ran into Taylor before you met any Sioux. Of course, most Sioux would notice that the beadwork on his fancy shirt says he's a squaw, but they might have been surly, anyway. Sioux don't think much of Chippewa. Funny outfit to be wearing out here in Lakota country. But that's his problem."

The girl frowned and asked, "What on earth is a Lakota?"

Matt shrugged, "Lakota, Nakota, Dakota, depending on the accent of the band. The Lakota Confederacy we just whipped includes what we call Sioux, the Cheyenne, some Arapaho and Blackfoot. After we find out which band is on the warpath, we'll see about getting you folks safely on your way to California. How come you didn't take the Transcontinental? Most folks ride the trains, these days."

She said, "I was thinking of taking the train, but it's rather an expensive way to travel. When I heard Captain Penderson and his friends were coming west by wagon, I bought passage with them. I have a hope chest and other things in one of the wagons. The railroads charge dreadfully for freight."

Matt suppressed a gallantry about her husband-to-be in California being a lucky man. She obviously knew she was pretty and it seemed a waste of time to flirt with a gal who'd been spoken for. He noticed a wisp of ash-blonde hair under her veil and glanced away. He hadn't had a woman for a while, and he figured there was no sense in torturing himself.

Windy Mandalian had circled out for sign, but was riding in now. He rode to join Matt, and after he'd been introduced to Phoebe and had tipped his battered hat to her, he said, "The grass is too grazed and the ground's too hard, like I said, Matt. When we get near the post, I'll ride in to Gray Elk's and see if any buck's been bragging. Cheyenne purely hate Delaware, and somebody might be counting coup for the squaws to admire."

Matt nodded and said, "I'll see that Crying Boy rates full military honors when we bury him. Be careful, though. You're the last scout we have. I don't suppose you'd consider taking anyone into Tipi Town to watch your back?"

Windy brushed a fly from his face. "Not hardly. Any buck who'd fool me would likely fool any other white, and they dummy up in front of you blue legs."

Phoebe Mills sniffed again and said, "That attitude you have toward them certainly gives them plenty of call to resent you, don't you think?"

The two men exchanged puzzled glances. The girl said, "You refer to them as *bucks*, like they were animals to be hunted!"

Windy just snorted. Matt said, "'Buck' is not an insulting term, ma'am. It's as close as we can get to a perfectly fine Algonquin word, meaning 'man.' You see, they don't use the same alphabet, so a lot of letters get lost in the cracks. That's why we can't decide if it's Lakota or Dakota. The Cheyenne word for 'man' could be 'buck' or 'huck' or maybe 'hawk.'"

"So you pronounce it as you do our word for a hunted deer?"

"That's true. But I never thought of it that way."

The girl nodded grimly. "I read about the way you hunt down Indians. It's no wonder some of them have acted mean, after what you soldiers did to them at Sand Creek and the Washita!"

"Sand Creek was ugly," Matt admitted soberly. "It was the Colorado State Troopers, not the U.S. Army, but I'll allow they shot more women and children there than they needed to. At Spirit Lake, a lot of *white* women and children died ugly.

Maybe some of the State Troopers at Sand Creek had that in mind."

"That's no excuse. *We're* supposed to be *civilized*! Are you going to say it wasn't the U.S. Army at the Washita Massacre?"

Windy said, "My turn, Matt. I was at Washita, missy, riding with George Armstrong Custer and the Seventh Cav. I don't know what you calls a massacre, but we lost nearly twenty men taking Black Kettle's camp that day."

"I see. So the Indians defended themselves, as anyone would. Are you going to deny that Custer killed women and children there, or that he even shot the poor Indians' ponies, afterwards?"

Windy spat downwind and said, "Nope. Some squaws and papooses got hit by both sides, since we was all firing into one another in a lot of smoke at point-blank range. I shot me a kid about eight years old at Washita. I ain't ashamed to say it. The little cuss was pointing a Henry rifle at me when I done it. As to shooting the ponies, we always shoot their ponies. A buck can't ride against anybody iffen he has no horse, ma'am."

"But you had no right to fight them at all! The papers said Black Kettle and his band were at peace when Custer attacked them!"

Matt Kincaid said, "Opposition papers, ma'am. No matter which party is in power in Washington, the other side says their Indian policy is wrong. Custer collected political enemies the way a dog collects fleas. He wasn't too popular with anyone, as far as that goes, but fair is fair."

Phoebe's eyes blazed under her veil as she snapped, "You call what he did 'fair'? Riding down harmless Indians trying to live in peace?"

Matt started to answer, but Windy said, "Let me, boy. I was there." Then he looked at Phoebe and asked, "How do you reckon you'd feel if some Injuns grabbed you, ripped off all your duds, and took turns with you until you went a mite crazy, ma'am?"

Matt said, "Windy! That's no way to speak to a lady!"

But the girl repressed a shudder and met Windy's eyes with a cold stare of distaste. The scout continued, "We found two captive white gals in that harmless Injuns' camp, ma'am. You see, we didn't kill *all* the women and children. Not even the squaws. We thought the two crazy white ladies was Cheyenne, too, until we hauled 'em out in the light as the gunsmoke cleared. One just stood stone-faced and not saying much. The other was sort of laughing and screaming a lot until old George Custer slapped her to calm her down and we got her story. It wasn't a pretty story, and Matt's right about a lady having delicate ears, so we'll say no more about it. But I do get riled when folks say we butchered harmless Injuns that cold winter day. The hysterical gal recovered and the last I hear tell, she's making a new life for herself, somewhere where nobody knows her. The other one's in a lunatic asylum, back East. They say she just sits and stares a lot."

Phoebe Mills rode in silence for a time before she shuddered and said, "That's not the way I heard the story of the Washita fight. But surely there *are* good Indians?"

Windy nodded and said, "Yep, just like there's good white folks. I aim to have supper with a Cheyenne gent I'd trust with my own daughter, this evening. But if I thought Matt, here, would let me show you what's under that tarp up ahead, I could show you what some *bad* Injuns done."

Matt said, "I think you made your point, Windy. It doesn't really matter whether Miss Phoebe believes us or not. She and these other folks aren't going to meet any Indians, good or bad, until we find out who killed Crying Boy and put them in a box."

# four

A quarter-mile to the southwest of Outpost Nine, two soldiers of Easy Company were on a secret mission. With an IG officer on the post, First Sergeant Cohen couldn't openly conduct a class in basic marksmanship. Every man in the outfit was supposed to have qualified with his weapons before coming out here. At the same time, the son of a bitch from IG was skimming through the files and making clucking noises about rifle drill. Four Eyes, the company clerk, was in mortal danger of a transfer to the Quartermaster Corps, and while Four Eyes couldn't have hit the broad side of a barn, even from inside, he was a good clerk, so what the hell.

Cohen had sent Four Eyes out to qualify under the tutelage of Pop Fegan, an otherwise undistinguished soldier who'd served as a sharpshooter in the Army of the Potomac and consistently scored over ninety percent with his Springfield. Pop was in his late thirties and would have been an NCO long ago if he could do anything but shoot and salute. Unfortunately, Fegan was a slow thinker as well as prematurely gray. The first sergeant had saddled him with a problem beyond his capacity in telling him to take Four Eyes out and qualify him on the q.t.

In truth, the task might well have daunted a brighter instructor. As Pop hunkered by the prone Four Eyes in the shallow draw, it was becoming obvious as hell that the company clerk and the Springfield Trapdoor rifle were not made for one another. Pop had set a line of bottles from the suttler's store a hundred feet up the draw. The bottles were a lot closer than any target was supposed to be, but Cohen had said to build up Four Eyes' confidence, whatever that meant. So far, the clerk had fired twenty rounds without hitting the first bottle, and if Four Eyes was feeling desperate, Pop was totally confused. It seemed impossible to an instinctive marksman that anyone could miss so consistently. As Four Eyes reloaded the single-shot weapon nervously, Pop spat and said, "You have to be *aiming* that durned rifle, old son. This time, don't aim at the space *between* the bottles. Take a little windage and bust one of the little bastards."

Four Eyes snapped the breech shut and squinted down the barrel, heart pounding against the sod he lay on as sweat ran down his brow. His thick glasses were starting to slip down his nose, and his hands were clammy and oddly numb as he tried to aim. He licked his lips and complained, "I can't get the durned old sights to work, Pop. You know I have bad eyes. When I focus on the bottle I can't see the sights. When I get the sights clear, the bottle is just a blur, dancing around out yonder!"

Pop put a hand on the clerk's shoulder and said, "Hold your fire and listen to me, dang it. I've told you this afore, but you ain't listening. Of course you can't focus clear on the sights and target at the same time. Nobody can. The target's a hundred feet away and the sight's right under your fool nose."

"Then what the hell good is it? How in hell is a man to line up on the durned target with such fool blurry sights?"

Pop sighed and said, "Forget the sights. Stare hard at the target. Pick a bottle and sort of study on putting a ball into it. The blurred outline of the sights will do you. They're *supposed* to be just shadows or such on the edge of your vision. You ain't shooting at no sights, you're aiming at a *bottle*. So *look* at the son of a bitch!"

Four Eyes squinted hard. He was nearsighted, and the bottle wasn't too clear a hundred feet away. So now *everything* was blurred, but he could make out the fuzzy black V of the rear sight, and the stubby I of the front sight seemed more or less centered on the swimming blur of brown glass out there, if only the whole mess would stop waving around like that. Four Eyes suddenly yanked the trigger. The heavy rifle bucked back against his shoulder and he flinched at the noise and concussion. He opened his eye again as Pop swore softly. Four Eyes hadn't hit anything.

Pop said, "You're flinching, damn it. Didn't I tell you not to flinch?"

"I can't help it. The durned rifle kicks like a mule."

"Hell, everybody knows that. It ain't no sin to tighten up when it slams into your shoulder, old son. But you're flinching *before* you fire. It helps to fire with your eyes open, too. I was watching just now. You know what's wrong with you, old son? You're afraid of that fool gun!"

Four Eyes shook his head. It made his glasses slip worse. He moved them back in place with his free hand before he said, "I'm not afraid of the rifle. I don't like the son of a bitch, but I'm not afraid of it."

"Then why are you acting so schoolmarm, Four Eyes? You fire that gun like a schoolgirl throws rocks. You throw your head back, close your eyes, and just let fly. You raise the muzzle to your right like you're trying to kill a duck. There ain't no ducks up yonder, boy. The bottles are over there, see?"

Four Eyes took another round from the cartridge case in the grass and fumbled it in, saying, "I don't think I fear the noise and kick as much as I fear missing, Pop. I know I'm fixing to miss, even before I pull the durned old trigger."

The older sharpshooter blinked as something he remembered from his boyhood surfaced. He said, "Hold everything. Let's just study on what you just said. I remember this time when I was just a fool kid back on the farm, afore I larnt proper shooting. I suspicion what we have here is a bad case of buck fever, Four Eyes."

The company clerk sighed and replied, "What we have here is a case of piss-poor *vision*, you mean! Everybody knows I'm half blind. What the hell difference does it make if I can shoot a gun or not? Nobody expects a durned old Indian to pop up out of my wastebasket in the orderly room. I'm a pencil-pusher, and a pretty good one. This nonsense is a pure waste of my time and the taxpayer's money."

Pop shook his head and said, "Ben Cohen said he wanted every man in the outfit up to snuff in case that IG man orders target drill afore we can get rid of him. He said I wasn't to bring you back until I was sure you had a fighting chance of hitting the far end of the rifle range, and damn it, Four Eyes, you just ain't trying!"

Four Eyes grimaced, braced himself, and fired his Springfield before he said, "All right. There! How's that for trying?"

Then his jaw dropped as they both stared in wonder at the

line of bottles down the draw. There was a gap in the row and the sunlight glinted on the glass shards in the grass all around. Four Eyes licked his lips and said, "My God, I *hit* one!"

He raised the trapdoor of his breech, ejecting the hot spent brass, as Pop said, "There you go. It's like I said. Buck fever. That last time you fired without thinking, didn't you?"

Four Eyes reached for a fresh round as he frowned and said, "I don't remember what I did. You were mixing me up and I was sort of pissed off at you and—"

"Hold her right there, old son. I suspicion we're on the right track. But you won't have me to cuss, when and if you have to fire for record in front of that IG man. Let's study this. You feel sort of sorry for yourself because you have to wear them glasses, right?"

Four Eyes thought before he shook his head and said, "No. I'm used to wearing glasses. I've worn them all my life."

"Then why do you keep defending your constitutional right to specs, old son?"

"I didn't know I did. What are you talking about, Pop?"

"You and your infernal pissing and moaning about your eyes, Four Eyes. Ever since we moseyed out here to bust bottles, it's all you've talked about. I've taught a lot of old boys to shoot, and let me tell you something. Nobody shoots good right off, and everybody bitches. They bitch about the wind and the light. They allow as how the barrel must be bent, or the sights out of line. They suspicion the ordnance depot of issuing ammo left over from the War of 1812. It feels plumb foolish to miss a target, and it's only human to lay the blame somewheres."

"I'm not blaming this damned old rifle for my poor shooting, Pop."

"I know. It's unusual as hell. I've met damn few men in this man's army who have good words for these old converted muzzle-loaders. Half of the goddamned Injuns have repeating Spencers; and these Springfields *do* come with warped barrels and bent sights. Yet you lay all the blame on your own self, like you sort of *enjoy* it. You know what I suspicion, Four Eyes? I suspicion you don't *want* to learn to soldier."

Four Eyes snapped, "Aw, hang some crepe on your nose. Your brain just died! It's not my fault my eyes are bad. I had scarlet fever when I was a kid and—"

"You're full of shit," Pop cut in brutally. "You've got a

great excuse for ducking chores you don't cotton to. I don't see how you passed the physical, but even if you cheated, you must have been able to see *some* durned thing the sawbones held up to you. You sure as hell can see to spell my name on the duty rosters when you're sitting safe and snug behind your desk in the orderly room."

"Oh, hell, I don't assign the duties and you know it, Pop."

"Shut up. I ain't done talking. My point is that a man who can see to read and write can see them infernal bottles yonder. They're damned near close enough to *bayonet*! So let's stop whimpering about our poor little eyeballs and git this show on the road. Wait, don't fire until you hear me out, goddamnit! I'm tired of saying it, but I'll say it again. I want you to take three deep breaths, let the last one half out, and hold it whilst you slowly *squeeze* the trigger instead of jerking it. Don't worry about when the gun goes off. Let her surprise you both. That way you won't tighten up or flinch as you fire, see?"

Four Eyes said, "I've been trying, damn it! The damned old bottle out there keeps bouncing on and off my front sight. If I'm not lined up when I fire, won't I miss?"

"Hell, you've been missing since we come out here. I'm trying to larn you to *hit* the sons of bitches! Trust me, old son, no man born of mortal woman can hold a rifle steady as a rock on target. It's going to waver on you, even if your name is Buffalo Bill. But if you're lined up close enough to matter when the gun goes off, you'll hit her nine times outta ten. The target's bigger than your front sight, see? Just breathe deep like I told you and pay no mind to the flash and recoil afore it happens. Keep your damned eye on the damned target as you squeeze off the round, and keep the eye open for a change! Come on, Four Eyes. It's almost noon and I'm sort of hungry. Just hit one more bottle and I'll be able to face the top kick with a clear conscience."

Four Eyes almost sobbed aloud as he peered down the barrel at the madly bobbing bottles. He knew he was going to miss again, and it hurt so to have the others jeer at him, or, worse yet, pretend they didn't notice he was a pathetic parody of a soldier and a man. It had always been like that. He'd hoped, when he joined the army, he'd get away from smirks and knowing looks. He'd never wanted to be the sissy of his town, and everybody knew a soldier was tough. Some of the boys who'd laughed at him, back home, had slapped him on the back and told him he was "all right" when he joined up. But if he'd escaped his hometown reputation as a bookworm, and the cruel taunts about the way he threw a ball, it had only been to feel even more inferior among new comrades. His treacherous eyes were watering and he couldn't see a thing as he tried to follow Pop's instructions. He blinked his eyes to clear them as, without warning, the Springfield bucked against his shoulder.

Four Eyes groaned in frustration as he recovered from the savage kick. He braced himself for another laconic observation from his tormentor. But, to his surprise, Pop was saying, "I'll be damned. I *knew* you could do her, once you paid attention."

Four Eyes blinked his eyes clear and saw that he'd hit another bottle. He realized he'd been holding his breath, and let it out with a sigh of relief, trying to remember what he'd done.

Pop Fegan said, "I don't know about you, but I reckon we'd best quit while we're ahead. Let's police up your brass and head back for grub. Remember now, if Cohen's satisfied when I allow you hit a couple of bottles, I don't want you mentioning how many rounds we spent doing it, hear?"

Four Eyes nodded and started picking spent brass from the grass without answering. The ordeal was over for the time being. He saw no need to point out that the bottle he'd hit had been two spaces down the line from the one he'd been aiming at. Now if only that goddamned IG officer would leave without demanding further proof of his ability, he'd be in the clear for a while. Who the hell expected a company clerk to shoot an Indian, anyway?

In the kitchen next to the enlisted men's mess, Sergeant Erwin "Dutch" Rothausen was desperately trying to control his temper. It wasn't easy. Mess sergeants were expected to detonate easily, and the three-striper from Pennsylvania took professional pride in his short fuse. Dutch had never actually murdered a KP while on duty, but he was careful not to let word of this get around. He was aware of the other cooks and KPs standing at attention as the IG snooper, Lieutenant Colonel Bradshaw, inspected the mess facilities. Dutch didn't want them to think he was a sissy as he faced the IG snoop, but there were limits to how far even a mess sergeant could sass a field-grade officer.

The short colonel was saying, "I see you disinfected this table with lye after using it to dress that Indian's wounds last night, Sergeant."

Dutch said, "Yessir," as he wondered what the hell the bastard wanted. It was almost noon, and the bugler would soon sound chow call. How the hell were they going to feed the men if this silly son of a bitch kept asking questions? There was nothing here for the nit-picking bastard to nail them on. Dutch prided himself on a well-run kitchen almost as much as he did the temper tantrums it took to keep it that way. He noticed that the prick from IG was wearing white gloves. Going to run a finger over some pots and pans, was he? Well, let him. If the bastard could smudge that clean white cotton on the bottom of a stove, the KP pusher would suffer a slow and lingering death.

Bradshaw grimaced down at the damp white wood of the table and mused, "That Delaware scout died early this morning, Sergeant."

Dutch said, "Yessir. I know. We took the bullets out and dressed his hurts as well as we were able, but it happens."

"Uh, doesn't it bother you that a man died on the same table you use to prepare food for the men?"

Dutch said, "Begging the colonel's pardon. He didn't die here in my kitchen. He died in the scouts' quarters."

"Yes, but he'd been shot and rolled in dirt and he must have bled as you worked on him in here, eh?"

Dutch's face was impassive as he said, "Yessir. He shit his britches, too. The colonel will notice we cleaned up after him with lye and holystone. That table is cleaner right now than it was when it came from the carpenter. We poured boiling lye on the floor and laid fresh sawdust, too."

Bradshaw nodded and said, "I'm sure I could eat off your work table, Sergeant. It just strikes me as odd that you use the kitchen as an aid station, and dress wounds with the same implements you use in preparing meals."

Dutch said, "We have no medical officer or dispensary here, sir. We use the kitchen in an emergency because it's the cleanest place on the post."

"I see. You're a follower of that germ theory of Professor Pasteur, I take it?"

"I don't read French, sir. Back home in my father's butcher shop, I was taught that meat keeps better if it's kept clean. We always boiled our knives and scrubbed down the chopping blocks three times a day. Any butcher knows better than to keep a dirty shop."

Bradshaw nodded and said, "Well, we know that Delaware never died of infection. The captain tells me you took out half of his liver and a kidney. Ah, where did you study surgery, Sergeant? Were you a medic in the War?"

Dutch shook his head and said, "No, sir. Not exactly. Of course, I pitched in from time to time when the regular sawbones were busy. We took a lot of casualties at Cold Harbor—"

"Just a minute, Sergeant," the IG man cut in. "Are you saying you act as the company surgeon with no medical education at all?"

Dutch felt the back of his neck redden, but he managed not to swear as he replied, "I learned meat-cutting from my father as a boy, sir. I learned a few things about cutting into living critters since I joined the army. I cleaned and dressed that Indian's wounds and I sewed him up as good as I knowed how. A real doctor might have done it prettier, but we don't have one here."

"I understand. In other words, the men of Easy Company depend on an unskilled butcher to take care of them if they get wounded in action."

Dutch snapped, "I'm no such thing as an unskilled butcher, Colonel! I'm a damned *good* butcher, and if there's a better chef in this man's army, I ain't met up with him!"

Bradshaw laughed and said, "I'm sure you are, Sergeant. I ate last evening and this morning in the officer's mess. I'm not gigging you, son. I can see you're as much the victim of a lax situation as the men you, uh, do your best for. You're aware, of course, that it's against army regulations for anyone but a qualified surgeon to perform major operations on a wounded man?"

Dutch shrugged and said, "I know the rule books as well as most, sir. Last night, when they brought that shot-up Delaware to me, I didn't think he wanted to hear he'd have to wait until Regiment sent a surgeon out here. He was bleeding pretty good and he allowed it hurt."

"I understand, Sergeant. But you *did* perform major surgery and he *did* die. Isn't it just possible he'd have done better under the knife of a qualified physician?"

Dutch shrugged again and said, "We didn't have one. He

was as good as dead when I opened him up, so he'd have died in any case by the time a real sawbones could have gotten out here. I done what I could and you can put her down any way you like, but I'd do the same for you if they drug you in here gutshot."

Dutch had lapsed into a sullen silence, meeting the older man's gaze, before he realized he'd forgotten to tack on a few sirs. The IG officer hadn't missed them. He wasn't paid to miss anything. But Madison Bradshaw was army enough to know about mess sergeants' tempers, too, and what the hell, it wasn't this enlisted man's fault.

The IG man looked around as if he wanted to try his white glove on one of the hanging pots. But he didn't. He said, "I'd like to see your books, now, Sergeant Rothausen. I'm sure we'll find all your purchase and requisition slips in order, but they expect me to look, anyhow."

Dutch nodded and said, "Right this way, sir."

He'd had Four Eyes double-check the books for possible errors, and he'd kill the little bastard if this prick questioned a dotted *i* or a crossed *t*. He was probably going to pass inspection, he knew. So why didn't this nosy bastard get the fuck out of his kitchen and let him feed the real soldiers?

It was getting hot as well as bright outside. So Warner Conway allowed his eyes to adjust to the dim, cool light of the orderly room before he spoke. Ben Cohen got to his feet behind his desk, but the captain said, "As you were, Ben. I see we're alone."

"Yessir. I sent that half-blind clerk of mine out to qualify before that IG notices he's sort of confused about which end of the rifle the bullet's supposed to come out of. I don't suppose the captain would allow a few suggestions about the files?"

Conway said, "Forget it, Ben. I told you I've seen more outfits get in trouble trying to cover up for the IG than it's worth. Bradshaw's the least of our worries. If he gigs us, he gigs us. What are they going to do, pass us over for promotion again? I was hoping to find you alone, though. Any word on Kincaid or Taylor?"

They both knew that of course the lookout would have told them the moment so much as a cloud of dust appeared on the horizon. But Cohen shook his head and said, "No, sir." He knew what was eating the Old Man.

Conway took a seat at Four Eyes' corner desk and fished

out two cigars. He held one out to the first soldier, who accepted gravely as he stepped over to light the captain's smoke for him. Conway waited until Cohen had resumed his own seat before he said, "I guess young Corporal Dorfler's had some time to sweat, under arrest in quarters, eh?"

Cohen nodded and said, "Yessir. My wife's not speaking to me this morning."

Conway sighed and said, "I know the feeling. Matt Kincaid's not a married man. He'd have doubtless thought twice about putting Dorfler under arrest if he had been. What are we to do about this mess, Ben?"

Cohen took a drag on his own cigar before he replied, "I've been thinking about that ever since Maggie told me she wanted a divorce again, sir. I don't see what we *can* do. The boy was off his post and he got caught in front of God and the IG. God might forgive him, but the IG won't."

Conway grimaced and half-closed his eyes as he recited, "'Deserting one's post in the face of the enemy shall be punished by death or such other punishment as the court-martial shall decide.'" Then he added, "The offense calls for at least a special court-martial, so I won't be the presiding officer. I guess I have enough pull at Regiment to get him off with reduction in rank and a good stiff fine."

Cohen said, "I told my wife that, sir. She threw a plate at me while she explained that a private docked two-thirds of his pay for six months can hardly expect to keep a wife out here."

"I know that feeling, too. My Flora didn't throw anything, but it does seem we'll face a female mutiny on this post if we send that silly little bride back East. Damn that Kincaid! He should have thought before he clouded up and rained all over that kid!"

Cohen examined the ash of his smoke carefully as he said, "Begging the captain's pardon, Lieutenant Kincaid had no choice. We were all standing around with a dying man on the ground when the idiot came up, buttoning his britches, and as much as admitted he'd been screwing when he should have been guarding."

Conway said, "I tried to tell *my* wife that. She called me a brute anyway. It's not like Dorfler actually caused any trouble, Ben. Windy and his Delaware would have ridden into that ambush out there, in any case. Sure, the kid was off making love to his wife, even as you and I, but—"

"Begging the captain's pardon, I do not make love to my own or any other man's wife while I'm standing guard! I think the men know this. They also know that while everyone else was at his post, the corporal of the guard was off his post, literally fucking off and literally caught with his pants down! It's your command, sir, but I've seen men shot for just being caught asleep on guard. I don't see what else Lieutenant Kincaid could have done. He sent him back to his quarters instead of locking him up. Many an OD I've served under might have shot Dorfler on the spot. I know *I'd* never have sent him back to a naked lady for the rest of the night!"

Conway nodded and said, "All right, the fat's in the fire and what's done is done. The dumb little bastard deserves a general court-martial and a DD. But, now that we've said that, how in hell are we going to get him off, Ben?"

The first sergeant shrugged and said, "If that IG man didn't know we had him under arrest to quarters, we could likely wash our own linen, sir. Dorfler's popular with his squad and not a bad soldier, when he hasn't got a hard-on. The men would be satisfied if I made him dig latrines and peel spuds until everyone forgot why he was on my shit list. Of course, they're expecting him to lose his stripes."

"Damn it, Ben, I can get that deal from Regiment! The TJA would let me give him company punishment to save the paperwork of a trial, I suppose. But Dorfler's on his first hitch, so he has no fogies. How in hell is he supposed to support a wife on a base pay of thirteen dollars a month? That's all we can give him as a private, isn't it?"

Cohen flicked the ash and took another drag as he considered. The Old Man was all right, for an officer, but the Sergeants' Club frowned on letting the brass learn too much about how the army really worked. Officers caused less trouble when you let them think they were in charge. And the captain was one of those well-meaning hairpins who followed the book.

Cohen said, cautiously, "The captain allows me to run this orderly room my own way, right?"

Conway raised an eyebrow and replied, "Within commonsense limits. What do you have in mind, Ben?"

"Uh, speaking man-to-man, sir?"

"Of course. I told you I waited until I could speak to you alone. You know I've always trusted you with the petty details, Ben."

Ben Cohen knew. He knew no officer born of mortal woman would ever know the risks a good NCO staff took to keep him out of trouble, either. He said, "Since the captain trusts me to hold this outfit together, I'm going to ask him to trust me a mite further on matters that needn't concern anyone in officer's mess."

"I see. Like the time you stole those supplies from Fox Company in time for inspection?"

"Sir, I'm sorry you found out about that. But since you seem to be needlessly concerned, we never stole the gear we needed for that inspection. We just sort of borrowed it and then we got it back to Fox Company in time for *their* inspection."

Conway laughed and said, "I stand corrected. I was under the impression some NCOs from Fox got bent and bruised in the process. I had no idea their supply sergeant was so cooperative."

Cohen smiled back. "He didn't want to be, sir. But in the end, me and a couple of the boys I rode over in the wagons with managed to persuade him. Can we get back to here and now, sir? That other inspection is ancient history. I'm more worried about the one we're having now."

Conway nodded again and said, "Right. As I follow your drift, you want me to turn Dorfler over to your tender mercies and not ask too many questions. I'll go along with that, if you think it'll work. But can I tell my wife I'm not really an ogre?"

Ben Cohen looked uncomfortable and said, "Begging the captain's pardon. Women *do* talk and we *do* have an IG man among us. I can't tell anyone what to say to their own missus. I, for one, aim to keep my Maggie in the dark, painful as that may be to contemplate."

Warner Conway got to his feet with a relieved sigh. He had no idea what his Machiavellian top kick had in mind, but he knew Ben had a plan. He felt a little left out and wistful. But, like Ben, he knew that was one of the prices one paid for being a commissioned officer.

Cohen had some forms out and was working on them when Four Eyes came in with Pop Fegan. Pop said, "Well, I got this old boy shooting better than he used to, Sarge. We come back 'cause it's time for grub. But iffen you want us to go out agin . . ."

To Four Eyes' relief, the burly sergeant growled, "Never

mind all that. We've got work to do. Pop, you run over to the quarters and fetch Corporal Dorfler. What are you waiting for?"

Pop said, "I'm halfways there," and ducked out the door. Cohen looked up at his clerk and said, "Get out some blank paybooks. It's only fair to warn you that we're about to commit a federal felony."

Four Eyes said, "I'd rather do that than mess around with that fool rifle. Who are we felonizing, Sarge?"

"Dorfler. We're going to hide his real records and paybook. Then we're going to bust his ass on paper. He'll plead guilty and accept company punishment to avoid a court-martial. So I'll need a paybook showing he's been reduced to the rank of buck private in case that nosy IG man asks to see it. When Dorfler gets here, I'll explain why he has a lot of well-deserved shit details ahead of him on his off-duty time. Meanwhile, since he's a good squad leader and we need one, he's to serve as an acting corporal with the rank of private. Get to work on it."

Four Eyes went to a filing cabinet and rummaged through it as he asked, "Ain't this sort of complicated, Sarge? You aim to give him his stripes back as soon as that IG snoop leaves, don't you?"

"Not right away. Let the others see the horny little bastard serving with bare sleeves for a while. It won't kill him, and men who do their duty will feel better about it if they think he paid for his shirking."

Four Eyes went to his own desk with a puzzled frown. He sat down and said, "I'm missing something, Sarge. Why do we have to doctor his paybook and records if you aim to bust him and then give back his stripes?"

Cohen looked disgusted. "If we *really* break him, in the middle of this damned economy drive, it could take him a year to get the stripes, even if we promoted him again tomorrow. Meanwhile, he has a wife to feed. Jesus H. Christ, do I have to draw you a picture? You're supposed to be a company clerk!"

Four Eyes shook his head as if to clear it. Then he brightened and said, "Oh, I get it. We're going to tear his stripes off in front of everybody, but meanwhile he'll still really be a corporal and he'll still be getting a corporal's pay on the q.t.!"

"Something like that. Make out the new paybook, damn it."

Four Eyes went to work, but asked, "Hey, Sarge, while I'm forging all this stuff, why can't I say I'm qualified with that durned rifle?"

Cohen said, "Because you can't, you idiot. If the IG asks you to show him how well you shoot, it won't matter what it says on your papers. Let's not take chances we don't have to. If he finds one odd thing in the files, he might look for others."

Four Eyes said, "It sure seems mean, Sarge. You won't let me fix my own rifle score, yet you cover for a boy who really done wrong. How come you like him more than you like me?"

"Shut up and do what I told you. I don't like Dorfler all that much. The captain and Miss Flora want me to get him out of the mess he got hisself into."

"The captain ordered you to let Dorfler off, Ben?"

"Shit, you know he can't do that. He won't know what we've done, if we do it right. Just make up a duplicate paybook and forget about it if it's too complicated for you to follow."

Four Eyes said, "I can see what we're doing. I'm not that dumb. But won't we get in a mess of trouble if the officers ever find out? What am I to tell that IG man if he asks about Dorfler?"

Ben Cohen growled, "You're to say nothing. You don't know nothing. Tell the bastard to ask *me* any questions he pesters you with."

"You reckon you can skin him, Ben?"

Cohen shrugged and said, "I'll have to. If I can't, he'll sure as hell skin me."

The IG officer, Lieutenant Colonel Bradshaw, had set up shop in an unused room in the BOQ, with its own doorway leading out to the parade. He'd borrowed a map table and some bentwood chairs to conduct his inquisition. As Private Malone sat stiffly in one of them between Bradshaw and the open doorway at his back, Bradshaw recognized him as the meat and potatoes of a thorough inspection. Any officer could see that Malone was a company fuck-up on the first sergeant's shit list. Using these malcontents was distasteful, but useful. They tended to know all the dirt their superiors had swept under the rug, and they tended to jump at the chance to inform on the orderly room.

Bradshaw smiled fondly at Malone and said, "Well, I can

see by your paybook that you're an old soldier, Malone. I suppose you've gone through many an IG before, eh?"

Malone licked his lips and said, "I have, sor. And, faith, I've never understood thim. I've reported to ye as ordered, but ye'll have to be tellin' me what ye're wanting of me."

Bradshaw said, "Surely you know that I'm interviewing each enlisted man separately and in confidence, Malone. Anything you say to me today will be strictly between you and me, understand?"

"Ye mean like this was confession and yourself was a priest, sor?"

"That's close enough. As you know, under ordinary circumstances, an enlisted man with a gripe has to go through channels. You have to ask your squad leader's permission to speak to the sergeant and so forth up the line. I know some of you men think this is clumsy and unfair, but—"

"If ye please, sor," Malone cut in, "I've been in the army long enough to know the reasons. Sure, the orderly room would look like a railway station if every man with a question for the captain was to just dash in whenever he felt like it."

Bradshaw raised an eyebrow and said, "Right. On the other hand, the War Department is not unaware that the chain of command can sometimes make for certain injustices. It's not easy to complain to your CO about a sergeant who's been picking on you, when you have to ask that sergeant for permission to speak to the CO. These surprise visits and private interviews are designed to uncover such abuses."

Malone nodded and said, "I know that, sor. There was a first sergeant selling weekend leave when I was at Fort Sill. The last I heard of him, he was serving time at Leavenworth, thanks to an IG officer like yourself."

"Ah, then you know why you're here and what this is all about, Private Malone."

"If ye please, sor. I don't. Sure, there's been none of that in Easy Company. I've served in many an outfit, good and bad. Easy Company is the best I've seen so far. And I'll lick the man who says it isn't so!"

Bradshaw suppressed a smile as he stared down at the papers in front of him and said, "Your loyalty does you credit, Private Malone. Frankly, I'm surprised to find you so content with your lot. The records show you've pulled more company punishment than anyone else in the outfit."

Malone sighed and said, "In God's name, that's the truth,

sor. My parents raised me dacent and I try to stay the same, but when I've had a couple of drinks of a Saturday . . . Och, if I hadn't joined the army, it's in prison I'd be this day. I don't know what it is that makes me do the things I do when I've had too much of the creature, but God and these darling officers and noncoms have their hands full and that's a fact."

Bradshaw allowed himself a chuckle and said, "Your honesty and candor are refreshing, Malone. I take it you have no complaints, then?"

Malone shook his head and said, "Och, I've plenty of complaints, sor! The company's not up to strength, and even himself has to pull OD. The pistols they've issued us are second-rate, and many an Indian would scorn the auld single-shot Springfields we have. Our mail is ever late and the rations never arrive on time and the damned auld quartermasters hilp thimselves to all the good stuff anyway. I'm long overdue for new boots and me saddle tree is busted up and all that's holding me on me horse is faith and bailing wire. I've a patch in the seat of me best pants and me socks are out at heel and toe."

The IG man waved a hand and said, "I've made a note of the supply problem here, Malone. That'll be all, if you've no personal complaints."

Malone got to his feet, but said, "Yourself would take it personal if ye had to ride patrol in me saddle, sor." Then he saluted, turned on his heel, and left.

The IG officer consulted his list to see who was next. Another soldier dashed in and seated himself without bothering to salute or give his name. Bradshaw frowned across the map table at him and decided to forget it, for now. He vaguely remembered seeing the man before. The newcomer was wearing fresh blues and had red hair. The IG officer glanced at his roster and asked, "Private Fegan?"

The youth in the chair said, "No, sir. I'm Bob Bishop. My friends call me Red."

"I'll call you Private Bishop. You're not on my list, Bishop. Aren't you one of those recruits I rode out with yesterday?"

"Yessir. I heard you were taking complaints, and I sure do have a mess of them."

"I see. I've been questioning the men in order of seniority with the company, Bishop. Did you ask your first sergeant's permission to see me?"

Red looked startled and said, "Permission? I never heard

nothing about permission. Ain't you here to find out the way they keep abusing us, uh, sir?"

The IG officer stared silently at the malcontent for a long, hard moment. Then he said, "You're new. So I'm going to explain it once. Nobody in this man's army *ever* goes over his superior's head. The men I've called in here to interview haven't had to get permission because when the IG wants to talk to a man, his superior has nothing to say about it. But when a man wants to approach the IG on his own, he's supposed to go through proper channels, just like he'd approach any officer. Do you understand me, soldier?"

"I guess so, sir. Does that mean you don't want to talk to me?"

Bradshaw started to nod. Then he shrugged and said, "All right, as long as you're here, let's hear what kind of trouble you've managed to get into in less than twenty-four hours."

Red looked relieved and began, "Well, sir, the first sergeant is picking on me. Ain't it true that no NCO is allowed to hit us poor privates?"

"It's officially against regulations. Who hit you?"

"Well, nobody really hit me, but the first sergeant offered. He said he'd take me over to the tack room and whup my ass if I didn't do as I was told."

"I see. What was it he told you to do?"

"Aw, hell, sir, that rascal put me and them other new boys at the head of every duty roster the minute we got here. I'm pulling KP right now, and as soon as I get off I have guard duty. I ask you, is that fair?"

Bradshaw shook his head in wonderment and asked, "You're on Kitchen Police right now, under Dutch Rothausen, and you've snuck over here less than an hour after grub call? You must like to live dangerously, soldier! Who in blue blazes is washing the pots and pans right now?"

"That's another thing I wanted to tell you about, sir. That old Dutch and the first sergeant are ganging up on me. I told them in the kitchen that I was willing to peel spuds and sweep, but I have sensative hands and that lye soap makes 'em itch. But they told me they had a sink that was just made for me, and—"

"God give me strength," the IG officer breathed softly. Then he said, "Private Bishop, I'm going to save your tail, if only to preserve my image as a father confessor. I'm going to say I sent for you this afternoon. But for God's sake, don't ever do this again. Don't you realize that you're AWOL?"

Red blinked in surprise and said, "I'm still on the post, ain't I?"

"Soldier, there's a man under arrest in quarters just a few doors down. He was on the post when he left the guardhouse to play slap-and-tickle with his woman. You're absent from the kitchen without leave. If any officer or NCO wanted to be as nasty as you say they are, they could place *you* under arrest, too. I'd better give you a note to your mess sergeant."

Bradshaw took a scrap of foolscap and penciled a few lines as he added, "I'm only doing this because I remember being young and foolish once, myself. You've got a lot of growing up to do, soldier." He handed the slip with the date and time above his signature to Red and said, "Now get back where you belong, and for God's sake, keep your mouth shut until you have something to say. Frankly, I don't think you understand this break and you deserve a good spanking. But I'm a soft-hearted man and I foresee a grim future for you in any case."

Red left without saluting, wearing a frown. It was just as he'd figured. All the damned officers were in on it together. That IG bullshit didn't fool him. They all covered up for each other. A poor enlisted man had no chance in the durned old army. It was worse than being a nigger. At least a fool nigger could say he was free, these days. A soldier was as bad off as a slave had ever been before the War. But, what the hell, even a slave could run away. Maybe if he could talk Pud and Wilson into coming along, they could steal some grub and horses and just light out. They said even a cowhand could make a dollar a day out here, these days. Who but a fool would spend a hitch in a chickenshit outfit like this if he didn't have to?

As Red approached the kitchen near the gate, he saw Dutch Rothausen standing in the doorway with his hands on his hips and a thoughtful look on his face. Red swallowed the lump in his throat and waved the yellow scrap of paper in his hand, suddenly remembering some terrible stories the KP pusher had told them about the heavyset mess sergeant.

But then the lookout on the tower above was shouting, and some guards were running over to open the gate. The curious mess sergeant came out to have a look as Red approached. Red said, "I had to go see the IG, Sarge."

Dutch nodded absently, and said, "All right. You've seen him. Get back on those pots and pans." Then Dutch saw what was coming in and groaned, "Oh, shit. We just got done feeding the outfit and now we have to grub the fucking patrols! It looks like they picked up some feather merchants along the way. How the hell am I supposed to feed civilians, too?"

Red didn't know it, but Dutch was secretly pleased. He seldom got to show off his real skills, and he knew the captain would expect the best for visitors.

Flora Conway was pleased, too. The fourteen men and women from the wagon were naturally served refreshments in the officer's day room, with Miss Flora presiding as hostess.

Her husband and the other officers were over at the command post making marks on a map or something. But the civilian guests seemed a bit awed and uncomfortable. Save for the attractive and obviously well-educated Miss Mills, and the strangely dressed Colonel Hawkins, the wagon-party people seemed simple farm folk who weren't used to fine silver and delicate china. Dear Sergeant Rothausen had somehow managed a buffet of hot and cold hors d'oeuvres while the visitors bathed and changed from their dusty trail clothing, and dear Miss Mills had offered to pour the tea. Flora was a little surprised to see a man who called himself a colonel drinking tea from his saucer, but of course it wasn't the place of a refined hostess to question her guests' table manners. Captain Penderson and the other farm folk seemed able to manage their cups in the usual fashion.

Warner Conway came in with young Mr. Taylor. The captain said, "I see you've made our guests comfortable, dear. I'm afraid you folks are going to have to spend the night, at least, with us. We just tried to contact Regiment on the wire. My second-in-command, Lieutenant Kincaid, is gathering fresh men and mounts to find out what's going on."

Colonel Hawkins lowered the saucer he'd been inhaling to ask, "What does your headquarters have to say about this Injun scare, Captain?"

"We don't know," Conway replied. "Apparently the wire's been cut. I'm sending Kincaid down the road to find out where and by whom. Meanwhile, you'll be safe enough here."

Penderson frowned and said, "We're a half-month behind as it is, sir. We only average twenty miles a day, and at this rate we'll be crossing the Sierra Nevada dangerously close to the first fall snows!"

Conway nodded sympathetically. "Lieutenant Kincaid told me you'd gotten lost, sir. But another few days won't make that much difference. I'm more worried about you meeting hostiles near at hand than I am about possible frostbite in the distant future."

Colonel Billy Hawkins snapped, "Nobody was lost, dang it! I told your sassy shavetail I was leading these folks over a cutoff I've heard tell of."

Conway smiled thinly and said, "We'll have to compare notes on that before you leave, sir. If there's a pass over the Front Range that we don't have on our ordnance maps, I'm sure your information will be most useful to the War Department."

Hawkins changed the subject by asking, "Just what tribe seems to be on the warpath, Captain? Neither your scout nor that sassy young officer of yours seemed to be able to tell us as we rode in with them."

Conway said, "We don't know. That's why we've sent out another patrol. Our chief scout thinks they may be Cheyenne. He's over in that nearby tipi ring, right now, trying to find out."

Phoebe Mills poured a cup of tea for Conway as she asked, "Are those Indians we passed Cheyenne, Captain?"

He said, "Cheyenne, Arapaho, some Red River Breeds, and a couple of squaw men I'd like to run off if they'd let me."

Colonel Billy Hawkins said, "It's too bad they ain't Kiowa or Comanche. I could give you boys a hand if you had some of my blood brothers over there."

Warner Conway raised an eyebrow and asked, *"Nognitzitzin hano, ka?"*

Colonel Hawkins looked blank and asked, "What did you say?"

Conway caught his wife's warning eye and looked away as he replied, "I just tried some of the Comanche I picked up on the Staked Plains. I suppose you speak it with a different accent, eh?"

"That's right, by gum. You know how every band has a different way of talking. I knew you were spouting something that sounded sort of Comanche, but I reckon the boys I rode with that time pronounced a few words a mite less singsong."

Conway shrugged and sipped his tea. It was not his job to expose the so-called guide's foolishness, if the people who'd hired him couldn't see it. He was responsible for their safety until, and only until, they were beyond his jurisdiction. Washington wanted people out here. If the Homestead Act had been restricted only to the wise, the West would still be largely empty. There were still thousands of acres of land to be cleared and settled east of the Mississippi. Draining a swamp or restoring an abused farm offered far less danger, albeit far more work, than chasing golden dreams through Indian country.

Lieutenant Colonel Bradshaw came in and was introduced all around. The IG man took a seat across from Phoebe Mills and to Flora's left, next to the captain. As the pretty blonde immigrant served him across the table, Conway asked if he was through interviewing the enlisted men. The IG officer sighed and said, "Hardly. But I don't like to interfere with men on duty. I'll get the guards and such as they come off."

Conway nodded without answering. The bastard meant to spend another night here, did he? So be it. If he hadn't found anything worth gigging by now, he was wasting his own time.

As if he'd read the captain's mind, Bradshaw said, "I just saw your adjutant, Kincaid, off. He took some of the men I meant to talk to this afternoon with him. But I suppose restringing the telegraph wire is more important than my puttering about here."

Phoebe Mills asked, "Are the soldiers in any danger, sir?"

The question was aimed at Bradshaw rather than at the commanding officer, so the IG man met Conway's eyes as he said, "I doubt it, ma'am. Young Kincaid took about two dozen men with him. I found it a mite confusing, Captain. He didn't seem to be leading any particular platoon."

Conway nodded calmly. "Matt gathered a mixed crew of fresh off-duty riders, Colonel. I realize it must seem a bit informal, but we have to improvise out here."

Mr. Taylor chimed in, "My boys were ready and willing to ride out again, but Matt said they deserved a rest."

The IG officer sipped his tea and said, "I understand. How you gents run your patrols is not a matter for my department." But then he added, "I noticed Kincaid took young Dorfler along. I thought he was under arrest in quarters."

Flora brightened and glanced at her husband, but Conway's profile was to her as he quietly replied, "He's still under arrest,

Colonel. But we seem to be cut off from headquarters, we're under strength, and meanwhile, Dorfler is a good squad leader. I suppose Matt felt he'd be of more use to us on the trail than languishing about the post out of action."

Bradshaw shrugged and said, "It's your company, Captain. I don't suppose it's occurred to you that a man facing a general court-martial might see having a fast horse and his sidearms as a golden opportunity?"

Conway frowned and said flatly, "No, sir, I don't. If we'd expected Corporal Dorfler to desert, we'd have locked him in the guardhouse instead of sending him to his quarters. The man has a wife here on the post to come back to, even if he wasn't with an officer and other men, and even if he was fool enough to light out alone with Mr. Lo on the prod."

"I suppose so. It occurred to me that other men have deserted a wife for less reason. I notice you still refer to him as a corporal."

"He *is* a corporal, until a court-martial says different, sir."

"Don't you think he'll be convicted?"

"Frankly, I do. But he hasn't been convicted yet, and as I've said before, we're under strength."

Phoebe Mills had been trying to follow the conversation. She was aware that the two men were growling at one another about something, but she wasn't too certain as to what it was. She asked, "Who is this Dorfler and what did he do?"

Conway glanced down and said, "Army matter, ma'am," in the stubborn-little-boy voice his wife recognized as embarrassment. She smiled at the younger woman and said, "I'll explain it to you later, dear heart. You'll be meeting poor Wilma Dorfler later."

"Oh, it's her husband who's in trouble, then? What did he do? Is it a military secret?"

The IG man was no more willing than any other officer and gentleman to go into such details in mixed company. But he was more used to social patter than were most officers, so he smiled at the blonde and said, "The lad behaved irregularly on guard duty, ma'am."

"Heavens, is that all? From the way you men were talking, I thought he was in real trouble."

Nobody answered. Conway put his cup down and got to his feet as he said, "My apologies, all. I have to get back to the orderly room. I'm sure you travelers will be comfortable. But if there are any problems, you'll find me in my office."

The IG man and Taylor remained behind as Conway left. But Flora excused herself and followed her husband outside. She caught up with him out front and said, "You silly old growly bear, you had me very worried about those naughty children."

Conway sighed down at her and said, "I'm worried, too, honey. I don't see how I'm going to get out of breaking the boy, at the very least."

"Pooh, aren't you and Matt giving him another chance?"

"He's back on active duty, for the moment. But that IG snoop in there is waiting to see what I mean to do about him."

"That's silly, dear heart. He's not the commanding officer here. You are. What could he do if you just let the poor boy off with a good scolding?"

Conway shook his head. "Dorfler's *had* a good scolding. I'll catch more than that from Regiment if they get an IG report about lax discipline. Can't you get it through your pretty head, Flora? Dorfler committed a capital offense."

"Oh, piffle. He stole a kiss. Who on earth could hang a man for that?"

"The U.S. Army. Nobody's mad at him for making love to his wife. He was off his post during an emergency. But don't worry about them hanging him. I'm sure we can get him off with a fine and reduction to private, if I put in a word for him."

Flora pursed her lips and said, "Warner Conway, you'll do no such thing. I told poor Wilma I'd see that the charges were dropped! For heaven's sake, they barely have enough to live on as it is! I told the poor child I'd speak to you about promoting him to sergeant."

Despite himself, Conway laughed. "Flora, I love you. You are the most adorable lunatic this side of the regimental commander."

She said, "Well, I know it's hard to promote men with that mean old President Hayes pinching pennies back East. But I'll forgive you if you'll promise not to take the boy's two pathetic little stripes away."

She sounded as though she meant it. Conway glanced uneasily around and said, "Look, Flora, I wasn't going to tell you, and I want you to keep this to yourself, but I did have a word with Ben Cohen."

Flora clapped her hands and said, "Oh, Maggie will be so pleased. She doesn't really like to sleep alone, and now that her man is on our side . . ."

"Damn it, honey," Conway cut in, "you're not to say a word to any of the other people on the post about this. I don't even know what Ben has in mind. I just mentioned the matter and he said he'd see what he could do."

"I understand. It means old growly Ben will pull one of his sneaky sergeant's tricks. Remember the time he got us those bottles of champagne for our anniversary party, dear? By the way, I've never quite understood where those bottles and that turkey came from."

"Don't ask. There are things best left unmentioned in officers' country. I don't want you talking about Dorfler to the other women, either. I mean it, Flora."

"Not even Maggie? She's really terribly cross with poor Ben."

"I know. She's got a big mouth, too. Look, kitten, I know the two of you are just busting to comfort that young girl, but we're in the middle of an IG inspection, and it's better to let those kids sweat than to really mess things up with Colonel Bradshaw sniffing for blood."

Flora glanced back at the doorway and said, "Oh, he seems to be a nice man, dear. I don't think he really wants to cause anyone any trouble."

"Honey, it's his job to cause trouble. He's supposed to report me if we're missing a tent peg. For God's sake, don't try your charm on *him*!"

"Whatever do you mean, dear heart? Have you ever seen me look at another man?"

Conway sighed and said, "Honey, you don't *look*, you flirt outrageously. Fortunately, I know you well enough to just feel sorry for them. But leave that poor short colonel alone. Dorfler's only hope is that Bradshaw will leave under the assumption that we're doing something about the fool kid. So don't encourage Bradshaw even to think about it. If he mentions Dorfler at all in his official report, not even Ben Cohen and the Sergeant's Club will be able to save the boy's hide."

Inside, the IG officer they were worried about was talking to young Mr. Taylor. Bradshaw said, "I assume your Lieutenant Kincaid is a man who keeps his wits about him. Frankly, he's surer of himself than I'd be in his position."

Taylor looked puzzled. "I don't follow you, sir. Matt has met Mr. Lo before, and he's got enough men with him to handle the average war party."

"Quite. He's also riding with an armed man at his back who's facing a general court-martial."

Taylor looked incredulous and said, "Dorfler, sir? I doubt very much that the kid would have any reason to aim his weapon at his own officer's back!"

"You don't, eh? I'm glad you feel so confident of your men. More than one of us has caught a stray round rather mysteriously in a firefight. And as I understand it, Lieutenant Kincaid is the main witness as well as the arresting officer in Dorfler's case."

# five

Out on the open prairie, five miles or more from the post, Matt Kincaid had his own reservations about the hastily thrown-together patrol he was leading. Windy Mandalian was probably more useful at the moment conducting his own investigation back in Tipi Town, but Matt would have felt more comfortable with the savvy scout on point. Matt hadn't wanted to pull any of the fresh men off work details assigned to them by the forbidding Sergeant Cohen, so that had left him with few to choose from. He'd stolen one of the new men from guard detail, since Private Wilson had been supernumerary, and was more useful out here on the trail than lounging in the guardhouse. The other two had been on KP and stable detail, and hence as unavailable as if Cohen had sent them to the moon. He had Wilson riding close, where he could keep an eye on him. Wilson seemed a bit older than most recruits and he sat a horse well. But you never knew what a new man would do when the balloon went up.

He had three of the regular company fuck-ups with him this afternoon. It couldn't be helped. The wild Irishman, Malone, rode point, five hundred yards ahead. Malone had good eyes and was a fair soldier, when he was sober. Stretch Dobbs trailed far to the rear as getaway rider. Stretch wasn't a bad soldier. He probably didn't pull more dumb stunts or try to get away with anything any other man in the outfit didn't, but he had a problem he seemed unaware of. He stood six foot seven in his socks, and no matter where he was or what he was doing, the first sergeant couldn't help but notice. Matt had told Stretch more than once that a soldier who stood out in a crowd had certain advantages as well as disadvantages. Tall soldiers won more medals, since nobody overlooked them when they did right. But tall soldiers who tried to sneak into formation late, or were sneaking a smoke on the far side of the parade when they were supposed to be somewhere else, spent a lot of time digging pit latrines. Dobbs couldn't seem to grasp this. He was probably a bit dull-witted as well as willing and able. He'd have made a perfect Prussian infantryman.

Riding near the untried Wilson *was* an ex-Prussian soldier: Private Wolfgang Holzer. Matt kept him near at hand because while Holzer was a spit-and-polish automaton who obeyed every command he understood, he didn't understand English very well. The German immigrant had been grabbed almost off the docks by a recruiting sergeant who should have been ashamed of himself. He had apparently signed his enlistment papers in the sincere belief that he was filing on a homestead claim out West.

Off to Matt's right rode the troubled Corporal Dorfler, guarding the flank of the central column. Matt knew the old man and the first sergeant were cooking something up regarding Dorfler. He wasn't sure he wanted to know what it was. As the arresting officer, he couldn't back off. He hoped the kid understood. If he didn't, that was tough. Meanwhile they both had a job to do.

Corporal Kildare had ridden out with Matt the night before, and like Matt, he sat a fresh mount with a tired butt. He'd told Kildare to knock off for the rest of the day, but Kildare was eager. He probably hadn't heard that President Hayes had vetoed another military appropriation, or that the chances for promotion were better in the Mexican Army, for the foreseeable future. Kildare had a girl back East, and he was waiting for another stripe before he sent for her. Matt hoped they wouldn't be too old to have children by the time Kildare got it.

They were following the wagon trace and the telegraph line, of course. Both ran string-straight over gently rolling prairie, so one could see for miles, and for all those miles, the wire seemed to be up. The afternoon sky was a cloudless bowl of cobalt blue. The prairie met the sharp horizon the exact color of a mountain lion's hide, and the rises all about reminded Matt of the quietly tense muscles of a big cat.

He noticed that the new man, Wilson, was breathing hard for a man riding at a walk. He glanced over and saw that the recruit was ashen-faced and blue-lipped. He reined in beside Wilson and said, "Lean forward over the swells and try to get your head as far down as you can without falling off. It's mountain sickness. You'll get over it."

Wilson remained upright as he licked his blue lips with a puzzled frown and said, "Mountain sickness, sir?" as he stared blankly around them at the nearly flat prairie.

Matt explained, "We're over a mile above sea level, soldier. It takes a spell for a man or a mount to get used to the thinner air. Where are you from, Wilson?"

"The Carolinas, sir," the recruit said. "I reckon growing up in the Tidewater left something out of my education. I'd heard it was hard to catch one's breath in hill country, but this sure feels silly."

Matt smiled slightly. "I know. I'm a Connecticut Valley boy. I felt pretty weak the first few weeks out here. Now I only notice it when I boil an egg on the trail. Takes five minutes out here to boil a three-minute egg."

Wilson took a deep breath and said, "I thank you for telling me, sir. I feel better now that I know I'm not coming down with some ague." Then, to his credit, Wilson asked, "May I ask what this funny air means to my mount, sir?"

Matt said, "Indian ponies, raised out here, don't seem to notice. Our remount critters soon get used to the altitude, like anyone else. Although the War Department will send green troops out here on sea-level horses to look foolish chasing Indians. These horses are all acclimatized, and of course they stand a couple of hands taller than your average Indian pony."

Matt waited, testing, and Wilson nodded and said, "I see, sir. That gives us the advantage in a long chase."

Matt nodded and said, "Right. Mr. Lo can outrun us for the first couple of miles, riding lighter. After that, the longer legs of our grain-fed mounts wear them down. Back in the late sixties, the Pony Express played tag with Indian ponies for a good eighteen months and never lost a mail pouch. You've probably read a lot of nonsense about the noble redskin's noble stallions, especially since the Little Big Horn, but you don't beat a well-bred saddle horse on a half-wild scrub. There'd be no point in breeding horses if you could. Let me ask you something while we're on the subject, Wilson. I've explained about the air being thinner out here. Assuming that horse you're riding is used to it, what *is* there left for you to worry about?"

Wilson thought for a moment. Then he nodded and said, "Chills, sir. I noticed your stables were a mite fancy and clean, even for army. These critters have to be kept dry and rubbed down proper so the thin air won't stiffen 'em after a workout. They likely need more water than usual, too."

Matt nodded and said, "Yes, water is a problem out here, and one place Mr. Lo has the advantage. His half-wild stock is used to living on dry grass and alkali water. How are you feeling now? I see a little more color in your face."

"I'll make it, sir. Now that I know what it is, I'll remind myself to breathe deeper."

Matt looked around and saw nothing of interest. He knew the recruit was all right, and chatting with the enlisted men wasn't his normal custom. But his curiosity was aroused. He said, "You don't have to answer this, soldier. I read your enlistment papers, and if you want to say this is your first hitch, we'll say no more about it."

"Sir?"

"You don't talk like a recruit, Wilson. You sit your mount like an old cavalryman, too."

Wilson shrugged and said, "I did some riding in the Wilderness Campaign, sir."

"I see. What rank did you hold in the Confederate Army, Wilson?"

Wilson looked away and murmured, "It was a long time ago, sir. I took my oath to the Union after Appomattox, if that's what you're worried about."

"I'm not worried about you, Wilson. Our company bugler's an old reb. An ex-officer of the Army of Virginia saved my tail against Mr. Lo last summer. If it's any comfort to you, I was too young to make the War. It was over long before I graduated from the Point."

"Yessir," Wilson replied. "It was a long time ago for everybody. I took this job because I needed it. We lost our plantation in the War, and soldiering is the only other skill I have."

"You were an officer, weren't you." It was a statement rather than a question.

Wilson nodded. "It was a long time ago, sir, and I know my place. You won't find me putting on airs or fighting the War all over in the suttler's bar."

Matt nodded and said, "Carry on, soldier," as he spurred his mount a length forward. The horizon was still empty and the overhead wire was intact as far as he could see. Mr. Lo wasn't even making smoke talk. The wire could simply have broken by itself. But sooner or later they'd find where it was down, and then they'd fix it and ride back. Army routine was like that. Dull as dishwater, six days out of seven. It was the seventh you had to worry about. A man could adjust to routine boredom. Many a dead soldier had. The real strain of soldiering was fighting to stay alert when not a goddamned thing was going on. He glanced over at poor Dorfler, who'd just learned that lesson the hard way. Matt couldn't remember how many nights he'd stood guard, bored and wishing that something, anything, would happen. He knew that many a soldier had fallen asleep or left his post during a long, tedious tour on guard. Most times, you could get away with it. He'd have never noticed when Dorfler had slipped into his quarters for those stolen moments, if the scouts hadn't picked that time to ride in all lathered and shot up. But the kid had lost his gamble. The odds had been a thousand to one against his being caught, but that was how it happened.

Matt heard a shout and forgot about the unfortunate Dorfler as he swung his gaze to the left flank. An Indian in full feathers and paint sat a spotted pony on a rise about a mile to the north. The Indian wasn't moving. Corporal Kildare had been the one on that side who'd shouted, and now Kildare was riding up the slope toward the Indian at full gallop, alone!

Matt shouted, "Kildare! No!" And then Wilson had broken ranks and was following Kildare! Matt spurred his own mount after them, calling back, "Cover down on the road, goddamnit! Corporal Dorfler, take command and hold!"

Kildare and the trailing Wilson had an impossible lead on Matt as the three of them sped up the slope at the impassive Indian. Matt saw that the buck was wearing the blue paint of a Cheyenne Crooked Lancer. As the over-eager Kildare approached rifle range, the Indian swung his mount around and dropped over the far side of the rise with a derisive, leisurely wave. Kildare followed, cresting the rise at a dead run as he drew his pistol, but Wilson had reined in and dropped lightly to the ground, rifle in hand, to follow on foot.

Matt stopped near Wilson's horse and did the same. He gained on the ex-Confederate as he legged it up the slope with his own rifle, either because he was in better shape or because Wilson was becoming cautious as he approached the skyline. Matt knew it was the latter as he caught up and they both moved on, a few yards apart, in a crouching run. Wilson glanced Matt's way and said, "I tried to catch him, sir."

Matt said, "I can see you know the form. Belly by that soapweed down the ridge and cover me. I'm cutting to the right."

As he moved on and up, Matt heard a fusillade on the far side and swore softly. As he dropped to his knees to crawl the last few yards, a riderless horse tore over the ridge between him and Wilson. It was Kildare's mount. Matt didn't follow it with his eyes. He knew it would head down to join its stablemates, and that one of the men with Dorfler would tend to it.

Matt took a deep breath and rolled himself over the ridge fast, not looking until he had his own outline below the blue sky behind him. He spotted a clump of soapweed and slithered behind it, then he raised his head. A half-dozen Indians were trotting their ponies over another rise, far out of rifle range. One of them waved as they dropped out of sight again. Matt got wearily to his feet and walked slowly down to the blue-clad figure lying facedown in the grass. He knew, before he knelt to feel Kildare's throat, that the kid was dead. Nobody had ever looked as dumb and dead.

He looked back up the slope. Wilson was still belly-down in that other clump, covering him, as Matt had told him to. At least one soldier in this man's army knew enough to do as he was told.

Matt walked up to Wilson's position and said, "Stay here and cover him. They may have ideas about his hair. They didn't get it and I don't want them to. I don't have to tell you what he did wrong, do I?"

Wilson said, "No, sir. I knew what he was doing wrong. That's why I went after him. I'm sorry I didn't wait for orders, sir. I lost my head. It won't happen again."

"I don't mind a man thinking on his own, as long as he thinks right. I'll get his pony and we'll lash him to it. I'll be back directly, Corporal Wilson."

"Corporal, sir?"

"Acting corporal, second squad, first platoon. Your platoon sergeant will be Gus Olsen. He was in the War, too—on our side, but you'll just have to manage. God knows when we'll manage confirmation and pay for you, but as you can see, Mr. Lo just left us with a vacancy on the TO. What's the matter, don't you want the job?"

"Of course, sir. But I just got here. I never saw an Indian before!"

Matt looked back down the slope and said, "You moved right when you did. That's more than that poor son of a bitch can say."

They found the place where the Indians had cut the wire, two miles further to the east. Stretch Dobbs climbed up and spliced it. If he thought it was an exercise in futility, he didn't say so. It was all they could do, in any case. Mr. Lo could cut the wire again whenever he felt like it; they all knew that. Privately, Matt hoped the original cut had been meant only to set up the ambush. Mr. Lo didn't really care if the white men talked to one another over the Singing Wire. He knew there wasn't much that Regiment could do about another dead soldier unless Washington ordered them to. Windy Mandalian said Sitting Bull and some of the other medicine men subscribed to the *Army Times* and *The Washington Post*, so they knew Indian policy as well as anyone else did. It was unfortunate that none of those political hacks back East could subscribe to an Indian newspaper and find out what *their* policy was this summer.

The repair patrol got back to Outpost Nine after sunset and, of course, late for grub. But after they'd seen to their mounts, Dutch Rothausen fed them, swearing about the extra work as he sullenly served second helpings and threw in some apple pie meant for Sunday. Nobody had much to say about the body they'd brought back, lashed across Kildare's saddle. Matt saw that the men were going to be all right, so, after sharing a cup of joe with them, he left them to the tender mercies of the mad mess sergeant and headed for the orderly room to do the paperwork.

Corporal Dorfler followed him out and caught up with him on the dark parade. Matt stopped and said, "Well, Dorfler?"

The younger NCO stared uneasily up at Matt and said, "I, uh, was wondering if I'm still under arrest, sir."

Matt said, "You were placed under arrest, weren't you? I don't remember hearing that you'd been tried, do you?"

"No, sir. I guess they'll bust me, huh?"

"If you're goddamned lucky. I suppose you think that riding out with me this afternoon rates some consideration?"

"No, sir. I didn't do anything anybody owes me anything for."

"I'm glad you said that. You did hold steady under fire and you did carry out my instructions. So did everyone else, save for that poor fool, Kildare. If it's any comfort to you, I'd have busted his ass for that fool stunt, had he lived. Flank guards do not go into business for themselves in this army. Is there anything else you wanted to see me about?"

"No, sir. I just wanted to make sure it was all right to join my wife in our quarters."

"Have you read the bulletin board since we got back, Dorfler?"

Dorfler looked confused and said, "Bulletin board, sir?"

"Big square thing. In front of the first sergeant's doorway. They put things on it that a good soldier is supposed to read. Is this too deep for you, Dorfler?"

"Sir, I read the bulletin board every morning."

"Read it again. Sergeant Cohen's had all day to post things on it. I know this sounds terribly complicated, but they do that so that they don't have to look for a man when they want him for something."

Dorfler looked perfectly miserable as he said, "Yessir. No excuse, sir," and turned away.

Matt sighed and said, "Hey, Dorf?"

"Sir?"

"Go to your quarters and give my compliments to your missus. You have maybe fifteen minutes. I don't ordinarily read the board for anyone but myself, but you're pulling CO tonight. I know, because I suggested it to Sergeant Cohen myself."

"I understand, sir."

"No complaints?"

"No, sir. I thank you for giving me time to explain it to Wilma."

"Move it out, then. I'll cover for you exactly fifteen minutes from the time I reach my desk. I'm not doing this for you. It's a favor for your wife. She's not on my shit list. But in case you're wondering, Dorfler, you are."

Then he returned Dorfler's salute and strode on, annoyed at himself for acting so soft. It was hard not to feel sorry for the little girl alone over there in those enlisted quarters. He knew she'd spend the next few nights alone, too. He wondered if it would do any good to explain to her that it was for her Jimmy's own good. But he knew he couldn't. How in hell could you ride a man into the ground if his own wife knew you were trying to save his ass?

Matt found First Sergeant Cohen alone in the orderly room when he got there. He nodded and said, "Dorfler knows he's supposed to hold that desk down tonight, Ben. What are you doing here so late?"

Cohen said, "Well, sir, I thought I'd catch up on some paperwork, since I have no happy home of my own to go to, anyway."

Matt smiled and said, "Come on, Ben. You must have told Maggie your plan, even if you won't tell us."

"Plan, sir?"

"Oh, shit, I know I'm a fucking officer, but I'm not wearing new gold bars. I don't know what you have in mind, but for Pete's sake tell your wife."

Cohen sighed and said, "I can't, sir. She's taken that fool kid's weeping Wilma under her wing. She's already promised the fool girl that I'm going to save her husband's ass or die a slow, lingering death. I can't make our hazing stick if I give in an inch. Miss Flora's ganged up on us, too. Women just don't understand the way things have to be."

Matt nodded and said, "I'll be in my office. I want to know if Dorfler gets here even one minute after the hour. Is there anything else you want me to do, aside from riding his ass?"

Cohen glanced at the filing cabinet and said, "Well, sir, I do think we ought to pull his stripes. He can still pull his regular duties as an *acting* corporal."

"Yes, but Captain Conway's worried about the loss in pay. We'd have to ship his wife home if he was reduced to private, wouldn't we?"

Cohen looked uncomfortable and said, "The lieutenant asked for my suggestions, sir."

"Ben, are you pulling something contrary to the ARs?"

"Nothing any officer has to worry about, sir."

"I see. All right. You do what you think best and I'll stop asking questions. But for Christ's sake, be careful. By the way, what are the chances of getting permanent stripes for Corporal Wilson?"

"I'm working on that, sir. Kildare left a blank in the pay-book, but if anyone asks about seniority, we're in trouble. There's no corporal overdue in Easy Company, right now. But there are a couple of married NCOs at Regiment who've been waiting for their stripes a long time."

"In other words, Wilson will have to lead his squad on a private's pay for now?"

"I didn't say that, sir. I said I was working on it. Wilson's on his second hitch, remember?"

"Second hitch? For God's sake, he's only been in the U.S. Army a little over two months. His previous military service was in the Confederate Army!"

"Yessir. You know that and I know that, but my hand-writing's not that clear, and it's funny how a C.S.A. can look like a U.S.A. when you fill in the blank under 'prior service.'"

Matt laughed incredulously and said, "Damn it, Ben, that's outright forgery!"

But Cohen said, "Begging the lieutenant's pardon, it ain't. Under the ARs *and* civilian criminal code, forgery is the fal-sification of records for gain. Since anyone can see *I* haven't a thing to gain by getting another man his stripes, I'd say the only charge they'd have, if anyone ever found out, would be bad handwriting or maybe simple stupidity. Wilson isn't sign-ing his promotion papers. He's not supposed to see them before the promotion is confirmed or denied. Those fat-cat officers on the promotion board know how stupid us enlisted men are, and I sort of doubt they'd notice a *C* sort of scrootched on its side like it could be a U. Especially since they'd hardly be expecting to see it."

"Hmm. I can see that slipping past. But he was an officer in the Confederacy. His service record would sure look sort of weird, wouldn't it?"

"I don't see why, sir. I disremember what he said his rank was, the last time he served. The spaces don't call for much gossip. They just ask if a man has prior service. I'm assuming he must have served under the same serial number, since it's the only one I have on file. You don't have to worry about the details, sir. That's what I'm here for."

"Right. I don't want to know. I'd be curious to hear if you've pulled this sort of thing before, but you've lied enough to me tonight. I've got my own paperwork to tend to, Ben. Talk to you later."

Matt went into his own office off the orderly room and

struck a match, lit the brass lamp on his desk, and sat down. He took some stationery from a drawer and stared morosely down at it, wondering how to begin.

What did one say to the family of an idiot? "Dear Folks: Regret to inform you that your son acted like an asshole and fell for one of the oldest tricks in Mr. Lo's book"?

He took out a cigar box and placed a campaign ribbon on the green blotter by the accusingly blank paper. Every soldier serving west of the Big Muddy rated the red-and-blue ribbon awarded for the "Indian Wars," but Kildare's family might take some comfort in it.

He muttered, "What the hell," and took out another one for the girl Kildare had been writing to. He'd find her address when he got around to going through the dead man's kit. She didn't rate a letter or a ribbon under regulations, but she'd been waiting a long time.

He started to write. Then he swore and balled the paper up. He wasn't any goddamned author. He knew what he had to say, but how the hell was he supposed to say it to a dead man's kith and kin?

He was working on his third rough draft when he heard a soft rap on the door. The door was ajar and he said, "Come," expecting it to be Dorfler. He glanced at the banjo clock on the wall as he remembered he'd forgotten to keep track of the time. It was Dorfler, but the CO had the blonde woman, Miss Mills, with him. Dorfler said, "This lady asked to see you, sir."

Matt rose behind his desk and nodded as Phoebe Mills came in. He stepped around the desk and ushered her to a seat between the desk and the sod wall as the CO left.

The pale blonde waited until he'd taken his own seat before she said, "I wanted a word with you in private, sir."

"Call me Matt. What can I do for you, Miss Phoebe?"

"I didn't want to intrude when you and those others rode in with that dead trooper."

"Soldier, Miss Phoebe," he corrected her. "We're mounted infantry, not cavalry."

"Is that important?"

"It would be to Corporal Kildare. He died wearing infantry blue. I'm trying to write a letter to his folks about it. It's just starting to hit me. But let's get to what's troubling *you* this evening."

Phoebe stared thoughtfully at the little ribbons on the desk and said, "Our scout wants to press on. He says this fight is only between the army and the Indians. He says—"

"I know what Colonel Whiz-Bang says, Miss Phoebe. But if you want permission to leave, you came to the wrong man. In the first place, I'm not the commandant here. If I were, I'd still say no. It's pitch black outside and we still don't know what's going on. Those Cheyenne we met could have been just a gang of kids out for trouble. Or the whole Dakota Confederacy could be on the warpath. Pick anything in between and I'll sign it."

"Colonel Hawkins says the trail is cooler after sundown, and he says the Indians never attack at night. They have this superstition about fighting in the dark—"

"I read the same ridiculous magazine, Miss Phoebe," he cut in. "It's not true. Indians prefer cavalry charges in broad daylight for the same reasons Napoleon and everyone else always have. It smarts to ride into a ditch or a telegraph pole in the dark at full gallop. Indians creep up on you after dark, and they're very good at creeping. Most warriors count their first coup by stealing a pony or lifting some hair under cover of darkness. I'd better have a talk with your guide. Meanwhile, it's not costing any of you a nickel to stay here inside the walls. What's the big hurry? Is our army grub really that awful?"

"On the contrary," she said, "we've been treated very kindly. But my fiancé is waiting for me in California and he'll be very worried if we arrive late."

Matt pointed with his chin at the blank papers on his desk and said, "I'm trying to write a letter to a fiancée who was waiting, Miss Phoebe. I think she'd feel a lot better about Corporal Kildare being tardy than she's going to feel about anything I can possibly offer in the way of comfort. We have the wire up. Why don't you write a message and I'll see if we can patch through to Western Union."

Phoebe brightened and said, "Why, that's very thoughtful, Matt. I confess I never thought of it!"

"I know. I'm surprised Colonel Billy Bobtail didn't know the transcontinental telegraph has been up for some time. Here, why don't you take my seat and write away? I'll leave you in privacy."

"I don't mind. You're going to have to read my letter to send it, in any case, aren't you?"

"Yes, ma'am. Don't write anything naughty. I have to talk

to the CO anyway, and it's boring to watch a lady writing love letters."

He left her there as he stepped outside. He didn't really know what else he could do to make poor Dorfler uncomfortable, but he'd think of something. It was his job.

He was spared the chore as Windy Mandalian came in, saying, "They told me you was here, Matt. Heard you lost one this afternoon."

"Yeah. The old skyline trick. What did you find out over in Gray Elk's camp?"

Windy shifted his cud and said, "They say they don't know a thing, which is sort of interesting, when you think on it."

"You mean they're lying?"

"Don't suspicion so, Matt. Injuns have fibbed to me in the past, so I'm fair slick at questioning the rascals. You wasn't listening to me, boy. I said they hadn't *heard* nothing, or *seed* nothing. I mean, they didn't know about them kids we've seed skulking about to the west."

"Couldn't they be lying about that?"

"Sure they could, but why? If any of the kids from Gray Elk's band was playing over there, they'd *know* we seed 'em. Crying Boy waved to one, and the Cheyenne waved back. What would Gray Elk be trying to hide? The kids we scouted wasn't doing nothing. Why lie when all he had to say was, 'Sure, some of the little varmints was over yonder, hunting rabbit'? You know Gray Elk's granddaughter is sort of fond of me, and she has a couple of kids by God only knows who. I whittled and jawed with the little rascals, after I said a proper howdy to their mama. They like to tease me and call me their uncle. Her oldest boy says that maybe when he grows up he'll git to lift my hair. I suspicion he means it, the little bastard."

"What's the point, Windy?"

"The point is that if any kids from Tipi Town had been fooling around over here, he'd be bragging on it to the other kids. You know how they are. Little runts like to count coup, and all sorts of fool things count. A kid who'd snuck up close enough to arrow one of us would brag about it, even if he didn't shoot his fool arrow. I'm just about dead certain that them Cheyenne skulking about are from another band. I was setting there, jawing with Gray Elk in the flesh, when an Arapaho squaw come running in to tell us all about you boys riding in with a body. Everybody over yonder was surprised as hell, unless they're damned good actors."

"Back up. How do you account for Arapaho knowing about it before we sent word to you?"

"Shit, Matt, she was one of the gals who come over here regular to beg water from the kitchen. I suspicion the suttler's been more'n friendly with this particular one, but that's neither here nor there. She wasn't with no Cheyenne Crooked Lancers this afternoon. She was here at the outpost."

"I'd better have a word with the suttler. He's not supposed to trade with Indians."

"Hell, he ain't trading with 'em, he just screws 'em. Don't go messing up a good thing for another white man, sojer boy. I could fix you up with a nice little Cheyenne breed, if you wasn't so persnickety."

"Another time. If those troublemakers aren't from Gray Elk's band, who else do you have in mind, Windy?"

"Well, Medicine Wolf has his people over in the Pipestone Draw to the northwest."

"Medicine Wolf? He's supposed to be on the reservation, a good hundred miles from here."

Windy shrugged and said, "Hell, he knows that, Matt. He's not a mean Injun. He just likes to wander some. He was out under Red Cloud last summer, but he's signed the treaty and even made his peace with Gray Elk and the other friendlies. I don't think he's out looking for a fight. He's just hunting robes and digging pipestone and such."

"Right," Matt said. "They're all so sweet that butter wouldn't melt in their mouths. Those bucks who ambushed Kildare were Cheyenne Crooked Lancers, Windy. Not Arapaho, not Sioux. Cheyenne."

"Blue paint?"

"Damned right. I'm not color-blind. Arapaho wear green and Sioux wear red and I know a Crooked Lancer's feathers when I see them, too. Are there any other Cheyenne bands camped near enough to matter?"

Windy shrugged and said, "Don't know. I'd best find out. I'm fixing to be sort of surprised if either Gray Elk or Medicine Wolf are in back of this trouble, though. I knows 'em both."

"Why can't it be Medicine Wolf? He's fought us many a time before."

"That's what I just said, Matt. I fought the rascal. What happened to Kildare ain't his style. Medicine Wolf's a man of his word and a stand-up fighter. If he was sore at anybody, he'd say so. Then he'd come at you with ever'thing but the kitchen sink, and if that didn't work, he'd throw the sink. He's an old, proud warrior. He'd never mess with picking folks off Apache-style. I reckon I'd best ride over to the foothills and have me a word with Medicine Wolf. Some of his young men may be acting foolish and he'd want to know about it."

"You want to go alone?"

"Don't *want* to. *Have* to. It'd scare the shit out of Medicine Wolf to see a platoon of soldiers riding down on him. I can get in and likely get out. I won't tell 'em I'm coming and I'll be under the chief's protection as I leave. I'll let you know what he has to say."

"All right. When are you riding, Windy?"

"Sooner I git started, the sooner it'll all be over."

The scout left with no further discussion. Matt stared thoughtfully at Dorfler, seated at Cohen's desk. He couldn't think of a thing he wanted to say to the worried kid, so he went back to join Phoebe Mills in his office.

The blonde had finished her short telegram, of course. Matt took it from her and put it in his dispatch folder on the desk without reading it. She smiled shyly and said, "You're right. It is hard to write mush when you know a lot of people are going to be spelling it out a letter at a time."

He said, "At least you were able to write something. I'm still stuck."

She nodded and asked, "Would you like for me to try? I know how to spell, and a woman's handwriting might seem softer."

He said, "You don't understand. Officially, the captain is supposed to send the letters. I'm his assistant, so I get to make the rough drafts. Then he'll copy and sign. Besides, what could you write? You weren't there. You never met Kildare."

She picked up the pencil and said, "I was an English major. Why don't you just tell me about the boy in your own words, and I'll see to the spelling and punctuation."

Matt shrugged. "There's not much to say. Kildare behaved stupidly and started chasing Indians the way an untrained pup chases a cat. Coyotes use the same ruse to get a farm dog alone on the prairie. He rode right into a firing squad they'd set up on the far side of an unscouted rise."

"It's going to sound nicer if we just say he was brave,"

Phoebe pointed out. "Couldn't he have been leading a charge?"

"Why not? It's not going to bring him back, but you're right about it sounding better. Yeah, let's say 'killed in action against superior numbers.'"

"I'm going to say he *fell* in battle, gallantly upholding the honor of his regiment. I read that somewhere. It sounds ever so much less brutal than 'killed.' They'll want to hear how devoted his men were to him and how you officers respected him, don't you think?"

Matt nodded and said, "I know what they want. It's not the first time I've had to do this. It's a little tough to make up mush about a fool."

She said, "Just talk to me about the boy and his squad. Tell me what their job was and I'll try to make it sound important. I have the advantage of ignorance. Unlike yourself, I only feel sorry for the poor boy. I wouldn't know a good soldier from a poor one, so I only have to think of him out there on the prairie, all bloody and scalped."

Matt shook his head and said, "They didn't get his hair. The Cheyenne lit out before the rest of us could get near enough to matter."

"Oh, good. I'll mention that his comrades drove the Indians away to save his gallant form from further outrage."

Matt glanced at her rapidly moving hand and said, "You sure write fast and funny. Is that shorthand?"

"Of course. I'm just jotting down notes as we talk, and then I'll compose something loftier. I have enough on how he died. They won't want the gory details, and I don't mean to dwell on his death. You were going to tell me what sort of a boy he was. I'm going to try and fill most of the letter with how fond you were of him."

Matt snorted and growled, "He was hardly worth his stripes even when he listened to me. On his own, he was an idiot." Then he noticed that she wasn't writing. He leaned back and began to simply outline the late Corporal Kildare's job and the routine duties of the company. Phoebe made a mark from time to time. Matt was trying to be factual and laconic. He didn't know what he was giving away about himself and the way he felt about his men as he stared into space. Her voice was gentle when she said, "That's enough, Matt. I think I'll be able to explain what their son was doing out here, now that I've a better idea myself."

Matt nodded, wondering why his throat had a lump in it,

and decided he likely needed a smoke. The girl took another sheet of paper and began to write in longhand as he watched the way the lamplight played with her ash-blonde hair. She suddenly sniffed and dabbed at her face with her free hand. Matt said nothing, but she said, "Isn't this foolish? I never even met the boy."

He didn't answer. He knew his voice would crack, and she was right; the whole thing was silly. He'd been in the army long enough to know that the often mawkish sentimentality of an old soldier was the reverse side of his graveyard humor. Old soldiers stood at attention with tears in their eyes as the flag was lowered against the sunset, and toasted the memories of forgotten battles with husky voices because they weren't allowed to weep openly for a comrade they'd just seen killed before their eyes. The dead and wounded were dismissed with terse reportage. A man with a bullet in his gut wasn't expected to complain. The tears caught a soldier off-guard, unexpectedly, as he watched the colors being trooped, or heard the soft refrain of taps as he drifted off to sleep.

Damn, he was dying for a smoke. He knew she'd permit it, if he asked, but somehow it seemed wrong to ask, and he didn't know why. Something magical was happening and he was afraid to break the spell. So he sat in silence, watching her. Her softly illuminated features were focused down at the letter she was writing, and he knew she was unaware of his admiring and reflective gaze. He was wrong, of course. Phoebe Mills was very much aware of his eyes on her. She wrote very slowly and carefully. She was hoping she wouldn't blush when she finally finished and just had to look up and meet his gaze. What was happening? Why did this polite stranger's eyes make her feel so oddly? They were piercing eyes of gunmetal gray that seemed to reach deep inside a body, and she knew that a girl would have a hard time keeping secrets from Matt Kincaid. But what of it? She had no deep, dark sins to hide. What was she afraid he'd see?

Phoebe kept her eyes on the paper as she murmured, "I've just written a rough draft. I'll leave it to you and Captain Conway to fill in the address and so forth." Then she handed it across the desk to him, not looking at him. Their hands didn't touch as he took the scrap of notepaper. Why did it seem to shoot an electric shock through her own fingers as he took it?

Matt read the letter, giving Phoebe a chance to lean back

and compose herself as, now, she watched *his* face. Matt's eyelids were lowered, of course, as he read what she'd written. The lamplight softened the harsh treatment his clean-cut features had received at the hands of wind and sun and worry. She wondered how old he was, and if that dry crack near the corner of his mouth was windburn or if he'd hurt his lip that afternoon. She didn't think it would be seemly to ask, but she didn't know why.

He glanced up, catching her by surprise, but the gentle light was filled with mercy as well as other magic, and he didn't notice the sudden color of her flushed cheeks as he said, "You write a great letter of condolence, Miss Phoebe. I never could have made the kid look so noble." He paused for a moment, then continued, "I know I'm asking a lot, but . . . he had a girl."

"Oh, that *will* be a chore, won't it?"

"You don't have to. Officially, only the next of kin rate a letter from the CO. I thought I'd send her one of those fool ribbons, too. I guess you think I'm being sort of mushy, eh?"

"On the contrary, I think you're a very sweet and thoughtful man."

"Oh, hell. Sorry, ma'am, that just slipped out."

Phoebe dimpled and said, "I'd be proud to write a letter to his sweetheart. I'll just say more or less the same thing and throw in some of that mush you men all seem so afraid of."

She took another sheet of paper and started. Corporal Dorfler rapped on the jamb of the open doorway and said, "Begging the lieutenant's pardon, some riders are coming in. I thought you'd want to know, sir."

Matt glanced at the wall clock and rose with a puzzled frown. He said, "I'd better look into it. My apologies, ma'am. If I'm not back before you wish to go to your quarters, the corporal here will escort you to your door."

Phoebe nodded and Matt went out. He was on the orderly room veranda when the OD atop the parapet ordered the gates open and a double file of soldiers rode in with a Gatling gun mounted on a mule-drawn caisson. Matt stared at the brass barrels of the Gatling, gleaming in the moonlight, as the newcomers reined in. One detached himself from the rest of the detail and trotted over to where Matt stood, outlined by the open doorway behind him. The rider said, "First Lieutenant Fitzgerald, Heavy Weapons, reporting as ordered."

"Matt Kincaid, Company Ajutant. We weren't expecting

you, but of course you and your men are welcome, and we'd better see about making them comfortable." Matt turned to the door and yelled, "CQ! On the double!"

Dorfler popped out, stammering, "You ordered me to stay with the lady, sir."

"I know what I ordered. Show Lieutenant Fitzgerald's sergeant to the stables and tell the cooks to grub everybody. Then go get the top kick and he'll see about quarters and so forth."

As Fitzgerald dismounted, Matt said, "You'll refresh yourself in my quarters, of course, Lieutenant. Would you like for the CO to see to your mount?"

The new officer said, "No need for that. Old Baldy can stay where he is. I have him ground-trained."

Matt didn't answer as the heavy-weapons man joined him on the veranda. It was Fitzgerald's horse, not his. He'd met few experienced riders who'd leave a mount untended in the night air after riding all the way from Regiment. Hopefully the idiot knew something about *guns*.

As they stepped inside, Matt saw that Fitzgerald was a boyishly handsome man a little younger than himself. He didn't ask why the kid's campaign hat was gussied up the way it was, with the brim pinned to the crown by its crossed brass rifles; maybe he had some reason for wearing his hat like the Three Musketeers. Phoebe Mills had heard the commotion and was standing in the office doorway with her rough drafts. With an elaborate flourish, Fitzgerald removed his fancy hat as Matt introduced them. Matt said, "I'll have an escort for you directly, Miss Phoebe. Things are a bit confused right now, but—"

"Heavens," she cut in, "I'm certainly capable of finding my way to my quarters under a full moon."

Fitzgerald said, "I would be honored, ma'am."

Matt had had about enough. He said, "I'll be taking you to meet the CO as soon as I file your papers and figure out what's going on. Nobody told us you were coming, Lieutenant."

Fitzgerald reached into his tunic and withdrew a sheaf of transfer papers and dispatches in a pasteboard folder as he matched Matt's puzzled look with one of his own. He said, "They told us they were wiring you, uh, Matt. Didn't you receive the message from GHQ?"

Matt shook his head and took the papers as he answered,

"No. I'll check in a minute, but the wire's probably down again. Did they tell you about Mr. Lo's games with us this afternoon?"

"Of course. That's why we're here. The colonel had a fit when you wired about losing a man in that skirmish. It's all in that dispatch on top."

Matt opened the folder and ignored the temporary-duty slips of the twelve-man detail as he scanned the instructions from Regiment. He nodded and said, "Right. They've decided we could use a Gatling gun out here, and I'll not argue with that. But what's this about a punitive expedition against the Cheyenne? We don't know which band we tangled with, yet. We have a scout out, trying to find out, but—"

"I don't think GHQ is worried about petty details," Fitzgerald cut in. "My orders are to ride with Easy Company and just hose down any Indians you point out with Gatling fire."

Matt said, "I had that part figured out. I didn't think they'd sent a heavy-weapons detail to take photographs. But it's a little early for another Washita. We'd better find out how the Cheyenne Nation feels about a war this summer, before anybody goes off half-cocked."

Lieutenant Fitzgerald smiled smugly and replied, "I never go off half-cocked, Kincaid. My Gatling fires eight hundred rounds a minute, and it can be a very civilizing influence. I got the distinct impression that was how the colonel wanted his Cheyenne. Civilized!"

Phoebe Mills gasped and said, "Surely you gentlemen don't mean to fire on *good* Indians!"

Matt didn't answer. Fitzgerald laughed boyishly and said, "Don't you worry your pretty little head about it, ma'am. We all approve of good Indians. I happen to agree with General Sheridan's views on how you *make* any Indian a good Indian. He's always said the only good Indian is—"

"We'd better go see the captain," Matt cut in. But the girl had understood, and her face was pale as she stared in mingled distaste and dismay at both of them. Matt knew she was expecting him to take issue with the young twit's words, but the heavy-weapons man held equal rank, and the orders were from headquarters. There wasn't any point in arguing with Fitzgerald. He was only a symptom, not the disease.

# six

Windy Mandalian was spotted riding into the tipi ring at dawn, of course. But he was too close to Medicine Wolf's lodge for the Dog Soldiers to attack him without permission, so the weatherbeaten scout ignored the catcalls and threatening gestures as he steadied his mount. An arrow thudded into the sod in front of his pony, but the animal didn't shy. Windy had ridden this particular mount into Indian camps before. A pack of skinny yellow mongrels encircled him and growled as he reined in and dismounted in front of Medicine Wolf's tipi. The chief's lodge was patched with U.S. Army tenting, and the Stars and Stripes hung listlessly from one of the poles of its smoke ears. Medicine Wolf was off the reservation, but the flag announced that his heart was still good to the Great White Father.

Windy stood patiently, holding the reins of his pony. Some kids were peering shyly out from a nearby tipi. Windy knew their mother had told them to stay put. Windy didn't try to figure why. The band could be in a sullen mood or just worried about a white man in Pipestone Draw. White men weren't supposed to be on sacred ground, and the Cheyenne knew *they* weren't supposed to be here, either.

A million years went by. An ugly camp dog moved cautiously up to sniff at Windy's leg, teeth bared. Indian dogs seldom bit unless you kicked them, so Windy didn't. It was considered polite to call your dogs off a visitor, in Indian as well as polite white society. Windy made a mental note that if they weren't just feeling shy about something, they were acting downright inhospitable this morning.

The first dog was joined by another, emboldened by the stranger's inaction and the lack of instructions from its human masters. The second dog nipped experimentally at the fringe of Windy's leggings. The scout shifted his plug of tobacco and said conversationally, "If you're not careful, I aim to tell my hosts how partial I am to roast dog, you runty cur. You just go ahead and bite, if you've a mind to. But I'll remember you when I get to choose my supper."

A bearish man wrapped in a white buffalo robe ducked out of the chief's lodge and stood up, blinking in the morning sun as if he were surprised to see a white man standing there. The black eyes in the big Indian's wrinkled moonface were as hard as frozen lava, but he managed a slight smile as he said, "Heya, my heart soars to see my old enemy, Windy. Have you been drinking again? I see you have come alone to this place. Did you think this would be a good morning to die?"

Windy spat and replied, "Everybody dies, one day or another. I don't expect to die today. There's nobody around me but Cheyenne and other yapping puppies."

Medicine Wolf's smile became more genuine as he announced, "Hear me. I count coup. I have taken Crow hair and ponies. I have killed Pawnee. At the Battle of the Greasy Grass I killed one of your officers. I still have his horse. Would you like to see it?"

"No. If a Cheyenne can ride it, it must be a piss-poor mount. I gave a Pawnee squaw a pony once. Some Cheyenne tried to steal it. But they never. That squaw's pony was too spirited for a Cut Finger to ride out of camp."

"I believe the part about a Pawnee squaw. Pawnee women sleep with anybody. Since they are already diseased, it doesn't matter if they catch the crotch sickness all you Americans have. Is that why you all squat to piss, or is it because you are women who never learned to piss like men?"

"Don't know about the others. If you'll just kneel down and open your mouth, I'll show you I can piss standing up. Or would you just rather suck it?"

Medicine Wolf sighed and said, "It's a good thing for you I have the flag above my lodge this morning. You really carry the usual greetings onto dangerous ground, Windy. Have you eaten?"

"No. Are you offering?"

"You are standing before my lodge. I have to kill you or feed you; that is the Way. I don't think I want a war, right now. But one of these days, Windy . . ."

Then Medicine Wolf half-turned and called out in his own tongue. Two young squaws came out to spread a blanket on the trampled, dusty grass in front of the tipi. Medicine Wolf sat down and patted the wool at his side. One of the squaws took the reins of Windy's pony as the scout joined the chief on the blanket. Windy offered the Indian his cut plug of chewing tobacco. Medicine Wolf shook his head and said, "No. I said I would make you welcome. I didn't say I wanted to be friendly. I must think about that. First we will eat. Then you will tell me what brings you here."

Another, older squaw came out of the tipi and placed a communal bowl of parched corn and jerked antelope between them. Windy knew they had government rations that tasted better, to his way of thinking, but the offering was more for ceremony than for enjoyment. Medicine Wolf waited until Windy picked up a handful of parched corn before he said, "We don't have much real food to offer, these days. In the Shining Times we ate fat cow. Our women knew how to cook the things Matou put on Earth Woman's robe of grass."

"Yeah, I know," Windy said wearily. "Us white men came out here to shoot all your women and rape all your buffalo. Do we really have to go through all this bullshit, old son? We don't have much of an audience, and we know one another pretty well. If I don't get back pretty soon, the Americans are going to suspicion you of lifting my hair. You don't really want them looking for me out here, do you?"

Medicine Wolf frowned, spat out a mouthful of parched corn, and said, "*Pahah!* It didn't used to taste so dusty before I got used to flapjacks. You are a very rude person, even for an American. Why are you in such a hurry? Why should anybody think I'd hurt you? Haven't I made my mark on the treaty? I am not an evil person. If the Great White Father does not know this, you should tell him. Hear me, Windy. You know me. We have traded shots and brags. Have you ever known me to turn on a guest, even a foul-mouthed one I never invited to my tipi ring?"

Windy spat too, and said, "Fair is fair, Medicine Wolf. You could use a bath and you still wouldn't be pretty, but I've never knowed you to break your word, in peace or war. I told them that afore I rode out here."

"Then what is all this talk about the Americans thinking I would do an evil thing to you? Has somebody been saying bad things about me to the Americans? Heya! I'll bet it was Gray Elk! I told him he was an old woman when he refused to ride with me against Custer last summer! If Gray Elk has been saying bad things about me, I will get him. I don't care what the Indian Agent says. Hear me! I am a warrior! I have the right to defend myself!"

Windy said, "Simmer down. You got enough on your plate without another feud with Gray Elk. I was in his camp yesterday. He says he don't think you're on the warpath. He said you're an old fool, but a good person."

Medicine Wolf shrugged. "I don't care for him much, either. But if Gray Elk hasn't been spreading lies about me, who has? What is this about my being on the warpath? We are hunting. At least we would be hunting, if some damned white man hadn't driven all the game away from here. There used to be a fine stand of elk in this draw every year at this time. Now there is nothing. We shall soon be heading back to the reservation for the winter. What makes the Americans think we are on the warpath? Have I taken down the flag? Do you see paint on my face? What's wrong with you people? Can't you read sign?"

Windy said, "Hear me. The other night my Delaware and me were jumped by Indians in the dark. I could be mistaken about the color of their paint, but Crying Boy had seen them by daylight. He said they were Cheyenne."

"Bah, Delaware squat to piss."

"I have not finished. Yesterday they got a white man. Somebody cut the Singing Wire. When the soldiers rode out to fix it, they were ambushed by men wearing the insignia of the Crooked Lance Society. The Great White Father is expecting some explaining from his red children. So start talking."

The older man frowned and said, "The soldiers could have made a mistake. I don't like Delaware, but if another red man tells me to my face that he has fought Cheyenne, I think I might believe him if I could look into his eyes while he was speaking. When and where does Crying Boy want to meet with me?"

Windy had intended to ask trick questions. Either Medicine

Wolf was a better liar than anyone thought, or he hadn't heard. Windy decided to give up a pawn. "Crying Boy and the other Delaware who rode with me are dead. A white soldier is dead. So some Crooked Lancer is counting coup on three men. I am listening."

"Then hear me! What you say fills my heart with thunder. I am crying tears of blood. I don't care about the death of three old enemies. But I am president of the Crooked Lance Society in these parts. Nobody riding as a Crooked Lancer has any right to do so without telling me and the other elders of the society! You have made me very cross."

Windy nodded and said, "I hoped you might be. That's the main reason I rode out here to talk with you. If you say your band is keeping the peace, that's good enough for me. But some sons of bitches are out raising pure ned. Are there any other Cheyenne bands about that neither the BIA nor the army might know about?"

Windy knew that a less honorable man might jump at the out he'd just offered. So he tended to believe the chief when Medicine Wolf shook his head and said, "No. Gray Elk leads the only other Cut Fingers I know of within many days' ride. There are some Arapaho in the foothills to the west, but they wear green paint, as you know. They do not have a Crooked Lance Society. Could your Delaware and the soldiers be mistaken about the feathers and paint?"

Windy shrugged. "Everybody makes mistakes, but Lieutenant Kincaid don't make many as serious as that. What are we going to do about this mess, old son?"

Medicine Wolf made some secret signal and Windy noticed other older Indians drifting toward them, looking disinterested, as Medicine Wolf said, "I don't know. We have traded shots in honest battle, Windy. You have always been a good enemy. I think you speak straight when you say you don't want another war. What do *you* think we should do? Would they believe we were keeping our word if we just slipped back to the reservation and said no more about it, or do they want to use this business to humiliate us further?"

Windy stared down at the grass while the other elders joined them silently. There were a half-dozen of them. They hunkered down around the blanket, not looking at the white visitor. Windy spoke to Medicine Wolf alone as he said, "Hear me. The Americans don't want to rub the faces of good enemies in the dust. Your people have proven they are men. Nobody but a fool fights Those Who Cut Fingers when he doesn't have to."

Medicine Wolf realized the scout was speaking more politely now, in deference to his position in the band. His own voice took on tones of dignity. He wanted the others to understand this was no time for bantering between ex-enemies. He said, "Windy, you are almost a Real Person. We enjoyed fighting you. I would have been honored to dance before the people with your hair. I think you have a good heart. I believe you when you say you wish to keep the peace. We want to keep the peace, too. So speak and we will listen."

Windy said, "If you run for the reservation, it will look like some of your young men have gotten out of your control and that you and these other good men are frightened. I think you should all ride back to the outpost with me. You know Captain Conway has a good heart. Nobody else can attack you under the outpost's guns."

One of the elders snorted and said, "We don't need to be protected from anybody. We are men, not livestock."

Windy said, "I haven't finished. I'm not taking you back with me to keep somebody from stealing your ponies. I'm offering you an alibi. If you and Gray Elk are camped within sight of an army outpost, nobody can accuse your young men of being the ones the soldiers are looking for."

Medicine Wolf looked around at the other men. One of them looked at the sky as if he expected to see something up there, and said, "I will speak. I am Dancing Raven. I have been a Crooked Lance, and now I lead the Dog Soldiers here. When I was young I killed my grizzly, alone, with my knife. Last year at Greasy Grass, I killed two Americans with my rifle. Between these things, I have counted coup so many times it would take all day to recount them. I have many ponies and my wives are fat and beautiful. I own a Remington repeater. I have seen the Great Bitter Lake on the far side of the Shining Mountains. My medicine is good. I am not afraid to die. I am not afraid to fight another war. But I am not a fool. I am willing to leave the Americans alone if they will leave us alone. I will not be led to another peace talk like a puppy with a string around its neck. I have spoken."

Another man stood up and said, "Hear me. You all know my name. All of you know of my deeds, except for this

American, and I don't care what *he* thinks of me. My brother, Medicine Wolf, has made him welcome and I make him welcome, too. But he is not a Real Person, so I will get right down to our problem as I see it. I have made my mark on the paper, and the Great White Father said this meant we would never fight again. I am old enough to see the sense in this. There are too many soldiers, and our Dakota allies have all run away. If we fight the soldiers alone, we will die. If we don't meet them halfway, we will have no choice. They will say we are evil people and come after us, and there are many of them. Many. I think we should ride to the fort and tell them we know nothing about the fighting that's been going on. But I agree with Dancing Raven that we should not ride tamely in, with this American leading us. I will go there as a visitor, not as a prisoner. If any man wants to make me his prisoner, he will have to beat me in a fair fight and tie my hands and feet and carry me. Even tied, I would not walk where an enemy tells me to. I don't want to fight. This does not mean I can't. I have spoken."

As he hunkered down, another Indian started to rise. But Medicine Wolf held up a hand and said, "Forgive me, my brothers, but I will speak out of turn to save time and avoid a possible mistake. This American must go back before his friends come looking for him. We will all have our say after he leaves. Is this agreeable to everyone?"

There was a general nodding of heads, and Medicine Wolf told Windy, "Ride back and tell them these three things. First, we have not broken the words we made our marks next to on the paper. Second, we may ride over for a visit before we head back to the reservation, but it will be on the army's head if this gets us into a quarrel with the Indian agency or Gray Elk's band. Lastly, tell them that if we come at all, we will be coming at our own pace and in our own good time. We don't want any soldiers meeting us or scouting us. We will be very cross if anyone says something stupid about disarming us or searching our tipi ring for whatever it is you Americans always seem to be looking for under other people's blankets. Are my words agreeable to you, old enemy?"

"Half a loaf is better than a firefight," Windy said. "I'll tell the captain I believe you. He already knows I know you. I'll ask him to give you a couple of days to come in on your own."

"We don't like veiled threats, Windy."

"I ain't threatening, I'm telling. I don't run the army, either. So it ain't for me to say when and if you come in. But if you don't make it sort of soon, they'll likely come looking for you. You boys just do as you've a mind to. I'd best head back and show Uncle Sam my full head of hair."

Windy got to his feet, and the squaw who'd watered his pony led it shyly back to him. He told her she was pretty and mounted up to ride off, not looking back. This wasn't rudeness. Like other warrior societies, Cheyenne were insulted by a guest who seemed to worry who was behind him after they'd offered safe shelter.

Medicine Wolf waited until the white man was out of camp before he said, "Well, boys, we have quite a problem, don't we? Have any of you the least notion where that gang of kids ran off to?"

Dancing Raven shook his head and said, "American Tears was supposed to bring them back. Now he's missing, too. You don't suppose our young men have been up to something silly, do you?"

Medicine Wolf sighed. "Young men are always doing something silly. Don't you remember being young? I'm sure American Tears knows better. But if the kids have been counting coup, it means he hasn't caught up with them. Young Twisted Rifle is the leader of that puppy pack, isn't he?"

An embarrassed-looking elder nodded and said, "Twisted Rifle is my nephew. His father, Blue Bull, died of the spotted sickness seven winters ago. I have tried, but a boy needs a real father to grow up straight. I don't think the boys would hurt the clansman we sent after them, but American Tears may not have been able to cut their trail. I confess I have often taken Twisted Rifle hunting. I have taught him many ways to hide his sign."

Medicine Wolf frowned thoughtfully. "American Tears is a fine tracker. On the other hand, my own young kinsman, Red Lance, is with the gang. He is wild. He takes after my sister. But he is not evil. He would never hurt American Tears or any other member of his own band. Something very strange is going on."

Dancing Raven shrugged and suggested, "Maybe that American scout is wrong. Maybe some Arapaho are trying to be men. The soldiers could have make a mistake, or some Arapaho could have disguised themselves to look like us."

Medicine Wolf snorted disgustedly. "Why would anyone do that? What honor is there in counting coup on an enemy who doesn't know who he's fighting? I think we should ride in and show good faith. We will leave sign here, so the others will know where to find us when they come back. I am going to be very cross unless someone has a very good explanation for where they've been and what they've been doing."

A man who hadn't spoken until this moment asked cautiously, "If we find out it is our own young men who fought the soldiers, what are we going to do? Do you think the soldiers would still wish to fight us if they learned the boys acted without our permission?"

Medicine Wolf scowled and asked, "Who is going to tell them? Even if the boys have been bad, they are still Cut Fingers. Would you stand by and see one of your own die, hanging on a white man's rope?"

"Not while my heart still beats or my legs hold me upright!"

Another old man with liver-spotted hands and a dried-apple face struck himself on the chest and began to chant his death song. Medicine Wolf said, "Oh, shut up, Stone Hand. This is no time for making medicine. We have a very serious problem. If we don't find those young fools before the Americans do, we'll have ourselves another war. I don't know about the rest of you, but I'm getting very tired of having wars with the Americans. We keep losing them."

Dancing Raven said, "I agree, but is there any other path for us to follow, if the Americans catch our young men and try to hang them?"

"No," Medicine Wolf replied grimly. "I told you it was serious."

Windy Mandalian stopped atop a rise as he spotted the First Platoon of Easy Company to the southeast. He saw that they had spotted him, too, so he waved and rode to meet them. Matt Kincaid was in command, and he signaled his men to rein in and rest their mounts while maintaining their positions.

Matt had ridden out to search for Windy at the van of Second Squad, with First Squad out to his far left and Third Squad to the right. Matt usually stayed with First Squad and Sergeant Gus Olsen or Corporal Miller when he took the platoon out. But today he rode with the new and untried ex-Confederate, Wilson, who'd replaced the late Kildare as leader of Second

Squad. The keen-eyed Malone was out ahead on point, of course, with other outriders just visible on the horizons to the left and right, scouting the flanks. The regular platoon lieutenant was back at the post pulling OD, the main reason Matt had selected this particular one of the three platoons in the outfit.

Regulations called for a bugler and the showing of colors by a patrol this large. Matt was aware that their visiting IG officer might not approve, but that was just too bad. He was willing to offer a bit of spit and polish on the post for the prick; out here on the prairie, soldiering was a serious trade.

Matt allowed his mount to lower its head and graze as Windy rode down to report. Matt glanced at the sun and saw that Windy had timed it about right. He'd said he'd be back at Outpost Nine around noon, if he got back at all. They were about three hours' ride from home, and it was a little after nine. Windy joined Matt. The lieutenant raised his hand and drew a circle in the sky before pointing back the way they'd come. The men swung their mounts around but waited, as did Matt, for the outriders to take up new positions. Matt asked Windy how it had gone. The scout spat and said, "They're still sulking a mite. But the flag's still hanging on a tipi pole and there's a fifty-fifty chance they'll come in peaceful. I gave 'em forty-eight hours. What are you doing out here, Matt? I wasn't really all that lonesome."

Matt saw that Malone had loped by and was a quarter-mile closer to the post than they were. He signaled Walking Advance, and noted with approval that Acting Corporal Wilson had switched ends without asking fool questions. Technically, Windy was supposed to be riding at Matt's left, in deference to his rank. But Windy was a free thinker, as well as a civilian, and Matt didn't care who rode on his right as long as they weren't on parade. As they headed back, Matt explained, "The captain was worried about you. It gets worse. Regiment is after us to lean on the Indians. They've even sent a Gatling gun detail out to us. I'm not just out looking for dirty old men. This is supposed to be a show of force."

Windy snorted and replied, "Shit, who in blue blazes are we supposed to show off for? I just told you they say they don't want a fight."

"Are you sure the whole band was at home while you dropped by for a visit, Windy?"

"They tried to make me think so. I counted ponies as I rode in and out. Allowing for the fact that most have more ponies than one to a lodge, their remuda was a mite thin. 'Course, some of the bucks could have been out hunting in the foothills to the west. I didn't figure it would be polite to ask. I was itching to ask where American Tears was. But I never."

"American Tears?"

"Crooked Lancer. Mean and boastful. He's usually there when you visit Medicine Wolf's camp. The old man is the head Crooked Lancer in these parts, and American Tears is his second-in-command. You get the notion, listening to American Tears, that he's sort of confused about the order of their ranks. He generally rides a buckskin he's proud to race. I didn't see it amongst the others this morning."

"I see. Could he be leading a coup party without the chief knowing about it?"

"Hell, Medicine Wolf don't know *you're* here, does he? Like I said, the young men could be off hunting innocent. If American Tears is on the prod, we'll know it soon enough. He ain't just mean. He's dumb. He'll never in this world be able to keep his mouth shut, now that he's killed a white. He claims he lifted hair at the Custer Fight, but the details are sort of hazed over when he's asked for 'em. But he *talks* a good fight, whether he was there or not."

Matt remained silent as they rode on, allowing Windy to fill him in on everything at Medicine Wolf's camp in the scout's own somewhat roundabout way.

Matt was watching the skyline as they conversed, of course, so he forgot what he'd been about to ask Windy when Malone, way out in front, started pumping his rifle up and down over his head.

The other squad leaders had seen the signal, of course, and were already wheeling into a ragged skirmish line. Matt spurred his way to Wilson and said, "Dismount and hold here as reserve, Wilson." Then he rode on, not looking back. He heard Windy's hoofbeats as the scout began to catch up with him. He called out, "What the hell are you following *me* for? If you want to be useful, cut over to Wojensky and tell them to move straight ahead and occupy that ridge with Malone."

Again, not looking to see if his orders were obeyed, Matt loped over to First Squad. Sergeant Olsen saluted and said, "Sir! First Squad at your command!" So Matt rode past, calling out, "Follow me!" as he cut toward the southwest in line with the ridge ahead. As the two NCOs and eight men galloped after him, Matt heard the ragged crackle of distant shots. He had no idea what lay over the rise, but he meant to take whatever it was on the flank.

He glanced back and saw that the others were doing their jobs. Wilson's men had dismounted and formed a reserve screen in front of the two men holding their horses. Corporal Wojensky's men were afoot and moving up to join Malone on the rise, with Windy and another man trailing, still aboard their mounts.

Matt gauged the time he had before Wojensky made the skyline. He swung to his left and called back, "Over the rise, mounted and in file!" as they tore up the slope. He didn't rein in at the top. That was a foolish move that it took a long time to drum out of new men. Matt topped the rise at full gallop and kept going, sizing up the situation as he rode into it as a moving target.

Four prairie schooners stood boxed on the trail in the draw below. A couple of dozen Indians were circling the wagon box just outside of pistol range, firing and taunting as they rode. Matt had just sized up the situation and recognized them as Cheyenne when they, in turn, spotted him. He bored straight down and across the trail, putting the wagons and the Indians surrounding them inside the angle of the big el that First Squad formed with Third, at right angles on the ridge above. Matt reined in, pulled his Springfield off its spider, and dropped off his horse as he shouted, "Form on me in line of skirmish afoot!" and then he was already moving forward, teeth bared and rifle at port arms as he realized fully what the hell was going on. The Indians were attacking the Penderson party. That damned fool, Billy Hawkins, had led them out again, and Phoebe Mills was inside that wagon box, if she was still alive!

He glanced to his left. The others were dressed on him and moving as one long extension of his grim advance. "Spread out and cover down!" he snapped. "Be careful about those wagons, but fire at will."

The Indians had peeled away from the wagons and regrouped on the far side, reconsidering their options. Matt spotted someone waving a kerchief at him from between two wagon ends. They'd managed to pull some of the livestock inside, but some of the critters lay in the grass all around. That had been a bit of luck. The immigrants hadn't known enough to turn the wagons on their sides, but the carcasses had saved their foolish shins as the Indians fired between the wheels. Matt spotted a familiar saddle horse on its side in the tall grass, about a rifle shot out from the wagons. It was still alive and trying to rise. Matt shifted the rifle to his left hand, drew his Scoff .45, and shot the poor brute in the head when he got to it. Just beyond, Colonel Billy Hawkins lay on his back, staring up at the sun with a surprised expression. He was missing his right hand at the wrist, and his skull had been peeled from just above the startled eyebrows to probably the nape of his neck; Matt didn't roll him over to look.

One of the women from the wagon party stepped out, waving. Matt called out, "Get back in there, you damned fool woman! Everybody stay covered!"

Now that he was this close to the wagon box, he couldn't see the Indians, who were doing something on the far side. Up on the rise to his flank, Corporal Wojensky's men were waiting to find out, too. Matt called out, "Olsen, take five around to the left and meet me on the far side. The rest of you stay dressed on me."

So the squad parted like a protozoan as they skirmished toward the wagon box, with Matt moving widest to make the swing with all his guns lined up on Mr. Lo. He was dying to know if a certain young lady with ash-blonde hair had made it, but they'd talk to the fool immigrants after they'd taken time to get acquainted with the Indians who'd jumped them.

As Matt got out of line with the wagons, he could see that the mounted Cheyenne were edging back, undecided. A brave on a buckskin pony streaked with jagged blue lines was shaking a feathered lance and yelling something. Later, Matt would realize he'd been too interested in a distant Indian for his own good. But there wasn't time for him to think now. A brave on a pinto pony suddenly tore at him from behind the wagons, war club raised and singing his death song!

Matt swung the muzzle of his Springfield and fired from the hip, blasting the Cheyenne off his saddle pad as the heavy round took him full in the chest. The sound of the shot seemed to have a scattering effect on the Indians further off. They started riding in every direction but toward Matt. Matt cursed.

He knew they'd be long gone before he could remount his men properly. But what the hell, they'd put one on the ground and the immigrants were safe.

As he moved to rejoin Gus Olsen's men on the far side, Matt heard shots from the rise to his left and glanced up. A trio of the Cheyenne had made a foolish mistake and ridden up into Wojensky's range. Third Squad was smoking them up good, and all three were on the ground now, with their ponies shot out from under them. One rose to his feet, dazed, and started back down toward Matt's party. One of Olsen's men fired, but missed, and Matt shouted, "Hold your fire! I want some prisoners, damn it!"

The confused Indian stopped, looked back and forth, then threw down his coup stick and sat down cross-legged in the grass, resigned.

Up above, Wojensky had either heard or—more likely—figured out the same thing. Matt saw a couple of Wojensky's men moving down to take charge of the Cheyenne they'd dismounted. One of the Indians seemed hurt and out of business. The other took a swipe at Private Malone with his war club—not the best move he could have made. The big Irishman swatted him like a fly with his rifle butt, but when Wojensky yelled at him, Malone stopped kicking the downed man.

Matt stood thoughtfully and stared once around the entire horizon, making certain it was empty before he called out, "Secure the perimeter, Sergeant Olsen. I'm going in for a look-see."

He walked over to the wagon box, automatically reloading his trapdoor rifle before slinging it on his shoulder. Phoebe Mills met him between two wagon ends, with the thoroughly frightened Captain Penderson at her side. Matt removed his hat and said, "Morning. I'd ask you what in blue blazes you folks meant by leaving the post, if I thought you had any idea. Please don't tell me about that snow in the High Sierra. Damn it, we *told* you there were Indians out here. Who did you lose, besides Billy Hawkins?"

Penderson said, "Nobody. He saved us, Lieutenant. We spotted Indians ahead, and the colonel told us to box the wagons while he rode forward to powwow with them."

Phoebe sobbed, "Oh, it was awful. Poor old Billy rode to meet them, holding out tobacco, and they just shot him down like a dog. I'm sorry I ever said a word against the way you soldiers feel about them. I know how you feel. I hate them more than I thought it was possible to hate anyone. They're not noble savages. They're not even people. They're like mad dogs!"

Phoebe suddenly covered her face with her hands and ducked back inside. Penderson told Matt in a shaky voice, "We watched them cutting up the colonel. He must have been only wounded when they blew him out of the saddle. He, uh, died sort of noisy."

"You lost half your stock," Matt observed. "But I think we can manage to get you and your wagons back to the post. I take it you've given up on California for today?"

"Christ, yes. Your captain told us something like this was likely to happen, but Colonel Billy said . . . I'm sort of mixed up about that, Lieutenant. Our guide was obviously a fool. Yet, in the end, he saved us. It's sort of confusing."

Matt shrugged and said, "Not to me. Nobody's wrong all the time. The part that worries me is that nobody's *right* all the time. Hawkins is dead. Leave it be. We'll send you on your way with another guide, when it's safe for you to leave."

Windy Mandalian rode down from the rise and reined in. He said, "Old Wojensky sent me to ask what you want him to do next. We got us three prisoners. One of 'em's hit pretty good, but he'll live long enough to hang."

"Wojensky will keep. We'll scout about for sign and get these folks and the Cheyenne back soon enough. They are Cheyenne, right?"

Windy shifted his cud, spat, and said, "Yep. One of the little rascals is Red Lance. Medicine Wolf is his uncle. Wounded boy is Broken Pipe. Same band. The third one, the one old Malone just whupped, is called Funny Hair. He don't have much to say, but I recognize him. He's a breed. His daddy was a passing buffalo hider. His mama is Gray Elk's sister-in-law."

"Christ! Does that mean both Gray Elk and Medicine Wolf have broken the peace?"

"Nope. Means restless kids from both bands has joined forces to play Cheyenne Halloween tricks. Who'd you shoot, down here? I saw you put one on the ground."

Matt pointed and started walking as Windy followed, on his mount. They came to the dead youth in the grass and Matt rolled him over with his foot. The dead Indian's face was painted half black and half blue, with red stripes running down each cheek. Windy nodded and said, "Another one from old Medicine Wolf's band. His name was Twisted Rifle, and his mama sort of spoiled him. They got one of ours, too, right?"

Matt pointed across the brown grass and said, "Colonel Billy Whiz-Bang. He must have read James Fenimore Cooper a lot. They got his hand and hair. Not that it makes much difference, I suppose."

Windy shifted his weight and said, "Well, it was an even fight, then. One kilt on either side."

"Have you forgotten the three prisoners, Windy?"

Mandalian shifted his cud and said, "I haven't forgot the little bastards. You do figure I'm on Uncle Sam's side, don't you?"

"Get to the point, Windy."

"Well, the point is that I'd let them three kids go, if I was running things."

Matt stared up at the scout and said, "Are you drunk? The sons of bitches just killed and mutilated a white man, useless as he might have been."

"I know," Windy answered. "And as members of treaty bands, them three boys will hang, sure as hell. Even if the army turned them over to the Indian bureau, they'd have to be strung up. That's what the law says. A hostile band gets one chance to surrender and sign up for rations. If they get to killing us again . . ."

"Damn it, Windy, I know the Renegade Laws. Those kids we just captured knew them, too. If you want to play, you have to pay."

"That's true, old son, but let's study on the ante in this here game. If we take them boys in, the army will court-martial 'em and hang 'em high. That don't fret me much, but it's likely to make their folks mad as hell. Medicine Wolf ain't about to stand idly by as we hang his nephew. Gray Elk will be a mite put out if he hears we aim to hang a kid from his band, too. Right now, the bands is separated and barely talking to one another. Do you really want them two old chiefs combined agin us?"

Matt turned and stared up the slope to where Wojensky's men were guarding the three young prisoners of war. He noticed they were binding the wounds of the one they'd hit. He sighed and said, "I can't just turn three prisoners loose, Windy.

I'd catch a court-martial myself. It's a capital offense to give aid and comfort to an enemy of the U.S. Army, and if they're not enemies, I'll be damned if I can figure what else to call them."

Windy spat and said, "I know. There's three ways to do everything. The right way, the wrong way, and the army way. I can see the bind you're in. Just thought I'd mention it."

Matt nodded. "The fat's in the fire. Aside from us, we have these civilians as witnesses to what was either war or murder. Can't you explain our position to the two chiefs, Windy?"

Mandalian said, "I can explain it. But I can't make them see their way clear to stand still for a triple execution if I talked from here to doomsday. A chief ain't like a king, Matt. We've gotten into a lot of grief by acting like they was. Both Medicine Wolf and Gray Elk lead bands of folks who expect them to stand up for them and do what's right. I mean, what's right as Cheyenne see the right."

"Surely they know it's wrong to commit murder, Windy?"

"'Course they do. They'll likely declare war on us afore they hit us, riding side by side."

## seven

Captain Conway found that his wife had company when he went to his quarters at five to change. Flora was having tea with Phoebe Mills and Maggie Cohen. Conway nodded and said, "Ladies."

His wife smiled and asked, "My, what brings you home so early, wearing such a stern expression?"

"I have to put on my dress uniform. We're holding a court-martial this evening for those Indians Matt and Windy brought in." He nodded at Phoebe Mills and said, "I hope you've recovered from your trying ordeal, ma'am."

Phoebe said, "You've all been very kind, and only one of us met the fate of poor Billy Hawkins, thanks to your gallant soldiers. Tell me, sir, are Matt and the others to be decorated for what they did this morning?"

Conway looked puzzled and replied, "Decorated, ma'am? They'll be mentioned in dispatches, but nobody expects a medal for a routine skirmish."

"I'd hardly call what they did routine, sir! Heavens, Matt led his men over that ridge going lickity-split, and sent those rascals running just as we'd about given up!"

"I know what they did, ma'am. We just finished our staff meeting across the parade. I commended Matt and his men for a job well done, but at the moment, we're more concerned about the future."

Flora said, "Sit down and have a cup of tea before you dress, dear. I'm sure there's time, and we're dying to hear what you menfolk are up to. Everyone's been rushing back and forth so, since Matt's column brought these people in, and nobody's told us a thing about what's going on."

Conway drew a rosewood chair closer to his wife, and perched on it as he said, "Well, simply put, we've just been sweeping up the latest mess Mr. Lo made. The dead have been buried. The prisoners are under guard in the lockup. We've hoisted that Gatling gun up on the lookout tower and canceled all passes. The wire is down again, of course. So we're just playing by ear until we have a better idea what's going on."

Phoebe gasped, "Oh, we're cut off from the world by those savages?"

Conway smiled reassuringly and said, "I'd hardly say that, ma'am. The world is still turning, right under us. A few bush-whacking Indians are out cutting wires and looking for a safe shot at a stray white. But we're safe behind thick walls, and the nearby townships are forted up by now. We sent dispatch riders out to warn everybody."

Flora asked, "Did you send a rider to tell Regiment, dear?"

Conway shook his head and said, "No. It's a long, lonely ride, and I saw no need to risk a man's life just to tell Regiment we're still here. They know where we are. It's on the map."

"But, dear, how are they to know the Indians are on the warpath if we don't get word to them?"

"In the first place, I'd hardly say Mr. Lo is on the warpath. Windy thinks it's a small band of wild kids, led by a rogue called American Tears. In the second, Regiment has to know the wire's down again. They *are* holding the other end of the string, you know."

"Phoebe brightened and said, "Oh, doubtless the army will send a big column to rescue us, then, won't they?"

Conway smiled and said, "Hardly, Miss Phoebe. They put Outpost Nine out here to handle local outbreaks. They know we have the men and ordnance to stand off the whole Dakota Confederacy, if push comes to shove. I know you just went through a very frightening experience out there on the trail, but Indians are guerilla fighters, not stand-up soldiers given to advancing with fixed bayonets behind an artillery barrage. I've no doubt a battalion of regulars could reduce this position, but I'd be a mite surprised, and so would Regiment, if prancing, dancing Indians put a dent in our defenses."

Flora nodded at her worried young guest and said, "Dear

Maggie and I have been forted up like this before, dear heart. There's nothing to worry about."

Maggie said, "Sure, ye should have been out here after what happened to Custer and thim poor yellow legs. Do ye remember how some of the new wives carried on, mum? Faith, I thought I'd catch me death from laughter to see Rosie Swensen under her bed when I came calling. And in the end, we learned the Indians had all fled to Canada and were nowhere near at all, at all!"

Conway nodded in agreement and rose, saying, "I'd love to stay and chat, but, my apologies, ladies. Colonel Bradshaw's expecting me back, all gussied up."

He left the room. Maggie Cohen leaned forward and asked, softly, "Have ye spoken to himself about the Dorfler children, mum?"

"I know they're up to something," Flora replied. "I think we should just let the poor dears work it out their own way."

Phoebe Mills looked puzzled and asked, "Who are the Dorflers?"

Flora put a finger to her lips and warned, "Not so loud, dear heart. We're speaking of a young corporal and his wife. The silly boy got himself in trouble, and his poor little wife is worried that our growly bears will send her home."

Then Flora brightened and added, "Oh, Maggie, I just thought of something. They *can't* send poor little Wilma home *now*!"

Maggie slapped her thigh and said, "Oh, me eyebrow, that's true! What a darling time the Indians picked to make trouble. Faith, in all this frush and fluster, there's a chance the men will lose track of the charges against her Jimmy."

"Your husband has never lost a scrap of paper within living memory, Maggie. But Jimmy Dorfler's offense does seem less important now, with real action going on."

Maggie said, "You let me worry about papers, mum. You're right about himself. But his clerk, Four Eyes, lives in mortal fear of me, for some daft reason. I'll just wait until Ben's out of the orderly room and—" She stopped and smiled up innocently as Warner Conway came out of the bedroom, wearing his dress sword and beribboned tunic as well as a sheepish smile.

Flora said, "You look very imposing, dear. I told you turpentine would take those stains out."

Phoebe Mills stared at the decorations on his chest and said, "My, you've certainly won an awful lot of medals, sir. How on earth did you ever get so many?"

"Idiocy, ma'am. Are you sure these buttons will hold, Flora? It feels a mite snug. I don't know if I'm getting fatter or if this fool tunic is shrinking."

"I'm sure it's the laundering, dear. You know dress blues are supposed to be dry-cleaned, but what are we to do but sponge it with cold water and hope for the best? I wish you'd told me you needed it this evening. I'd have steamed it for you. Why are those Indians standing trial *here*, anyway? The last renegades you caught were sent back to headquarters for trial."

Conway nodded and said, "I know. Trying them here and now was the IG officer's idea. I guess he wants to feel useful, now that it's not safe for him to travel. I'm not even sure a general court-martial will stand up to appeal under these conditions. We're supposed to have a panel of field-grade officers."

Again, Flora saw that her younger civilian guest was bewildered and quickly explained, "A field-grade officer is anyone higher than a captain, dear. I don't know why they say everything so complicated, either."

Conway laughed, unaware of how boyish he looked to his adoring wife when he dropped his stern facade, and said, "Well, it's not our problem if he's made a mistake. Matt and I both pointed out that we don't hold the rank needed to pass a death sentence, but he says he knows all sorts of regulations, and even if he's wrong, it'll be on his head. As the ranking officer, he gets to deal the cards. He gets to pay up if he's made a mistake, too."

Phoebe Mills said, "Now I'm really confused. Is there any doubt about those Indians being guilty? I thought the trial was simply a formality before you hanged them."

Conway looked a bit awkward as he replied, "I know this sounds silly, ma'am, considering that you and the other witnesses were there. But under military law, a man is innocent until he's been convicted."

"Surely there's no chance they won't be convicted, sir?"

"I don't see how that could happen, ma'am. They were caught red-handed."

"Then what on earth is the problem? Don't you want to see those savages properly punished?"

"'Properly' is the key word, ma'am. Under certain circumstances, such as an emergency in the field, any officer can convene a drumhead court and execute for certain charges on the spot. But if you mean to have a full-dress general court-martial . . . well, I, for one, think it ought to be done right. I suggested we hold those three young bucks for now and let Regiment and the BIA sort out what's to be done with them. But, as I said, Colonel Bradshaw's probably bored."

"Is Matt—I mean, Lieutenant Kincaid—sitting as a judge?"

"Yes, ma'am. Along with that other first lieutenant, Fitzgerald. Colonel Bradshaw will be presiding, with Lieutenant Taylor as prosecution and Windy Mandalian as defense."

Flora, who really knew more about the army than she let on, asked, "Is that proper, dear? Windy is a very nice man, but he's a civilian."

Conway said, "Matt pointed that out. He also protested being asked to sit in judgment, since both he and Windy were witnesses to the boy's actions, and he wants to take another patrol out, anyway. But Bradshaw got a bit huffy and that's that. It'll all be over in a few more hours, and as I said, Bradshaw's the only one who'll be in trouble if he's overstepped the bounds of his authority."

Flora started to say that in her opinion, three young Indians might also find themselves paying for the IG officer's mistake, but she kept the notion to herself. She knew her dear Warner often thought she was too soft-hearted for an army wife, and she was determined, this time, not to feel sorry for anyone.

Conway excused himself again and went to the door. As he opened it, he paused and frowned. Flora knew her man well enough to read his expressions, even from the back. She shot a warning look at the other women and rose to join him as he stood in the doorway, head cocked to one side.

She could hear it, too, now. She asked, "What is it, dear heart? It sounds like distant drums."

He shrugged and said, "That's about the size of it. They must have heard about it over in Gray Elk's camp. Somebody's beating a tomtom. I don't see what good they think it will do, but you know Mr. Lo when he gets excited. Keep your head down, honey. I'll be back as soon as the trial is over."

* * *

Matt Kincaid was arguing with Lieutenant Colonel Bradshaw when Conway arrived at the officer's mess the IG man had selected as the chambers for the impending court-martial. Conway saw that the others had all arrived ahead of him, thanks to his chatting with the ladies. But Taylor, Fitzgerald, and Windy were listening in awkward silence as Matt spoke to his superior in tones that bordered on insubordination. Bradshaw nodded to the captain as he came in and said, "I'm ready to begin, Captain Conway. Shall we send for the prisoners?"

Before Conway could answer, Matt snapped, "You don't seem to be listening to me, Colonel. I just said I was formally protesting this improper trial. I'll put it in writing, if you like. I see no need at all for us to drumhead those kids. They're not about to go anywhere, and they're wards of the U.S. Government. I demand they be turned over to the BIA via GHQ."

Bradshaw smiled thinly and said, "Can't you hear those tomtoms, son? We don't seem to be in any position to hand those renegades over to higher authority. The articles of war are quite clear on how one deals with a treaty tribesman who's broken his parole. What's come over you? Why are you so concerned about the greasy little bastards? You sound like one of those bleeding hearts from the Mission Society."

Matt snapped, "Begging the colonel's pardon, he's talking like an asshole! If you'd been out there with us this morning instead of looking under the bunks for lint, you'd have seen me put a Cheyenne on the ground!"

Captain Conway sucked in his breath and said, "You're out of order, Lieutenant! Nobody in Easy Company talks to a superior like that while I am in command! Do you read me, Kincaid?"

Matt shrugged and didn't answer as he glared at the IG man.

Bradshaw smiled and said, "I'm big enough to allow a junior officer to express an opinion. But now that we've heard the lieutenant's views on the matter, shall we take our seats and get on with it?"

The others started to take their places. Matt stood his ground and said, "I'm not sitting as a judge. I'll appear as a witness, but *I* know the articles of war, too. The panel is supposed to be made up of disinterested officers. I'm not disinterested. I exchanged fire with the sons of bitches. I was the arresting officer. You can't order me to sit in judgment."

Bradshaw stared thoughtfully at Matt for a long, unblinking moment before he said, "There are a lot of things nobody can make you do in this man's army, Kincaid, but they can sure make you wish to Christ you had." Then he said, "Very well, since Lieutenant Kincaid seems unwilling to serve on the panel, we'll simply have to consider him a witness. I feel we have enough of a court to get by, considering the circumstances. Is anyone ever going to bring the prisoners from the guardhouse? One would think the TJA would have had them here by now."

Mr. Taylor glanced at Matt for guidance, but didn't get any, and saw that he was on his own. He licked his lips and said, "If it please the court, the prosecution needs more time to prepare its case."

A less experienced man would have asked Taylor what the hell he was talking about. Bradshaw's eyes narrowed as he nodded and said, "So you're siding with your fellow junior officer, eh? You could be making a big mistake, Mr. Taylor."

Taylor met Bradshaw's eyes steadily as he said, "I've no idea what you mean, sir. I need time to take statements and decide which witnesses to use. I'm sure the colonel wants an orderly procedure, and it's likely to be confusing if everyone involved is called."

"Don't be ridiculous. You know we only need a half-dozen sworn statements that the damned redskins were taking part in that attack when they were captured."

"I know that, sir. That's why I need more time. Aside from the civilians in the wagon party, there were over thirty men with Lieutenant Kincaid. Some of them saw what was going on and some of them might not have. I need time to have a word with everyone before I prepare my list of witnesses to be called."

Windy Mandalian said, "I need more time, too, Your Honor. I ain't all that up on Injun law, so I'd like to read that treaty they might have busted. Then the boys need a translator and—"

"Goddamnit, Mandalian, you know you speak Cheyenne!"

"Well, I don't know as I speak it good, and in any case, Mr. Taylor here can't hardly cross-examine without a translator of his own, can he?"

"Why can't *you* translate, damn it?"

"Would that be fair, Colonel? I'm supposed to be defending those young rascals. How in tarnation can a man defend a man by telling on him when he puts his foot in his mouth?"

"I'm afraid I'd have to protest this scout as my translator, sir," Taylor put in. "No offense, Windy, but you are sleeping with Funny Hair's kinswoman, you know."

Windy sighed and asked, "What can I say? I'm a weak-willed old cuss, and she do move nice on a blanket. Regiment has a couple of scouts as can talk Cheyenne. Mebbe you'd best wait until we can get in touch with GHQ, right?"

Bradshaw turned to Conway and said, "I hope you can see they're ganging up on me, Captain."

Lieutenant Fitzgerald said, "*I'm* on your side, Colonel. I'm from GHQ, and I'll be damned if I can understand what's going on!"

Conway ignored the brown-nosing heavy-weapons man and said, "I can see how it might appear that way to you, sir. But I'm sure the boys are just doing their duty as they see it."

"So? You intend to back your junior officers?"

Conway shrugged and said, "I can't stop you from taking it that way, if you intend to, sir."

"You know goddamned well how I intend to take this, Captain. Are you aware I still haven't filed my report on this company?"

"Yessir. I expected you to file a report on us. That was why the IG sent you out here, wasn't it?"

"I could take that as a snide remark, Captain."

"Sir?"

"Don't fence with me, goddamnit. I know the way you soldiers in the field feel about headquarters johns. You think you're a bunch of fucking heroes. You resent us coming out here to make sure you're doing everything by the book."

Conway smiled thinly and said, "Easy Company is going by the book this evening, Colonel. Does that upset you?"

"Listen to me and listen tight, you smug bastard! IG *wrote* the fucking book! The rules and regulations of this man's army are exactly what the IG says they are, and no guardhouse lawyer is going to pull what you three think you're pulling!"

Windy Mandalian stretched and said laconically, "Hell, make it four. I ain't sure what they're doing to you, but if it means we ain't about to hang three kids with their folks raising pure ned just outside the gates, it sounds like a good idea."

Bradshaw said, "Don't worry, Mandalian, I'm going to include you in my official report, and if you ever get a job even pushing a broom for the War Department, after I'm done, I don't know my job as well as I thought I did."

Windy shrugged and said, "Shoot, I could make more herding cows, old son. But ain't you putting the cart afore the horse?"

Bradshaw looked blank, so Windy continued, "That's a war drum they've took to banging on, out there. By now, Medicine Wolf will have heard we're holding his nephew for the necktie party you seem so set on. I wouldn't be so boastful about eating cucumbers and doing wonders until I figured how the hell I was ever getting out of here with all my hair, if I was you."

Lieutenant Fitzgerald laughed incredulously and said, "Don't worry, Colonel. My men and I are anxious to see the Cheyenne attack. That's why we brought our Gatling gun."

Cocking an eyebrow at him, Windy asked, "Didn't your gunnery sergeant tell you, sonny?" Then he saw the puzzled frown on Fitzgerald's face and went on, "Nope, I guess they never. They're likely still hoping to find it, unless it fell on the trail, coming out."

Fitzgerald asked, "What are you talking about, Mandalian? What fell out of where?"

"Your firing cog, of course. I was talking to your boys whilst they was hoisting the Gatling up on the tower. They tried to dry-fire the action after they got her in place. That's when they found out they'd lost the part. That big brass bastard sure looks pretty, sitting up there in the sunset, but as of now, it won't fire one round. They can't even get the durned old arming crank to turn."

The evening star hung in a purple sky as Flora Conway crossed the parade with Maggie Cohen and a bemused Phoebe Mills in tow. Maggie was carrying a heavy kitchen canister she refused help with. Phoebe had no idea why she was tagging along, but she had nothing else to do, the night was young, and she certainly wasn't going to get any sleep with all this banging of drums and boots stomping all about on the parapet above.

Private Wolfgang Holzer was walking his post in a military manner in front of the lockup, mercifully unaware of how much he resembled a clockwork toy soldier. The twelve general orders were among the few English phrases he could understand as well as say, and the first one read, "I shall walk my post in a military manner, keeping always on the alert and reporting to the corporal of the guard anything and everything that takes place on or near my post." So, as Holzer saw three ladies headed his way, he eyed them warily, trying to form enough English in his mind to (1) find out what they wanted, and (2) manage to pass on the information to the *verdammt* corporal of the guard the next time he came by.

Holzer stamped to the corner of the lockup, pivoted like a puppet on a stick, stamped back to the door, stopped with an almost audible click, and presented arms to the captain's lady. He didn't know if he was supposed to say "halt" or not. Even Holzer could see that "Halt, who goes there?" was a bit officious under the circumstances.

Miss Flora smiled at him and said, "Good evening, soldier. We've brought some medicine and chicken broth for the wounded prisoner."

"Bleaz, *mein Damen*?"

"Oh, dear, you're that German boy. I suppose we'd better speak to the corporal of the guard."

"Bleaz, *mein Damen*?"

Maggie Cohen sniffed, then shouted loudly, "Corporal of the guard! Post number three!"

Private Holzer winced as the big woman's bellow echoed through the night. He had no idea what he'd done wrong now, but it sounded serious.

Acting Corporal Wilson came from the nearby guard room at a trot, one hand bracing the Schofield .45 on his hip. He slowed to a walk with a puzzled frown as he saw the three women in front of the lockup. Flora Conway explained, "I have some broth and painkiller for the wounded lad inside. Would you be good enough to let us in?"

"Ma'am, those prisoners are *Indians*," Wilson said.

"Heavens, don't you think I knew that? I'm sure Dutch Rothausen did a fine job of surgery on the one who got hit. But I've nursed many a gunshot wound, so I know the pain and thirst seem worse after sundown."

Wilson smiled softly. "Yes, ma'am, I remember the first time I got hit, a long time ago. I could have used some chicken soup. But does the captain know you ladies are here?"

"You can certainly tell him, if you like. Nursing an injured prisoner is hardly forbidden under the ARs. Won't you open up for us?"

"I'd be proud to, ma'am, if it was only up to me," Wilson said. "But I just made this temporary rank and, no offense, I'll have to ask the OD."

Flora sighed and said, "You'd best put that canister down, Maggie dear. Who's on OD tonight, Corporal?"

Before Wilson could answer, Matt Kincaid came into sight, wearing an OD brassard. Flora waved to him and said, "Oh, Matt, dear, we seem to have a problem getting this door open. What are you doing on OD? I thought you just pulled it a night or so ago."

Matt nodded to Flora and the two other women and told Flora, "I think your husband wants to keep me as far as possible from that puffed-up IG. What's this about, Miss Flora?"

She explained again about her errand of mercy. Matt said, "Well, I see no harm in it. Although, frankly, I see no good in it, either. Do you have the key, Wilson?"

"The ex-Confederate nodded and produced a key ring. Unlocking the massive ironbound wooden door, he swung it open on its groaning hinges. Matt led the way in. A coal-oil lamp hung from the beams between opposing cages. To the left, two young Cheyenne squatted sullenly and silently, eyeing the visitors like trapped wolves waiting to be skinned. The wounded youth lay alone on a pallet in the other cage. As Wilson fumbled with the lock, one of the others growled across in Cheyenne, "Hear me, Broken Pipe. They are going to let their squaws torture you. Remember, you are a man. Remember, men don't scream."

The wounded boy rolled his back against the wall and stared up, stone-faced. Flora dropped to her knees at his side and smiled down at him. She asked, "Do you speak English, son?"

"I am Broken Pipe. I am not afraid. If I felt better, I would fight you. But I am weak from bleeding too much. My head feels funny when I try to rise. Do what you will, old and ugly woman."

Maggie set the canister down and muttered, "Faith, if he was mine, I'd wash his mouth out with soap. You're wasting your religion as well as your time, Miss Flora."

Flora put her hand on Broken Pipe's shoulder and he flinched like a nervous colt at the cool touch of her pale fingers. "I'm not going to hurt you," she reassured him. "I see the dressing on your chest is holding, so we'll just leave it alone. Does it itch?"

"Yes. It feels like there are ants under the bandages. Does this please you, ugly old woman?"

"Yes. I know it's uncomfortable, dear, but the itching is a good sign. It means the wound is clean and your body is trying to repair itself. I have some broth for you. You need salt and liquids. But first I want you to take some of this medicine."

The Indian watched, sincerely puzzled, as she pulled the cork from a small brown bottle and said, "They won't let me leave you alone with a spoon. But this will get you through the night if you take a sip every few hours. Mind you don't drink it all at once. It will make you vomit. Can you sit up?"

Broken Pipe made no move to rise as he stared up at her. It wasn't true that she was ugly, but her pale features were unsettling to him. She looked like a spirit woman in the dim light. He licked his lips and said, "I don't think I want to drink your poison."

Matt moved around and said, "I'll haul him up for you, Miss Flora." But Flora shook her head and murmured, "No. Can't you see he's frightened? We'll manage, Matt, dear. Won't we, son?"

"Why do you call me your son? You are not my mother. Heya, you are a crazy old American woman!"

Flora leaned forward and put her free hand behind the Indian's nape.

"Careful," Matt muttered.

"Pooh," Flora said. "He's not going to fight with me, are you, son?"

The Indian allowed her to raise his head with one hand and place the neck of the bottle against his lips with the other. The liquid felt strong and bitter going down, so he knew it was probably good medicine. He propped an elbow against the blankets he lay on and stared up at her warily as she stoppered the bottle and placed it beside him, saying, "There. You'll feel less discomfort in a few minutes. Now we're going to give you some broth."

She opened the canister and Maggie knelt beside her to hand her a ladle. Broken Pipe sniffed suspiciously. It smelled delicious, and he was thirsty. Flora held a ladle of broth to his face and said, "Now open wide, dear."

The Indian suddenly laughed. Then he let her feed him a

ladleful before he struggled into a more upright position and said, "I am not a child. I can feed myself, you crazy old woman."

Flora handed him the ladle and sat back with a satisfied smile. Behind her, Phoebe Mills watched, standing at Matt's side. She murmured, "He's only a little boy. He can't be more than fourteen, can he?"

"They start them young," Matt said. "That's when Mr. Lo is at his most dangerous."

Shaking her head, she said, "I can't believe those were children we fought out there on the prairie this morning. I'm sure this one just tagged along with his older brothers."

"Take a look at the others across the way, Miss Phoebe."

She turned, peering through the bars in the dim light. Then she turned away with a shudder and said, "It's frightening. They look so young and harmless without their feathers and paint. Are you really going to . . . you know?"

"That's what the law says. Laws are made by old men sitting alone in musty rooms back East. Things look different when you're out here in the real world, don't they?"

"I'm trying to remember that I hate them. They really did some hateful things to poor old Billy Hawkins. Do you suppose, if they'd taken us before you and your men arrived . . . ?"

"Yes, ma'am. They sure would have. Even our own kids can be pretty cruel, and these boys were led by a really nasty brute. But I understand your feelings. Out there in a firefight, an Indian is an Indian. Locked up and at our mercy, they turn back into people. Mighty young people, at that."

Broken Pipe had swallowed all the broth he was capable of. As he handed the ladle back to Flora, he smiled weakly and said, "I still think you are crazy. But that was good and I think you are a good person, even if you are crazy."

Maggie Cohen growled, "Don't you know enough to say 'thank you,' me bucko?"

Flora said, "Shush, dear. I'm sure he just did, in his own wild way. I don't suppose we could leave this canister and ladle for him, Matt?"

"No, ma'am. Nothing made of metal. I'm stretching the rules by allowing him to keep the bottle."

Flora smiled wistfully down at Broken Pipe and said, "Well, you just try and get some rest, son. I'll be back later to see how you feel."

The bewildered youth lay back, staring up at her while she

put the lid back on the canister. She said, "There's so much left, Matt. Do you suppose those other boys across the way would like some?"

"Forgive me, Miss Flora, but they've been fed and I've got my rounds to make."

"Well, maybe the boys in the guard room would enjoy it. It seems a shame to let it grow cold and go to waste."

Maggie reached out and took the broth. As Flora started to rise, the wounded Indian reached out and touched her skirt shyly. She smiled down at him, and Broken Pipe said, "Hear me. I do not understand you. I understand what your men are going to do to us. That is war, and war is not hard to understand. Hear me, I count coup. This morning I helped one of your people die. The other day I shot at another. My bullet may have been the one that put him on the ground."

"I know. You've been very naughty."

"You knew these things? Yet you came here to comfort me? You call me son?"

"Well, dear, your own mother's in no position to comfort you tonight, is she?"

Broken Pipe's eyes glistened in the lamplight. He blinked hard and fought to control the slight quaver in his voice when he said, "I will never see my real mother again. I still don't know why you wish to call me your son, but I will not laugh at you anymore. I have spoken."

Flora patted him on the shoulder and got to her feet as Matt leaned forward to help her. As they were leaving, one of the other Cheyenne was standing at the bars across the way. He stared hard at Flora and said, "I am called Red Lance. I wish to say something."

Flora paused with a friendly, puzzled smile. "I have been listening," Red Lance began. "I am going to escape, of course. Will you tell me your name, American mother?"

"I'm Flora Conway, sir."

Red Lance nodded. "I will remember your name as well as your face. You should try and remember mine. Hear me. No matter what happens between our people, I will be your friend. Speak my name if you are taken by my people. Tell them you are under my protection."

Flora didn't laugh, as grotesque as the prisoner's words might have seemed. She nodded gravely and said, "I am pleased to be your friend, Red Lance. But what of your young comrade in the corner? He doesn't seem to be too pleased with us."

Red Lance glanced down at Funny Hair, squatting sullenly on his haunches, and muttered something to him in Cheyenne. Funny Hair shook his head and growled ominously. "He is half white," Red Lance explained. "He doesn't understand how Real People feel about war."

Flora nodded and, knowing poor Matt was anxious, led the way out. As Wilson locked the door again, she asked Matt, "Do you men really mean to hang those children?"

Matt said, "Somebody has to, sooner or later. I've been holding out for later."

"I know. My husband told me about the dreadful row you had with poor Colonel Bradshaw. I don't think he's a bad man, dear. He's just a bit strict."

"My men would hardly say I was easygoing, Miss Flora. But the ARs have to be interpreted with common sense."

"Well, I agree those boys are awfully young to die."

"Nobody's ever old enough to die, if you ask them about it, ma'am. My quarrel with Bradshaw isn't about whether they hang or not. It's a question of timing."

Flora cocked her head and said, "I think I understand. But I don't hear those drums right now. Do you suppose the Indians are starting to calm down after the first excitement?"

"No, ma'am. I'd say they've gotten over the first excitement, true enough, but they haven't calmed down. They're probably getting down to some serious discussion about those three young rascals we're holding in there."

# eight

Matt Kincaid stood alone atop the parapet, staring at the flickering lights of Tipi Town to the northeast. It was getting late, and he knew Indians usually turned in early and were up at cockcrow. From time to time, someone moved between him and the fires inside the tipi ring. Both sides faced a sleepless night, it seemed.

The moon was full and the prairie all around lay ash gray in its cool rays. That was a break. They wouldn't need the full company manning the walls until the next quarter, and by then, things should have calmed or been settled the hard way.

Matt heard the crunch of boot heel on sod and turned. It was Captain Conway. Matt stood straighter and said, "Sir?"

Conway said, "Knock it off. We're alone, you idiot. You know I had to lean on you for sounding off at a field-grade officer like that. Let's get back to serious matters. Windy just came in. He didn't try to visit Gray Elk over there, but he scouted around the camp enough to know that Medicine Wolf hasn't arrived yet. The whites, Arapaho, and other neutrals seem to have left Gray Elk's camp. I'm surprised the old man hasn't sent us a delegation by now. He obviously knows we're holding one of his young men, or he wouldn't be making such a fuss."

"They won't come to us with their demands until they've made up their minds what they are," Matt said. "Gray Elk doesn't bluff and he doesn't like to break his word. I feel kind of sorry for him, knowing the bind he's in."

"He is in a pretty pickle, isn't he?" Conway agreed. "As the leader of his band, he's expected to keep all of them alive and well. As a treaty chief, he's supposed to go by the mark he made for the Great White Father. Which side are you betting on him remaining loyal to?"

"There's no bet, Captain. If he's forced to choose between them and us, he's with them. Wouldn't you be, in his shoes?"

"I'm afraid so. I've been thinking, Matt. That IG report is going to be lousy, anyway. How much worse could Bradshaw make us sound if we sort of let those kids escape?"

"I'm not worried about looking like a horse's ass to GHQ, sir. But if you're asking for an opinion, Mr. Lo is short on gratitude and long on respect. Right now, some of Gray Elk's young men are making fire-eating speeches about blood and slaughter. I suspect the older men are trying to calm them down as much as they can without losing control. Gray Elk's probably telling them how well he stands with the Great White Father and suggesting negotiations."

"Hmm, that's what Windy told me, too. But we can't surrender the boys to an Indian ultimatum, no matter how delicately it's put. That would make us look worse than if they got away, which takes us back to my first idea."

"We're not holding proven warriors, sir," Matt pointed out. "They're ragged-ass kids, and one of them's wounded. Can't you see what men like American Tears would make out of us not being able to hold them? We're not controlling Mr. Lo with a handful of men and some leftover rifles because he admires our big blue eyes. Even braves like American Tears are more afraid of us than they let on, and we have to keep it that way."

"Then why in thunder were you fighting with Bradshaw about hanging the little bastards?"

"I said our job was to *control* Mr. Lo, not to drive him crazy mean, sir. Out of sight is out of mind. They'll still be upset as hell when we send those young bucks off to whatever. But if the trials and hangings are off in some hazy future, the chiefs will have time for some fatalistic told-you-so's, and other young bucks will have time to cool off a bit. Every time American Tears makes war talk, some Cheyenne parent is likely to ask him how come three kids got hanged the last time he talked so big. On the other hand, American Tears is surely going to make some nasty cracks at the older men if they just stand idly by and watch us string three Cheyenne up. Like I said, it's a matter of delicate timing."

Conway took out a cigar, lit it, and then reflected, "It's a mess, no matter how you look at it. You'd better turn in, Matt. I'll take over the guard for you."

"Sir?"

"Oh, I forgot to mention it. I'm sending you out again. Windy says the other band under Medicine Wolf should be heading this way about sunrise. I want you to take two platoons and head him off. Technically, he's not supposed to be this far from the reservation. I want you to point that out to him as delicately as you see fit."

Matt pursed his lips and thought for a time before replying, "I can see the advantage of keeping the two bands separated, and I think I can handle either one of them with two platoons. But even if we can get Medicine Wolf back to the reservation peacefully, it's going to take us a few days. You'll be here with one platoon and a broken-down Gatling. One platoon's an even match for Gray Elk's band over there."

"We've got these walls, even spread a mite thin around them, Matt. I don't think Gray Elk's up to an all-out assault against forted-up infantry."

"Not alone, sir. But you're forgetting American Tears. He's not going to be with Medicine Wolf, when and if we head that other band off. He's got a dozen or so riders we know of. He may be able to recruit others, now that he's started to look good. What if he joins Gray Elk while I'm off with most of our strength?"

Conway blew smoke out through his nose and said, "We'll just have to shoot the bastard along with anyone else who's dumb enough to attack us. Frankly, I think he's too yellow to give us a fair fight. But *there's* an Indian I'd really like to hang!"

"I just had a crazy thought, sir," Matt said. "If I can head Medicine Wolf off, do I have powers of negotiation for the company?"

"Within reason. You know GHQ will let us bend the rules a bit if it saves the taxpayers a campaign now and again. What are you going to offer him, immunity from penalties for leaving the reservation?"

Something like that, sir. I'll lead First and take Taylor's platoon with me, if that's all right with you."

Conway started to object, but then he nodded and said, "Good idea. We're still short those new officers and men they keep promising, but I can put Fitzgerald over Third and bring it up to strength with the garrison service personnel if things get silly here."

Peeling off his OD brassard, Matt handed it to his superior before he went to the nearest ladder and climbed down to ground level. He heard the sound of a woman crying and stopped with a frown. He saw that the door to one of the enlisted men's quarters was ajar and that the sounds were coming from inside. He knocked softly on the wooden jamb. There was a mouselike scurrying, and then Wilma Dorfler opened the door widely with a hopeful, tear-streaked face, saw who it was, and died a little. Matt took off his hat and said, "I couldn't help hearing, ma'am. Your husband will be riding out with me in the morning, but—"

"You're just hateful!" she blazed, bursting into tears again.

Matt said, "I know how you feel. But if you aim to be an army wife, don't ever talk to an officer like that again. They're not all as understanding as myself. As I was saying, your husband will be riding with me, come morning. What extra duty has Cohen given him tonight? I know he's not on guard."

Wilma dabbed at her eyes with her apron and sniffed, "He's on that durned old CQ again, and it's not fair. He pulled CQ *last* night, and one of the other wives was telling me a man on night duty gets the next day off."

"They do, when they're not pulling company punishment. Can I trust you, Miss Wilma? You look like a smart young gal, and I know you love your man."

She stared up at him, puzzled, and Matt went on, "You're pretty, and your Jim is only human. What happened the other night was as much your fault as it was his. Do you really want to be an army wife, Miss Wilma?"

"Of course I do! I married a durned old soldier, didn't I?"

"That part's easy. Any gal can marry a soldier. Being a good army wife to him takes more sense and strength than most gals have. Or most *men*, as a matter of fact. A good wife can make or break a soldier, and she has to be almost a soldier herself. That means she has to be, well, tougher than any feather merchant, male or female. Are you a tough lady, Wilma Dorfler?"

The girl dabbed her eyes, straightened up, and said, "I don't know. I 'spect I can try."

"All right. I want you to stop this sniffling and feeling sorry for yourself. Your man has enough to worry about without running over here every five minutes to kiss your tears away. So cut this kid stuff out and soldier like a grown-up woman. I'm going to lead your husband out against Cheyenne in the morning. I won't lie to you. He could get killed. Any of us could get killed. Are you ready to bite that bullet, missy, or do you want to run home to your mama and play house with dollies who never have another thing on their little wooden minds?"

The girl set her jaw grimly and said, "You're talking awful mean to me. But you don't see me crying about it, do you?"

Matt smiled and said, "I figured you were army. So here's what you're going to do. You're going inside and you're going to wash that face and make yourself even prettier. Then you're going to comfort your man, remembering that he's the one who's likely to get hurt, not you."

"Oh, you're going to let Jimmy come to me, sir?"

"Yeah, and I'll kick myself if you mess up again. I know this is not a proper thing to say to another man's wife, but you're a tempting woman, Wilma. If you were mine, I'd have a hell of a time leaving you alone, too."

"Sir! Whatever are you *saying*?"

"Hush. I know it's improper, but we're both army and it has to be said. Your Jim's a good soldier. It'll be up to you to help keep him that way. I don't care how you do it, but I don't want him sneaking back here every chance he gets. I want him fully dressed and ready to do his duty when that bugle blows in the morning. I don't want him worried about you sitting back here sobbing and lonesome. Do you think you can handle it, Miss Wilma?"

She smiled enigmatically and said, "You send my man to me and I can handle him, Lieutenant."

Matt nodded curtly and turned away. Damn, she was pretty. He chuckled as he realized what Dorfler must have been going through the past few nights. Matt crossed to the orderly room and went in. He found the miserable Dorfler seated at Cohen's desk. He said, "Go over to the guard room and get one of the supernumeraries to relieve you, Corporal."

"Does the lieutenant have another duty for me?"

"Yeah, but it can wait until morning. We're going out to round up some Indians. You'll be leading your squad. It's over, Dorfler. Go to your quarters and get some . . . some sleep."

Dorfler's jaw dropped. Then he rose and said, "I don't know how to thank you, sir."

"You can't, you fool kid. Get out of here before I change my mind."

Dorfler left, and Matt sat down at the desk with a frown. He took the duty roster and began to make changes, taking men of the two platoons he intended to lead off garrison detail and initialing each change. Ben Cohen was going to have a fit, but that was just tough shit. If the rumors he'd heard were true, he'd just improved the first sergeant's sex life, too.

First and Second platoons were lined up and ready to mount in the cold gray light, when the lookout shouted down, "Indians coming in under a white flag!"

Matt turned to Mister Taylor and said, "Hold at rest. I'd better join the powwow."

As he walked away, Taylor nodded at Gus Olsen and the sergeant bellowed, "*De*taiiil . . . *rest*! Anybody wants a piss call, speak now or forever hold your piss."

Matt saw the captain, Fitzgerald, and Bradshaw heading for the gate, too, as it swung open. The Cheyenne delegation consisted of a dozen men, on foot. One carried a pillowcase tied to a reversed lance. He stuck it in the ground just inside the gate. Two others spread a blanket on the dust for their leader, Gray Elk, to sit on. He did so, as a soldier ran over with a folding chair for Captain Conway. The captain sat, crossed his arms, and waited. Matt and the others stood behind him.

Gray Elk's name had nothing to do with his appearance. He was about fifty, but his braided hair was ebony and he'd wrapped himself in a blue blanket. His features were more oriental than those of most Plains Indians, and he could have passed for a Chinese mandarin in demeanor as well as appearance. He met Conway's eyes with no readable expression in his own. Then he said, "I don't see Windy. Is he scouting my camp?"

"He may be," Conway replied. "On the other hand, he may be looking for American Tears and those other renegades."

Conway had offered the opening deliberately, but the old chief was in no hurry. Staring past the captain at the lined-up mounts, he said, "I see you are ready to ride against somebody. I thought we were not supposed to have any more wars with you."

"We don't want to have a war, Gray Elk."

"Good. Give us back the young man, Funny Hair, and we shall say no more about it. Medicine Wolf will be cross with you about the others you are holding, but I will keep to my mark if I get my own young man back with honor."

Conway said impassively, "All three of them rode against the peace under American Tears. Is that how my brother keeps his mark?"

Gray Elk looked uncomfortable. "Hear me. We are not bad people. Those boys were just being boys. I don't care what you do to American Tears. He is not from my band. I think he must be crazy. He made our young men crazy, too. If you give them back to us, they will be scolded by their parents, and the Dog Soldiers will punish them if they start acting silly again."

Conway didn't answer. Without seeming to plead, Gray Elk continued, "Listen. Just give us Funny Hair. He is not a bad boy."

"He fought my soldiers. When they took him prisoner, he resisted."

"That may be true. He has wild blood on his father's side. But his mother is a good person. She is the sister of one of my wives. I will tell you truthfully, I am not going to get much sleep unless I bring that silly boy home to my sister-in-law."

Conway smiled, but didn't answer. The chief said, "You know how women are. Some of our women are after us to fight with you. They are afraid you people will hurt those boys with that cruel trick you have with a rope. I watched your people hang some of Little Crow's band when I was younger, up near Spirit Lake. Heya, that was a very nasty way to kill a man."

"Yesterday those innocent boys you're so worried about killed one of my people," Conway responded. "They peeled his scalp. They cut off his hand."

Gray Elk shrugged and said, "That is our custom. The man was dead. Nobody made him dance around at the end of a rope, soiling and wetting himself, did they?"

"No. They cut him up while he was still alive. What do you people do with the hands, anyway?"

Gray Elk seemed a bit taken aback. "I told you, it is a custom. We Who Cut Fingers have done this always. The old men say it is to keep the dead enemy's ghost from being able to draw a spirit bow and make people sick. The scalp, of course, is taken to honor the dead enemy at the purification dances when we take off our paint. These things all have to be settled properly after a fight. We are not like you. We can't hunt or touch our women until we've put all the spirits to rest by doing the right things."

One of the other elders said something in Cheyenne. Gray Elk nodded in reply and said to Conway, "You know our ways, Captain. What are we going to do about that foolish young man you're holding?"

"All three of them will have to stand trial," Conway replied evenly.

"*Wahah!* That means you're going to hang them!"

"Not necessarily. If they're found innocent, they won't be punished."

"But how is a court-martial going to find them innocent? We all know they did it, don't we?"

"It sure looks that way," the captain agreed. "But don't you see that they have to be punished? They have killed two Delaware scouts and two Americans, a soldier and a civilian. That's four lives someone has to pay for. Yesterday my men killed one of your people. We have three more in our lockup. Add it up."

"I don't like those figures. Hear me, I am not being unreasonable. If you had killed all four in a fair fight, while they were being silly, I could tell their mothers it was their own fault for listening to American Tears. How am I to explain that the three boys are still alive and that I am doing nothing, nothing, like an old woman, afraid of night noises as she sits alone in her lodge?"

Conway didn't comment on the fact that the ante had been raised to all three. He'd assumed that if he gave one, they'd demand all three. Gray Elk stared up at him for a long, unblinking time. Then the chief drew a knife and stuck his other forearm out, saying, "I don't think you understand. I am being very sincere."

The watching whites and a couple of the Indians winced as the old man slowly cut a long gash on his forearm, watching his own blood flowing as he went on, conversationally, "I never made my mark on the treaty because I was afraid of suffering. I have not been a friend to you because I am afraid to die. The young men laugh at me and call me an old weakling. Medicine Wolf has called me a woman. I have taken all this, and more, because I wish to keep my people alive and well. But hear me, if I can't keep my people alive and well by being your friend, I will have to be your enemy. If you don't let me leave this place with those young men, I will come back and get them, wearing my paint!"

The old man put the knife away and sat quietly, waiting for the blood to congeal while he waited for an answer.

Warner Conway said gently, "If you try to take our prisoners by force, many of your other young men will die."

Nodding sadly, Gray Elk replied, "That is true. That is why I come here, begging like a hungry dog. Sometimes it is better to feed a hungry dog than to have it bite."

"You won't have a chance. We have a Gatling gun. We'll mow you down like grass. What kind of a leader loses many men to save a few?"

The old man shrugged. "One who is expected to, by his people. You just don't understand. You Americans can do anything you like. We Who Cut Fingers have laws. I am not bad. I am not foolish. I know you have many guns. I know many of us will die. But what else can I do? I have to follow my people's customs. A chief does not leave his young men alive in an enemy camp. He has to try and save them. I am a chief. I have spoken. What is your answer?"

Conway said, "I have to produce someone for the Great White Father to punish. If you and Medicine Wolf want peace, let American Tears come in to be tried, and I will exchange the boys I'm holding for him. I think the army and the BIA would even settle for just American Tears. One of you for four of us. How do you like *those* numbers?"

"You people are cruel with your numbers," Gray Elk answered, his voice quavering bitterly. "You give us numbers. You say a family needs such and such a number of rations, as if all people liked to eat the same things in the same amounts.

But these number games don't interest me. I don't care if you catch American Tears and hang him. He is not from my band. I don't think Medicine Wolf would care, to be truthful. American Tears, as I said, is crazy and refuses to listen to his elders. But you are not holding American Tears. You are holding Funny Hair. I want Funny Hair. I want him now."

"Then help us catch American Tears."

The old man was thunderstruck. "*Help* you? You want *us* to fight a Cheyenne for you? You want us to turn on our own, while at this very moment you are holding three Cheyenne for a hanging?"

Gray Elk rose to his feet and said, "I am leaving. Everyone I talk to lately seems to be crazy. I am off to make medicine and put on my paint. If my young man is not home by noon, I will know you wish a war."

As the Indians marched off, Conway rose to his feet with a sigh and said, "I think they mean it. You'd better get going."

As Matt saluted and turned away, the IG man, Bradshaw, snorted and said, "That sure was a crazy conversation."

Conway just shrugged and answered, "I don't know. It made perfect sense to me."

Since Matt Kincaid was riding out with the bulk of East Company, and since Mr. Lo was on the prod, this time he flew his colors and took along the bugler, Reb McBride. The blue-and-white guidon fluttered at Matt's right, carried by Stretch Dobbs, who sat taller in the saddle than anyone else in the outfit. The bugler, of course, rode on Matt's left at the head of First Platoon. McBride, like the new Corporal Wilson, was a "Southron," but there the resemblance ended. Unlike the ex-officer from the Carolinas, McBride hailed from Texas and had actually been too young to serve in the War. You couldn't have told this by listening to him when he had a bottle of three-point-two beer in his fist and a Damnyankee (one word) to argue with. Reb was a good soldier and a fair bugler, but a pain in the ass at times about the Lost Cause.

Mr. Taylor led Second Platoon in echelon-left of First, so his left-flank outriders were out of Matt's sight, while Matt's right flankers were over the horizon for Taylor. Yet the two leaders were within easy hand-signal range of one another, and thus the combined outfit swept a wider field than either could have alone. Matt's line of march was along the trail to Medicine

Wolf's that Windy expected the Cheynne to use if they rode toward Outpost Nine and Gray Elk's band. Taylor's position, to the rear and over toward the mountains, was designed to cut them off if, seeing Matt's colors, they made an end run toward the foothills. Third Platoon could have made it a neater dragnet, riding back on the right, but no outfit ever rode out in full strength, since SOP called for at least one-third of the outfit in reserve and holding the base of operations.

Poor George Armstrong Custer's ghost was still trying to explain to the armchair generals why he'd mounted a three-pronged advance that fatal June day on the Little Big Horn, instead of leaving Reno or Benteen forted up behind him as a reserve. Of course, Old George had served in a much more confident army than they had today. These days, a commander who put all his eggs in the front-line basket would be busted—and fast—even if he won.

As they topped a rise two-thirds of the way to Medicine Wolf's camp, Matt spotted Windy Mandalian talking to his point rider on the next rise. Raising his hand to halt the outfit, Matt turned to Gus Olsen and said, "Take over and rest, Sergeant." Then he spurred his own mount forward, and trotted up to join Windy and the point rider.

The scout nodded tersely and said, "They've broke camp, Matt. Nothin' up ahead but cold embers and turds. They don't mean to come back. They bury their shit if they mean to use a campsite again."

"Damn it, Windy," Matt said, "I ordered you to scout ahead. I never told you to ride into a hostile camp alone!"

Turning to one side, Windy spat a brown stream of tobacco juice, then straightened and said matter-of-factly, "Don't try to teach your granny to suck eggs, boy. I'm a scout, not an idjit. I told you they was *gone*. I pussy-footed around slick as hell, till I seen they'd struck their lodge poles and put out the fires. I wasn't earning my pay scouting a mess of nothin', so I eased in to cut sign. I done her, too. They've rode out to the northeast, not bothering to try and hide their tracks. They're dragging everything they own on travois poles. A sissy gal could follow a trail like that."

"They seem to be making a beeline for the reservation, then. Do you suppose they hadn't heard about the capture and Gray Elk's war talk?"

Windy spat again and opined, "Doubt it. When Coronado

was scouting near the Grand Canyon for the King of Spain, that time, his Injun scouts told him another Spanish expedition was over to the east of the Mississippi, and he later found they'd told him true. Gossip is one of Mr. Lo's favorite hobbies, and they always know what's going on over the horizon. I remember this time I was sheltering with some Utes, up around Jackson's Hole, and they was chuckling about a Sioux chief getting caught in the act with his mother-in-law. The hell of it was that the two tribes were at war and killing one another on sight, yet somehow they knew all about each other's scandals."

"I see what you mean. We're a short ride from Gray Elk's camp, and both bands are Cheyenne. But you say Medicine Wolf's headed back to his reservation."

"Now hold on, damn it. I said no such thing. I said they lit out in that direction. Where in the U.S. Constitution does it say a man can only ride in one direction across open prairie? I *told* Medicine Wolf to ride in to Outpost Nine, so he'd have met up with us by now if he was out to stay on our good side."

"Couldn't he just be trying to drop the whole thing by getting back under the Indian agency and having a tight alibi when the army takes off the gloves?"

Windy shook his head and said, "That'd be sensible. It wouldn't be Cheyenne. We're holding two of his young men for a hanging. He wouldn't be a chief long if he started showing squaw-heart."

"So what's his play?"

"Well, it's obvious he's carried his old folks and kids from a camp he knows we know about. He don't want us to Washita them as he rides agin the outfit with his braves. I figure they'll head for the agency a day or so, then do one of two things. They'll hide their kin and chattels in some cottonwood draw and ride hard to join the fun and games. Or they may tell the Dog Soldiers to really lead the noncombatants all the way to the agency and set up an alibi camp. Medicine Wolf is slick, for a Cheyenne."

"I'm missing something. The Indian agency may be fooled into thinking Medicine Wolf's band was on the reservation while his young men hit us, but once the army and BIA compare notes . . ."

"He ain't planning to let us, Matt. If there's no survivors at Outpost Nine, nobody can compare notes with nobody. He figures to be sitting there, making Chief Joseph speeches, when they send out the usual full expedition to clean up and ask questions."

Matt nodded grimly. "Right. Do you suggest we try to head him off, or should we trail him?"

Windy shifted his cud as he stared at the shimmering eastern horizon. "I vote we dog his tracks. It's the long way 'round, but we can make better time on our mounts than he can, dragging all sorts of shit. There's no way in hell we can intercept a force we're not in contact with, on rolling prairie. No matter how we spread out, he could run around our flank and leave us sitting out here like big-ass birds, staring north as he's laughing his fool head off to the south. We can save us a couple of miles by cutting thataway. I know his trail don't fork less than three miles out from his old campsite."

Matt noted the way Windy had pointed to the north-northeast, and nodded to the point rider, who saluted and headed that way. Matt raised his hand, waited until Gus Olsen indicated that he was watching, and signaled the new line of advance.

As the men mounted up, Windy stretched and said, "Well, I'll head out for a look-see."

But Matt halted him. "Stay with me. I know where we're going. I'll need you to read sign when we get there."

"Hell, you can follow the tracks of a travois, Matt."

"I know. But I might miss the hoofprint of an unshod pony in thick buffalo grass. I don't mean to be riding off on a false trail while the Crooked Lancers drop out of the column, one at a time, to form up over the horizon and hit the post."

"Oh, you know that trick, eh?"

"I learned it from the Comanche, the hard way. So let's make sure the Cheyenne don't pull it on us. Ride to my right and tell me if you spot a single broken grass stem. They're depending on us, Windy."

# nine

Back at Outpost Nine, Lieutenant Colonel Bradshaw was interviewing Four Eyes, the company clerk. He'd arrogated Matt's desk off the orderly room, and, finding Four Eyes alone there, called him in for a "friendly chat." Four Eyes tried not to squirm as he sat across the desk from the IG officer. It wasn't easy. The older man looked like a big, sleepy cat regarding a mouse in a corner while it made its mind up whether a sudden pounce was worth the effort on such a hot and lazy day.

The IG officer leaned back with his elbows on the arms of Matt's swivel chair, his fingertips tented like a country parson saying grace. Four Eyes saw his own paybook on the green blotter between them, but since the colonel wasn't looking at it, Four Eyes didn't think he should, either.

Bradshaw smiled tightly and began, "I've just been going over your records, son. Isn't it curious that we both have the same family name? I've been wondering if by chance we might be distant relatives. Bradshaw is a fine old Ulster name."

Four Eyes licked his lips and said, "If you say so, sir. My folks were Scotch-Irish."

"That's what I just said, Lance Corporal. You see, we could be kinsmen. But no matter, it's my job to look out for your best interests in any case. Shouldn't your rank be full corporal? You have a lot of responsibility for a one-striper."

"Sir?"

"Come on, the company clerk handles all the papers. He knows where a lot of bodies are buried, eh?"

"If you say so, sir. The captain's put us all in for promotion, but President Hayes don't hold with spending money. Sergeant Cohen is overdue for his diamond, and he's the first sergeant. So I'll likely have to wait for *my* next stripe."

Bradshaw nodded pointedly at the papers on the desk and said, "Yes, especially since I see you've failed to qualify with your rifle the last three times you were on the range."

So there it was, like a gobbet of spit on the desk between them. First the veiled promises, and now the almost open threat. Four Eyes shrugged and said, "I've been practicing with my Springfield, sir. I hope to do better the next time we fire for record."

"One would hope so. Of course, I can hardly ask for a demonstration with the post under siege. I suppose I could take your sergeant's word that he's satisfied with your improvement. One hand washes the other, eh?"

"Sir?"

"I was just going through the files out front. I can't seem to find any charge sheets on young Corporal Dorfler, the one who deserted his post the other night."

Four Eyes stared, thunderstruck, and blurted, "You went through Sergeant Cohen's files, sir?"

Bradshaw chuckled and said, "I know how first sergeants feel about their files, son. But I don't think he'll really bite me, do you?"

"I don't know, sir. I know neither the captain nor Lieutenant Kincaid ever open a drawer without Ben's say-so. Matter of fact, I've never seen an officer in Ben's files before. They generally ask for what they want and Ben gets it out for them."

"I know all too well how most companies are run, son. That's why they gave me this job. I hold a law degree and I'm an expert on military administration. That's how I know about the way the Sergeant's Club files things in its own inimitable way. Getting back to Dorfler . . ."

"Uh, he went out on patrol this morning, sir."

"While he's supposed to be under arrest to quarters? How interesting. I found no mention of his offense in his paybook."

"Uh, company punishment don't go in a soldier's record, sir. I do know Dorfler's been catching pure ned from Ben and the adjutant. I 'spect they've let up on him, now that Mr. Lo is on the prod."

"No doubt. Company punishment is a company matter, and I'd say no more about it. But I couldn't help noticing you made out a new paybook for him, on fresh paper. Your handwriting, son. Of course, you were only following orders, right?"

Four Eyes looked down and said, "No, sir. I do remember making out a new paybook for him a while back. You see, I spilled some ink on the old one. I made a fair copy, sir. There's nothing in that new book that shouldn't be there."

"Who do you think you're bullshitting, son? I've spent more time pissing in the latrine than you've served in this man's army! We both know you were told to make up a new paybook so that if Dorfler was fined or reduced in rank you could enter it in that dummy, let things cool off, and produce the old paybook as if nothing had ever happened."

Forcing himself to meet the older man's gaze, Four Eyes shook his head stubbornly and insisted, "The new book is a duplicate of the old one, sir. Since you just read it, without leave, you know there's no recent entries, so there can't be anything irregular going on."

"I told you I was an old hand at this game," Bradshaw said. "All right, I can see they intended to go through the motions if I insisted, and then forgot about it when I didn't mention the matter again. We'll put the Dorfler matter aside, at least until he gets back alive. I noticed something else in the files just now. I see that the company has paid for some damage to civilian property out of the orderly room slush fund."

Four Eyes nodded and said, "Yessir. Some feather merchants in town said somebody from the outfit busted up a saloon. The slush fund is discretionary cash collected by the first sergeant every payday. It don't come from Uncle Sam. Ben has a mason jar on the table, and as the men get paid they drop some loose change in it. They don't have to. It's for emergencies, like busted saloon glass or a man having to be sent on emergency leave with no pocket money."

The IG officer rolled his eyes heavenward and sighed, "Please don't explain everything to me, soldier. Let me guess once in a while. I know about those mason jars. I've caught more than one first sergeant putting the unrecorded cash in his hope chest, too."

"Not Ben Cohen, sir. He keeps a record of the slush funds, and accounts for every nickel to the adjutant. If he hadn't writ down that withdrawal, you'd never have known about it, right?"

"It's still sloppy, and some of us in IG don't approve of such semi-legal finances. But let's assume the sergeant did in fact pay for some damage some of his soldiers did in town. That leaves us with the very interesting problem of *who*. I'd like an answer, soldier."

"Sir?"

"Come on, damn it. If you laid out money for a busted-up saloon, you have to know who busted it up. I couldn't find any record of the brawl or whatever. How do you account for this?"

Four Eyes said, "It's not my job to account for it, sir. I'm only the company clerk, not the adjutant or the first sergeant. It's not for me to hand out company punishment. So I don't. I can't tell you who got into a fuss with some feather merchants, but I do know that any man Ben caught at it must have been made to wish he hadn't done it."

Bradshaw shook his head and said, "That's not good enough. The ARs allow the company to take unrecorded disciplinary action against a man for minor infractions. What we have here is a civilian claim against the U.S. Army, paid to said civilian satisfaction, without a goddamned thing on paper that means anything remotely legal. I don't care if the offending soldier walked it off or dug a hundred holes in the ground. If the U.S. Army paid out one nickel for his offense, the money is supposed to come out of his pay. So somebody, somewhere, should have a notation to that effect in his paybook. I can't find it. Who was it, son?"

"I don't know, sir."

"You handle the mail and you sit right next to the first sergeant, don't you?"

"Yessir."

"And you expect me to believe that a hot-under-the-collar saloonkeeper made a bitch about broken glass, and that the first sergeant paid him off, and that you have no idea what happened or who did it? You'd have to be mighty stupid not to know, wouldn't you?"

"Yessir. No excuse, sir."

Bradshaw nodded ominously and said, "You're making a

big mistake, son. I know they told you a good soldier backs his outfit. But not during an IG inspection, if he knows what's good for him. You realize that I could put you in my report as unfit for combat?"

"I can fight if I have to, sir."

"Not according to your range scores. How soon do you suppose you'll make your next stripe in a QM depot? Come to think of it, how long do you suppose you'll keep the one you have, if you're transferred to some outfit that already has all the clerical help it needs? You're not qualified to do anything else, you know."

Four Eyes faced his tormentor with a stubborn jaw and courage he'd never known he possessed as he said, very calmly, "I know what you can do to me, sir. I don't see how I'll ever stop you, either. But I've told you all I aim to. So you'll just have to do as you see fit."

Bradshaw made a mental note that the company's morale was good, however sloppily it was run. He smiled and said, "We're both doing our job, son. Your loyalty does you credit, and I'm not going to give you a hard time. I'll get what I want from somebody else. There's always somebody else. Carry on, Lance Corporal. You're dismissed."

Four Eyes rose with a relieved look and saluted. But before he could leave Matt's office, they both heard an outraged bellow from the orderly room next door. Then Sergeant Cohen appeared in the doorway, scowling horribly as he yelled, "Some crazy son of a bitch has been at my desk! I'll tear his fucking head off and shove it up his ass! I'll cut him into little pieces and mail him home a sliver at a time, and after that, I'll kill him!"

Then Ben spotted the IG man seated at Matt's desk. It did nothing for his disposition. He gaped in horror and said, "That's Lieutenant Kincaid's desk you're sitting at, Colonel!"

Four Eyes moved out of the line of fire as Bradshaw said, "That's all right. I'm sure your adjutant won't mind, and if he does, it's too bad. I outrank him by three grades."

Cohen said flatly, "Get out of that chair and out of this office, you . . . sir."

Bradshaw laughed incredulously and asked, "Are you crazy? Can't you see these silver oak leaves on my shoulders, Sergeant?"

"I don't care if you're wearing four silver stars and a ring in your nose, goddamnit! That's Lieutenant Kincaid's desk, not yours, not nobody else's. I'm asking you polite to move your ass, sir."

"And I'm telling you to go straight to hell!" Bradshaw flared, adding, "No goddamned enlisted man born of mortal woman tells a colonel where he can or cannot sit. Do you really want to push this, Sergeant?"

Cohen reached for his holster, drew his Scoff, and said, "If I have to, sir. I asked polite. Now I'm asking serious."

He sounded like he meant it.

Bradshaw rose, ominously calm. "I suppose you understand what you're asking for, soldier?"

"Yessir. I'm asking you to behave yourself. We're both old army, sir. We both know you are way out of line. You had no right to barge in here unannounced and go through other people's things. You had no right to make yourself at home in another officer's office. That's his personal desk. He could have personal things in the drawers, but I'll take your word you haven't stolen anything if you'll kindly get the hell out of here!"

Bradshaw drew himself up and said, "I promise you, Sergeant, I intend to report this insubordination to your commanding officer, and if he doesn't bust you on the spot, I'm taking it all the way to the top!"

Cohen nodded. "You do that, sir. Then I'll insist on a full court-martial before I surrender my stripes."

"Don't worry. You'll get one."

"Yessir. Then I'll have to tell your fellow field-grade officers what an asshole you are. Number one: No officer of any rank or for any reason ever enters enlisted country without sending a noncom ahead of him to call the people inside to attention. That's in the ARs, if you want to look it up. Number two: No officer or noncommissioned officer is allowed to open a drawer, footlocker, or whatsoever unless the soldier who owns what's inside it is present and has been told his things are being searched or inspected, and why. You can look that up, too, sir."

"Goddamnit, I'm making an inspection for the IG!"

"That may well be, sir. But the Inspector General in the flesh is supposed to follow the ARs, and you haven't followed them worth shit. Nobody, repeat *nobody*, enters any orderly room without knocking and receiving permission to enter said goddamned orderly room. The President of these United States does not have the right to enter any officer's office or quarters without his permission, and I don't remember hearing you ask Lieutenant Kincaid's permission to use his office. So if you won't leave willing, I'm placing you under formal arrest."

"Arrest? You can't arrest a commissioned officer!"

"I can if I have reason to suspect him of being a burglar, sir."

"Burglar? You wouldn't dare! You must be drunk."

"No, sir, I'm in charge of keeping order here, and you're the one who's making all the trouble. So what's it going to be?"

"We'll see about this," Bradshaw muttered as he left, stamping his feet peevishly. Cohen smiled thinly and put his gun back in the holster.

Four Eyes was staring at him in utter horror. He said, "Ben, you can't talk like that to a fucking officer!"

Cohen said, "I just did."

"I heard! What do you figure he'll do now?"

"Oh, he'll rage over to the old man and have a fit, I suspicion. Then the captain will calm him down and explain the facts of life to him. I'll probably get chewed, but the son of a bitch was in the wrong, and after everyone calms down they'll figure that out. So what the hell. You can't let them walk over you, kid. There's no way in hell to run an orderly room right if any asshole officer who feels like it comes in to poke through things that are none of his goddamned business."

Four Eyes said, "He's really going to be out for blood now. He was just trying to get me to rat on you, but I never."

"Hell, I never expected you to, kid. Simmer down. I think we've educated him some. You've got to learn about officers, Four Eyes. They can make you nervous, if you don't know their limitations. He's got everybody scared because they think he can give us a bad report. But I figured out a long time ago that the bastards *always* give a bad report."

Cohen grumped out to his own desk with Four Eyes in tow, still saying dumb things about military courtesy. Cohen sat down and said, "Screw the IG. I've been searching high and low for that new man, Bishop. The one they call Red. If I didn't know better, I could swear he wasn't on the post. Where the hell could he be hiding from me?"

Sitting down at his own desk, Four Eyes asked, "Could he have ridden out with the others, Sarge?"

"Not hardly. In the first place, he's supposed to be pulling KP. In the second, he's not assigned to either platoon."

"He's sort of mixed up about a lot of things, Sarge," Four Eyes suggested. "I was talking to his pal, Pud. Couldn't he have sort of tagged along with them? Pud says he thinks he's the U.S. Cavalry."

Cohen looked disgusted and growled, "Jesus, you really are an orderly room john. Nobody 'tags along' in this man's army, damn it. There's a corporal to every eight men, and even a corporal can count to eight without taking his shoes off. Where were you when the outfit rode out? Didn't you hear them call the roll and check each rider off?"

There was a knock on the door. Cohen yelled, "It's open!" and the civilian hostler from the stables came in. As a civilian, he knew Cohen wasn't allowed to bite him, but he'd been in the army during the War, and first sergeants still made him nervous. He said, "Well, I tallied the horses like you asked when you dropped by the stables a while back, Sarge."

"And?"

"Well, we seem to be missing that white-faced gelding that Lieutenant Fitzgerald rode out here from GHQ. I think he calls it Baldy. We searched high and low for the brute, and the long and the short of it is, he ain't here no more."

Cohen shook his head and moaned, "Oh, shit."

The hostler asked, "Do you want to tell that heavy-weapons john, or do I have to, Sarge?"

"I'll handle it," Cohen said. "Don't worry, I'm a born diplomat. You won't be held accountable. You reported it to me at first light, remember?"

The hostler looked blank. Then he grinned and said, "Right. You're a good man, Sarge. What do I say if that sassy heavy-weapons man comes looking for his mount?"

"Tell him to see me. He won't be going for a canter around the park with Mr. Lo lurking outside the postern, anyway. Go on back and finish your card game in the tack room. I told you you were covered, damn it."

The hostler left and Four Eyes asked, "Do you think he's deserted, Sarge?"

"It's a mite early to tell. Did you ever run away when you were a kid, Four Eyes?"

"How did you know that, Sarge?"

"Hell, every kid runs away at least once. Most times, their folks never know about it. They get a couple of miles from home and then the excitement starts to wear off as they study on where they aim to spend the night and what they're going to have for supper. When they get back and their mama asks where in tarnation they've been, they just say they lost track of the time while they were out playing pirates, right?"

Four Eyes grinned sheepishly and reminisced, "I was off to be a buffalo hunter or maybe a lion tamer if I could meet up with a circus." Then he sobered and came back to the here-and-now. "But old Red's a grown man, riding a horse and packing a gun, Sarge."

"You're right about him being mounted and armed. We'll wait and see how grown-up he is. He was on the post at morning report. Lieutenant Kincaid won't be back for a while. I see no need to bother the captain about it before I have to."

"But what about the mess sergeant? Ain't Red Bishop supposed to be on KP?"

"Of course he's supposed to be on KP, damn it. How did you think I knew he was missing? Dutch was sore as hell when he came to me about it. But Dutch won't say anything to the fucking officers. I told him not to."

"You sure are sticking your neck out for that recruit, Sarge."

"I know. The silly son of a bitch is going to pay for it, too, if and when he comes back. The point is that we have to give him the chance to see the light. You do see how we'll have to log it, if it goes on paper, don't you?"

Four Eyes said, "Sure. Going on Dutch leave aboard an officer's horse sounds mighty naughty, Sarge."

Cohen shook his head and said, "Dutch leave, my ass! The charge would have to be desertion in the face of the enemy! The outfit is officially on combat alert. If the Indians don't get the silly son of a bitch before the army does, he'll hang, sure as shit!"

"Hell, Sarge, a lot of old boys have deserted the army and got away with it, haven't they?"

"Maybe. The MPs haven't time to look for every fool kid who forgot to come back from town. But they'll make the time for a man who deserts an outpost under siege aboard a stolen officer's horse. There's no place in these United States that poor bastard can feel safe. So let's just hope he wises up to that before I have to turn him in. What time is it?"

"Eleven going on twelve, Sarge. Why?"

"We'll give him until retreat formation before we put it on paper."

"Can't it wait until bed check, Sarge? There's no roll call at retreat."

Cohen shook his head and said, "I'm his top kick, not his mother. We've got our own asses to think of. Besides, if he's not back by sundown, he won't be coming back at all."

"A boy could do some serious thinking in the dark, Sarge."

"I know. But it won't matter. He might have gotten through the Cheyenne going out this morning, but he sure won't get through them coming back after dark."

Matt Kincaid stared thoughtfully down at the trampled grass. "All right," he observed, "it looks like the whole band swung south here, toward Gray Elk's camp. How do you figure it, Windy?"

Mandalian shrugged and said, "They haven't split up after all."

"I can see that, damn it. Medicine Wolf is heading in to Outpost Nine with all his baggage. But if he means to shelter his noncombatants with the other bands, why did he make this six- or seven-mile detour?"

Windy said, "He likely didn't aim to meet up with us afore he had 'em all forted up in Tipi Town. You've got to stop trying to think like an Indian, Matt. It ain't possible. *I* figured he was sending his squaws and elders toward the reservation, too. But as you see, he ain't. He may have planned to. They likely argued back and forth about it as they rode this far. Then some old squaw convinced them there was no sense jawing about it no more and, as you see, they all cut south together."

Mr. Taylor had ridden over from his own command, which was halted in the middle distance. He asked what was up, and Matt pointed at the travois marks and said, "We're going to have to catch up with them. I'll want you on my left flank, just in bugle range. We've got the speed on them. So when we get them on the skyline, I want you to dismount and hold. I'll try to ride around and cut them off from the post. If they stop in a bunch, we'll know they're willing to talk it over. If the bucks peel off on their ponies, I'll go after them. You'll move in and pin down their dependents. Warn your men to behave as they hold them. I don't want anyone shooting some noisy squaw or a kid with a toy bow."

"What if they really want to fight us, Matt?"

"I doubt they'll be that foolish. You'll have to use your own judgment. Naturally, if it's to be them or us, it'll have to be them. But for Christ's sake, don't gun down anyone not wearing paint unless they're actually pointing a gun at you and yours. Don't let your men fire at will. Assign a sharpshooter from each squad to pick off any idiots who actually resist. Tell them to aim low if they have to fire at all. Give them time to fuss and yell back and forth. Remember that a squaw hoisting her skirts is telling you she wants to surrender, not that she wants to get laid. I don't have to tell you the army's views on rape. But you'd better make sure your men know my views on scalps and other souvenirs. Move it out, Taylor. We've got some ground to cover this afternoon."

As Taylor rode off, Matt spurred his own mount forward and followed the trail south between the bugle and the colors. Windy rode up to fall in with the point rider a quarter-mile ahead, so Matt knew he didn't have to watch the grass, but he did anyway. The sun was almost directly overhead, and the trail wasn't easy to spot, with no shadows to outline the occasional hoofmark or travois line on softer ground. He spotted a horse apple and saw it was fresh. The flies had found it, but no cowbirds were pecking at it, so it had only been there a few hours at the most. He resisted the impulse to have Reb McBride blow canter. They were moving at a slow, mile-eating trot that wouldn't jade their mounts, yet had to be faster than the Indians' pace. He knew a pony dragging a travois had to move at a plodding walk.

*Careful,* he warned himself. *You're doing it again.*

Windy was right about a white man trying to think like an Indian. It could lead to wrong conclusions. Neither race was smarter or dumber, he thought, but they didn't think the same way. It probably confused the Indians, too. Matt knew, objectively, about some of Mr. Lo's notions. But he didn't *feel* them. For example, he understood perfectly well that the Black Hills and the Blackfoot Indians were misnamed by his own kind because of the language barrier between English and

Sioux. He knew that the Sioux used the same word for "black" and "blue," not because they were color-blind, but because, to them, black was simply a deep shade of blue, or blue was a light shade of black, just as a varied number of completely different hues were lumped together by whites as "brown." So *Paha Sapa* translated into English as "Black Hills," even though both white and Indian eyes saw them hazy slate blue in the distance, like the Blue Ridge Mountains back East. The so-called Blackfoot Indians wore blue moccasins. The Flathead Indians had perfectly normal skulls, and had been given their grotesque name by other tribes who *did* deform their skulls in childhood. Few tribes called themselves by the names the government had them listed under. Sioux, Crow, Snake, Apache, even Cheyenne, were nicknames passed on via hazy translations, often from their Indian enemies. Learned professors wrote about "customs" they really didn't understand, and politicians made laws and regulations based on the professors' assumptions and mistakes. The Indian, of course, was just as mistaken in many ideas he had about the whites. Men of goodwill, on both sides, had died, and would die, because other men of goodwill mistook a friendly gesture for a threat. Matt knew that neither Gray Elk nor Medicine Wolf had the vaguest grasp of law as the white man saw it. Many a well-meaning Indian agent or army officer could be just as obtuse about Indian customs. Neither side was completely right or wrong; they were just . . . different.

Matt saw that Windy and the point rider had stopped on a rise ahead. He held up his hand to halt his men as he called to the sergeant, "Take ten. Windy's found something."

He rode forward with a puzzled frown. He knew they had to be a good two or three hours behind Medicine Wolf's band, and the two men out ahead didn't act like they felt themselves in any danger.

He loped up the rise to rein in beside Windy. The scout pointed with his chin.

"Oh, my God!" Matt groaned, as he saw what lay in the next draw.

A soldier in fresh blues lay facedown in the grass. They'd taken his boots, his hat, and his weapons, as well as his scalp and right hand. Windy was dismounting, so Matt did the same. The outrider took their reins to hold their mounts away from the smell of death.

Windy reached the cadaver first, hunkered down, and touched a finger to the peeled skull. As Matt joined him, Windy said, "Kilt just an hour or so ago. His britches are still wet, too."

Windy rolled the dead youth over. Red Bishop's bloody face and oyster-gray eyes were filmed with dust and grass stems. Windy said, "I've seed this gent afore. Ain't he from Easy, Matt?"

Matt nodded and said, "His name was Bishop. He just came to join us. What the hell could he have been doing out here alone? How far are we from the post?"

"Less'n twenty miles. Mebbe eighteen. They likely sent him out with dispatches and he got losted."

"I can't see the captain sending a green hand out on such a mission, but we'll worry about that part when we get back. The point is that we now know for sure that Medicine Wolf has taken off the gloves. I was hoping he'd powwow some, even if he beat us back. But the fat's in the fire now. He's bought himself a war whether he wants one or not."

"Now, don't go getting your bowels in an uproar, old son," Windy cautioned. "This boy wasn't kilt by the main band."

"What are you talking about? Look at those travois marks over there. He was killed right on Medicine Wolf's trail. What do you need, a signed confession?"

Windy stood up and said, "Look some more. I thought you knowed how to read sign, damn it."

Puzzled, Matt slowly circled the dead soldier, staring down at the ground. He spotted the sharp point of a shod army mount, superimposed on a dusty rut left by a dragging pole. He nodded and said, "Right. Bishop came through this draw after Medicine Wolf's baggage had passed through. He probably spotted the sign, green as he was. He might have dismounted to hunker down and study it."

Windy said, "No 'might' about it. He was off his mount when they caught him. Can you tell me why, now that you're so smart?"

Matt nodded and said, "It's simple. The boy would have been moving at a full gallop if he'd been mounted when they topped that rise and came down at him. You can see where a couple of ponies slid, moving down the slope at a run. Bishop's mount was here, standing. See where it tore up a clump of grass with its horseshoe? That must have been when it spooked as they fired. He was facing *that* way and—" He paused and looked around for a moment, then went on, "Right, he turned and ran, *away* from his mount. There's no spent brass. He never fired. He just panicked and took the first round in the back."

"You said he was new," Windy observed. "Look over here. Unshod pony circled to cut off the army brute. They took his horse as a trophy. Here's where they led it off. Empty saddle. Hoofmarks would be deeper if anyone was riding it. I'd say they headed due east, if that's all right with you."

Matt squatted to get a better angle on the trampled grass stems and said, "Yeah, they circled east, all right. I'd have expected them to trail Medicine Wolf. I read it as a dozen or more. Do you think it was American Tears?"

Windy nodded. "I don't *think* it. I *know* it. Any other war party would have followed the main band, but American Tears is a free thinker. He don't want a fuss with his chief, and even if he did, he's yellow. Medicine Wolf is headed for a showdown with the U.S. of A. Old American Tears don't cotton to odds like that. Him and his young rascals are out for easy pickings."

Matt nodded and started walking slowly back to his mount on the rise above, taking out a cigar and lighting up as he digested this latest development. As he was remounting, Taylor rode in again. Matt said, "You can see what they did. You'll be moving out after me, so detail a couple of your men to wrap him up and lash him aboard one of your ammo mules. We're riding east."

Taylor frowned and said, "East, Matt? We're about due north of the outpost, aren't we?"

"Yeah, and Medicine Wolf is headed that way with his main band. We have to nail American Tears, and soon. You know what's over to the east, don't you?"

"Sure," Taylor agreed, "but nobody's about to hit a whole town with a handful of bucks, Matt."

Matt said, "They won't ride into any town. They'll look for stray travelers or a lonely homestead a few hours outside of the main settlement. We have to catch up before they find more easy prey."

Taylor pursed his lips and whistled softly. Then he stared southward and asked, "What about the others back at the post, Matt? They'll have their hands full, holding off two bands of Cheyenne without us, won't they?"

Matt Kincaid nodded grimly. "That's true. On the other hand, the captain's behind a wall and expecting trouble. Trouble is his job. We were sent out here to protect the civilian settlers. Do you think some farmer alone with his wife and kids in some soddy will feel protected if American Tears comes to supper uninvited, Mr. Taylor?"

"Just hold your horses, damn it. I know we can't let those rascals hit unprepared civilians. But why can't one platoon or the other ride back to Outpost Nine and give them a hand? They're likely to need it, Matt."

The senior officer shook his head and said, "Neighborly thought, but bad tactics. You don't divide your command in the field if you can avoid it."

"Come on, Matt. How many riders does American Tears have with him, a dozen? Either of us could have him for supper with enough left over for dessert."

Matt stared across the draw where Windy was still scouting for sign. Turning back to Taylor then, he said, "Custer thought he was chasing thirty bucks with five troops of the Seventh Cav when he found out the hard way that a small band can fall in suddenly with God knows how many. Get back to your platoon and trail echelon to the north. Spread out as far as you can without losing contact."

Taylor said, "At your command, sir. But under protest. Our friends back at the outfit are sure going to feel lonesome when the main Cheyenne force hits them tonight."

"Protest noted, mister. But for the record, soldiers don't have friends. They serve with other soldiers whom everyone expects to do their duty. Move it out, Taylor."

Taylor wheeled his mount and rode off sullenly. Matt turned to the enlisted point rider and said, "You must have been following that discussion, soldier, so you know the new line of march. Ride over to Windy with his mount, and tell him to stop poking about in the grass and head for those settlements to the east."

Then Matt wheeled his own mount and headed back to where Stretch stood with the colors, resting his mount. The sun was hot on Matt's shoulders, and he was suddenly feeling older and more tired. He knew all too well what a severe choice he'd had to make. But it was the only choice he had. He knew Captain Conway would approve, if the outfit came through alive. The skeleton force at the outpost had to hold as best it knew how. The platoon had water, ammo, and provisions. The walls were thick enough to stop most bullets. Conway didn't have enough men to properly man the whole perimeter, even in broad daylight, but that was Conway's problem. An officer could only worry about the job at hand. So he told himself to forget about the outpost until he could get back to it.

But he couldn't forget. Down on the Staked Plains, he'd ridden into an isolated outpost after the Comanche had overrun it. It hadn't been the dead soldiers that had bothered him; you expected to see dead soldiers. It had been the scalped and multilated women that had made him feel so heartsick. And he hadn't even known those other army wives.

As he rejoined his men, Reb McBride snapped to attention, bugle cocked under his forearm, and Matt said, "As you were. Sergeant Olsen?"

Gus Olsen moved toward him, leading his mount, and asked, "Sir?"

"Have the men mount up. We're swinging east after hostiles."

"East, sir?"

"If I'd have meant south, I'd have said south, Sergeant."

Olsen saluted and started to turn away. But Matt said, "Gus?"

"Yessir?"

"I know you have a woman wondering if she should hold supper for you tonight. I guess that entitles you to a couple of questions."

Gus Olsen said, "No questions, sir. You just lead. Me and the boys will follow you."

Matt nodded and turned his face away. It hadn't helped one bit.

# ten

The sun had passed the zenith and was baking the western wall of Outpost Nine as Captain Conway circled the parapet. The dry sod roofing underfoot crunched crisply as he trod it. He knew all this activity was cascading flour-fine dust over the floors and furnishings below, and that the housekeeping would be a bitch for the next few days, but it couldn't be helped. He'd ordered every man who wasn't engaged in something vital up to man the walls, and he would have had more up here, if there'd been more. They were spread dangerously thin, at wide intervals. They were set to repel one rush, maybe two, considering they had six-shooters to back up their single-shot Springfields. If any two men in a row were picked off, it would leave a dangerous gap that an opportunistic enemy would be all too quick to take advantage of.

As he approached Dutch Rothausen, the mess sergeant snapped to attention, facing him. Conway said, "As you were, Sergeant. Keep your eyes out *that* way."

The cook said, "No excuse, sir," and braced his rifle on the sod bulwark again as Conway stared northeast over his shoulder. Neither man could make out any activity in Tipi Town. The lodges shimmered quietly in the harsh sunlight. But though it looked deserted over there, the air throbbed to the monotonous thumping of a tomtom.

"Tedious, isn't it?" Conway muttered. "Have you made the aid station ready and assigned litter bearers, Dutch?"

"Yessir. The stoves are cold, like you ordered. We've plenty of cold coffee and sterile water standing by. I boiled extra brown sugar and less pork than usual in the beans we set aside."

"Good thinking. Cold grease in combat rations can get tedious. I'm not sure I want you up here, Dutch. You're the closest thing to a surgeon we've got. Did Sergeant Cohen post you up here, or is this your own idea?"

"If it please the captain, I thought I'd lend a hand up here until I'm needed in the dressing station. I've been known to shoot a possible."

"I've read your range scores, Dutch. I know how boring it can be just waiting around, too. I'll meet you halfway. You can sweat it out up here until the action starts. I'll give you one free shot at Mr. Lo. But then you're to move directly to the kitchen. You're a good shot, it's true, but you're a better sawbones, and no damned good to a wounded man up here. If you're hit yourself, we're really in trouble."

"But, sir . . ."

"Carry on, Sergeant," snapped Conway, moving away. He got to the next soldier who, having heard the exchange, didn't move away from the bulwark. Conway said, "Private Hollis, when Sergeant Rothausen drops out, I want you to dress to your right and cover his gap as well as this position. I'm sorry, I don't remember your last range score."

Hollis said, "I shot an eighty-six, sir."

"Good enough. They'll probably start testing us in a while. Gray Elk and his bucks know the deadline, so they'll circle at maximum range, trying to make us look foolish and waste some ammo. Don't fire at anyone less than two hundred yards out."

"But, sir, ain't the deadline *three* hundred yards?"

"Yes. But let's be big about it. Hitting a moving target at more than two hundred is a bitch, and Mr. Lo knows it. Any buck circling within two hundred is either serious or showing off more than I'll sit still for. Remember to aim at the pony, not the rider. Even at two hundred, it's not easy to hit an acrobat all gussied up in feathers and trying to do a war dance aboard a bronc. If you spill a Cheyenne and he runs for his own lines, let him go. If he heads for you, kill him."

"You don't want me to pepper a sassy Injun after I dismount him, sir?"

"Not if you don't have to. I'm not being sentimental. A

dead or wounded comrade draws rescue parties like a horse turd draws flies. Dropping the first couple is easy enough. Then more and more tear in to try and scoop them up until, next thing you know, some son of a bitch is sheltered close behind the downed men and horses, shooting up at you from cover and close range. I want to keep the action loose and undecided until Lieutenant Kincaid and the others get back. Understood?"

"Yessir. I'll just aim at horses for now."

Conway moved on. The next two men were old hands who seemed to know what was expected of them. Conway found Four Eyes at the northeast corner. He made a mental note to order him moved, but didn't say anything about this to the mousy clerk. He knew the kid needed all the confidence he could get. He repeated his instructions about the range and tactics, wondering if Four Eyes knew what two hundred yards was, and doubting that he could hit anything at fifty. At least Four Eyes offered the sight of a human head and rifle, here. The Indians had no way of knowing he was a weak link; Gray Elk would figure the corner men were the usual sharpshooters. Conway nodded in sudden understanding and asked, "Did Sergeant Cohen post you here, son?"

"Yessir. He said this was the last place they'd try to lean a climbing pole against the wall, but I've brought an extra pistol anyway."

"Ben Cohen's wider awake than me, this afternoon. How are you feeling? Nervous?"

Four Eyes smiled wanly and said, "I'm scared shitless, Captain. But don't you worry. I won't break."

"Nobody expects you to, son. Carry on."

Conway moved past three more men before he came to Ben Cohen, walking the other way. The first sergeant was commanding the north wall, not manning a stretch of it, so of course he was moving back and forth. He stopped and saluted as the CO approached. Returning the salute, Conway said, "We're thin, Ben. Any suggestions?"

Cohen replied, "I sent most of the men to the west wall, figuring the sun. That heavy-weapons section under Lieutenant Fitzgerald ought to hold the gate and tower on the east with little trouble, even if their dumb Gatling gun *is* useless."

"Good thinking. They don't know the Gatling has broken down, and even if they did, Gray Elk wouldn't want to charge the gate with the sun in his eyes. The south approaches are a little far for a wounded man to make it, crawling back to his tipi. This north wall, of course, puts the encampment over there in danger from a wild stray round or two in an all-out firefight. I think you're right about any real attack coming from the west, probably just before sunset. But I want some more men here anyway. The trouble with fighting Mr. Lo by the book is that he doesn't *read* the book."

Cohen shifted uncomfortably and replied, "I agree, sir. But where am I supposed to get the extra men? I've got one squad in reserve below, as you ordered. Everybody else is already up here."

"What about the civilian suttler and horse handlers?"

"South wall, sir. A couple of the ladies volunteered. I told them no."

Conway nodded absently, as he considered this. Then he said, "All right. Leave things as they are up here, for now. We'd better have the reserves up here as well, an hour before sundown and at least an hour after moonrise. Then send a squad at a time down to bunk four hours at a stretch."

"May I make a suggestion, sir?"

"Go ahead, Ben."

"The men can haul their rolls up here and kip out just as well. There's no sign of wind or rain, and if Mr. Lo plans a night attack—"

"Do it. About the ladies—I think we'd better issue arms to the ones who know how to handle them."

"I already did, sir."

"Oh, good. We'd better concentrate them in one place so we know where they are, if and when. Agreed?"

"Yessir. Miss Flora thought so, too. All the womenfolk are holed up in the mess hall. The older wives are showing the younger ones how to load and aim the guns I issued them. Miss Flora said they'd be handy to any wounded carried to the kitchen, and—"

"Sometimes," Conway cut in with a wry smile, "I wonder who's running this post. Carry on, Ben."

A head popped over the edge of the roof, followed by the rest of Lieutenant Colonel Bradshaw. The IG man dusted his knee with his hat. A frown was on his face as he joined Conway and said, "I've been waiting for your orders, Captain."

Conway eyed the short colonel warily, noted that the burly

first sergeant had moved out of earshot, and said, "Well, sir, we could use an officer on the south wall, but the last I heard—"

"All right, I've got a temper," Bradshaw cut in. "Temper is one of the privileges of rank. But I'm not a total idiot. I can always chew a sassy soldier's ass. Right now I'm more concerned with my scalp, so we'll talk about the sloppy shop you run another time. How does it look to you, Captain?"

Conway pointed at the distant tipi ring with his chin and said, "Not a peep out of them since Gray Elk left the party mad, sir. There's no smoke above the lodges, so they've banked their fires, too."

"Does that mean anything? What's that tomtom saying?"

"A man wearing paint doesn't eat cooked meat," Conway explained. "The squaws are set to strike the poles and move at a moment's notice, no matter how things turn out. There used to be an American flag on Gray Elk's smoke pole. It's not there now. The tomtom is making medicine. I've heard the beat before. The Dream Singers are asking Matou for guidance. Meanwhile, everyone is still arguing. We'll know they've made their minds up when the drumbeats stop or change."

Bradshaw asked what he was supposed to do on the south wall. Conway repeated the tactics he'd outlined to the other men, and added, as politely as he could, that an officer on that side was mostly just for the visual comfort of the greener hands and civilians. He said, "Pop Evans, the suttler, is an old Indian trader and squaw man, so he won't need to be told what to do. It's just as well. Evans doesn't think he has to take orders from the army, anyway."

"I know," Bradshaw said. "I asked to see his books and he told me to go to hell. Some of the men say he's been overcharging them at his store, by the way."

Conway shrugged disinterestedly. "It's hard to stretch thirteen dollars a month from one payday to the next. But Pop's all right. If it was up to me, the army would run its own canteen and general store. Since they have to license private merchants, they have saddled some outfits with real crooks. I'm sorry he won't show you his books, but I'll vouch for him not overcharging or asking interest on his tabs."

Bradshaw still looked dubious, but decided not to pursue the matter right now. As he was about to turn away, a distant voice called out, "Lone Injun coming in from the northwest!"

Both men swung around to watch as a Cheyenne in full brag bored in at a gallop, shaking a feathered lance and singing his death song.

Conway's voice was conversational as he told Bradshaw, "Crooked Lance candidate. Showing off. No coup feathers. Just a kid."

The Indian reined in a little less than three hundred yards from the north wall, and began to shout at them as he shook his lance like a rattle, making his blue-spotted buckskin pony dance in place.

"What the hell does he think he's doing?" Bradshaw asked.

Conway said, "I told you, sir. Showing off. See those others, over near the tipi ring, watching? The kid has made his brag, and they're letting him test us as he proves he's a man."

"What are we supposed to do?"

"Nothing, right at the moment. He knows he's close enough to look good, far enough to be a tough target. He's already inside our official deadline, so he's got one half-ass coup right there. Of course, those elders watching know the facts of life, too, so they won't award him a coup, but they'll have to listen politely as he boasts about it tonight in camp."

The Indian edged a bit closer, bouncing from side to side and keening like a woman in labor. Then he drove the tip of his lance into the earth and dismounted gracefully, to start dancing in a circle around the feathered lance.

Conway said, "That's a challenge. He's saying that if one of us wants to come out and fight, he won't run away."

"Jesus Christ, does anybody ever go?"

"Hardly. He's not really expecting us to take him up on it. He's only carrying a tomahawk."

"I can see that. He's rather tempting, even for an old desk soldier. What would happen if I went crazy and rode out to teach him a lesson?"

"His friends would be able to say it wasn't fair, since you'd naturally be packing a gun," Conway replied.

"I see. Then they'd swoop in and shoot me. Who'd get my hair?"

"Oh, the kid out there, of course. He's made the offer, so it'd be his fight. The men who killed you would each count coup for helping a comrade in danger, but your scalp and the main honors would go to that prancing idiot."

"It sure is a dumb way to wage war, Matt."

"I know, sir. I've never been able to figure out how they keep winning every once in a while. But remember, you're just watching a sideshow. Fetterman and Custer both found out they sometimes get down to serious soldiering during the main event."

The Indian stopped dancing, shook his fist, and remounted before plucking his lance from the earth and shaking it some more. Then he yelled and started riding at right angles to them. Bradshaw asked, "Now what does he think he's doing?" and Conway explained, "He means to circle us. That's considered brave, too. He'll make a full circuit of our walls at a safe range and then ride back to tell everybody how easy it was."

"Aren't you going to order your men to fire?"

"Lord, no. Letting him circle us is bad enough. If he circles under fire, he'll really look fancy."

But as the would-be hero swung around the northeast corner, a Springfield fired somewhere.

Conway groaned, "Oh, shit!" Then his jaw dropped as the Indian's blue-dotted pony tumbled ass over teakettle, spilling its rider in a cloud of dust!

"Hold your fire!" Conway shouted, as the Cheyenne got shakily to his feet, looked around for his lance, and suddenly started running for his life, leaving weapon and downed mount behind, as, all along the wall, the men of Easy Company jeered and laughed.

Conway laughed, too, and headed for the source of the rifle shot as he called out, "Who did that? It was either shithouse luck or damned fine markmanship!"

Four Eyes snapped the trapdoor of his Springfield shut and presented arms with his still-smoking weapon as he stammered, "I . . . I guess it was me, sir."

Conway was as surprised as the IG man at his side, but he simply nodded and said, "It was a beautiful shot, son. But next time let 'em get in a bit closer. Carry on."

The officers moved back the other way as the abashed company clerk turned to the grinning man nearest him and asked, "Did I do something wrong?"

"No," the other soldier laughed. "But you sure did it fancy. I thought you caught a mess of Maggie's drawers the last time we went out on the rifle range, Four Eyes. When the hell did you start shooting like that?"

Four Eyes frowned and said, "I didn't know I could. Out

on the range, with everybody telling me to breathe this way and squeeze that way, I seem to be all thumbs. But when that sassy Cheyenne rode by just now, I never thought about anything but *hitting* the son of a bitch!"

Four Eyes was still puzzled as he turned to stare north the way he'd been told to. Then he frowned, even more puzzled, and took off his thick glasses to wipe them as he muttered, "Everything sure looks fuzzy over there, all of a sudden."

But his glasses weren't dirty. The two officers had spotted the dust above Tipi Town, too. Bradshaw asked, "What is it?" as Captain Conway took his field glasses out of the case at his side and raised them to peer intently toward the Indian camp. "Matt and the others must have missed Medicine Wolf out on the prairie," he said.

"Another band has ridden in to join Gray Elk? How badly are we outnumbered now?"

Conway lowered his field glasses and said, "Very badly indeed. It looks like Medicine Wolf's enlisted some Arapaho from that other band to the west, unless Cheyenne have suddenly adopted a new fad in paint. I'd say we're good for a couple of determined assaults. After that, unless Kincaid gets back in time, I'd say we were in trouble."

The sun was low in the west as Susan Keller gathered her laundry off the line stretched between the sod house and the lodgepole pine corral. The homestead woman was only in her early thirties and could look pretty in a fresh frock, after a bath. But a film of dust covered her calico dress and mousy hair, and she was glad the day was almost over. She folded the linens carefully as she put them in the basket on the grass, but the laundered clothes felt gritty and she wondered, sometimes, if washing anything was worth it, out here.

She was almost finished when her husband, Peter, came around the corner and said, "I'll fetch that in for you, Mother. You look a mite tuckered."

Susan Keller smiled wanly and said, "It's been a long day, but thank heavens for the gloaming. Have you finished with the ploughing, Father?"

He picked up the basket and said, "Yep. Me and the mule both feel like it, too. Where are the kids? Don't they know it's nigh suppertime?"

Susan braced her hands against her spine and stared dreamily out across the prairie as she said, "They're probably over in the draw, hunting horny toads again. My, don't it look pretty, late in the day like this, when the light's all purple and gold?"

Peter Keller held the basket against a hip as he shrugged and said, "It's all right, I reckon. I know you wanted a flower garden this summer, Mother, but the kids ain't old enough to chore enough to matter, and if I don't get the winter wheat drilled in . . ."

"Hush, Father, you married a woman, not a silly. I know we'll have this place fixed up someday. And I don't mind it, really, when the chores are done for the day and the gloaming softens the land a mite."

Peter Keller wasn't looking at the land or the fading light. "I like the way the sunset plays with your hair, old woman. I guess it's just as well we don't have a neighbor within twenty miles. A pretty wife can be a bother to a jealous mind. I'd never get no work done if I had to stand here chasing men away all day."

"You old fool," she chided him gently, smiling. "Who'd ever bother with a dried-up old stick like me?"

He grinned widely. "We'll study on that later, after we get the kids to bed."

His wife blushed in the ruddy light, then smiled and waved as she said, "Here comes Jill and Buddy, now. I do hope they haven't caught more horny toads. I know they have no pets, but honestly, I'd as lief have a hoot owl in the house as another ugly horny toad."

The boy, Buddy, ran forward ahead of his little sister. Buddy Keller was almost seven and so he tried to look important as he called out, "We just saw some Injuns, Dad."

Peter Keller smiled down at him and said, "Injuns, huh? No horny toads?"

"Honest, Dad. Ask Sis if I ain't telling it true. We both saw them, over across the draw. We waved at 'em, but they never waved back. There was a whole mess of 'em. Do you reckon they'll scalp us, Dad?"

The homesteader chuckled and told his young son, "I don't think so. You'd best wash up. It's suppertime."

"Don't you believe us, Dad? They're really over yonder, like I said."

His little sister, Jill, took her thumb out of her mouth and said, brightly, "I waved to Injuns, Mama."

Susan Keller looked thoughtfully at her husband and murmured, "Pete?"

He sighed and said ominously, "Buddy, do you remember the talk we had about always telling the truth?"

"I *am* telling the truth, Dad. I'm not making it up, this time. I know there really wasn't a bear in the draw like I said, that other time. But, durn it, we did see Injuns over there just now."

"I see. I suppose they were all wearing feathers and war paint and riding big white horses, right?"

"They had their faces all smeared up funny, but we didn't see no horses, Dad."

"Buddy, go wash up. I want you to think about it, and then, after supper, we're going out back and have a man-to-man talk about these games of yours, hear?"

The boy headed for the soddy, head downcast, with his sister tagging behind. Susan looked toward the draw they'd been playing in and repressed a shudder as she murmured, "He sounded like he thought he was telling the truth, Father."

Her husband sighed and said, "I know. I'm going to have to punish him this time, if he sticks to his story."

"Father, he's only a little boy."

"We were all little boys once. It's time he learned, Mother. Seeing pirates and Indians out back is harmless enough, back home in Ohio. But out here, there *are* things like Indians, wolves, and such. The boy has to learn to separate fact and fancy. He's got little Jill seeing his play Indians, too. But we'll work it out after supper."

Susan followed her husband with a thoughtful frown as he led the way toward the soddy. Her spine felt suddenly tingly, as though someone were staring at her from behind. She stopped and whirled around. There was nothing there but waving grass tops, flame-orange against a lavender eastern skyline. She shrugged and trudged on after her man. Peter was right, of course. Buddy's foolish notion had her feeling crawly, as if he'd really found something wiggle-snaky over there in the draw.

Peter Keller ducked inside. Susan paused in the doorway for a last wistful look at the sunset. Then her eyes widened. "Oh, my God," she gasped, then ducked inside and said, quite calmly, "Peter, we have company, coming in from the west. You'd, ah, better bring your gun."

Keller blinked in surprise at the suddenly pallid features of his wife, but he kept it light, too, as he told the children, "You kids stay put in here." Then he took his double-barreled shotgun from its wall pegs and stepped outside. He said, "Stay out of sight, Mother. They may just mean to beg tobacco and grub." Then, even as he was saying it, he got a look at the long, ragged line of riders against the sunset and his legs went rubbery under him. Susan stayed at his elbow as she murmured, "What are we to do, Pete? There must be a thousand of them."

He said, "More like a thirty-man band. Uh, Susan?"

"Yes, dear?"

"I'm going to try. It's all a man can do. You know what I'm trying to say?"

"Yes, darling. I've always loved you, too."

"Thank you, Mother. Now get inside. You know what has to be done to keep them from taking you and the kids alive. But wait until it's certain."

Then, not looking back, Peter Keller walked forward, shotgun across his chest. He didn't know he was acting foolish. Nobody had told him the only chance a settler had against a hostile band was holed up inside his soddy. They'd told him the local Indians were friendlies, and that the army had them under control.

Peter Keller dropped to one knee and aimed his shotgun as he called out, "That's close enough, gol durn ye!" and Matt Kincaid reined in to shout back, "Can't you see we're the army, damn it?"

The settler sobbed aloud and fought to control himself as the world spun all around him in the treacherous light. Matt rode closer and dismounted, asking, "Are you all right, sir? What's happened? You look like you're sick."

Peter Keller tried to answer, but words wouldn't come. Matt was helping him to his feet as Windy Mandalian rode in across the Keller homestead, and reported, "They circled, like the sign said. I found other sign over in a draw to the east. Found a little white gal's hair ribbon and some kid tracks over there, too. What's going on here?"

Peter Keller laughed wildly and, remembering that his wife was at the same disadvantage as he had been, staring into the sun, called out, "It's all right, Mother! They're soldiers! It's the U.S. Army, not the folks we thought!"

Then he turned back to Matt and said, "I'm sorry I'm acting so crazy, mister. You see, my fool kids had us all spooked with talk of Injuns, and when I saw you all, I didn't know what to think. I'll skin that kid of mine for saying there were Injuns about, but first I mean to giggle on it some."

Windy said, "If your boy said he spotted Cheyenne over by that draw, he told you true, mister. I make it a dozen or more, and they were scouting you, up to just about the time they spotted us coming in."

Then Windy turned to Matt and added, "They don't have five minutes on us, Matt."

The lieutenant nodded and let go of Keller to remount. As he forked into his saddle he called out to Reb McBride, "Sound assembly, bugler."

"Don't you mean charge, sir?"

"If I'd have meant charge, I'd have ordered charge, McBride. I want Mr. Taylor and the outriders in, and I want them now!"

So McBride sounded assembly as Susan Keller and the children came shyly from the soddy. Matt touched the brim of his hat to her as the bugle's echoes faded, but he had no time for idle gallantries.

Turning to Gus Olsen, he snapped out, "Sergeant, detail a squad to secure that draw on the far side of this spread."

"Yessir," Olsen replied. "Does the lieutenant expect them to double back?"

"No, but it pays to be sure. We're not digging in here, Gus, but I do mean to assemble and hold until the light is better."

Olsen saluted, wheeled his mount, and rode away. Susan Keller called out, "We've coffee if you'll have it, sir. What do you mean about the light getting *better*? Forgive me if I'm being silly, but doesn't it usually get *dark* after sundown?"

Matt had a moment now, so he smiled down at her and the children as he explained, "There's one way to fight in daylight, ma'am. Another way at night. This half-and-half at twilight is more dangerous than either. I don't mean to ride my men outlined against a red sky, with every draw as black as ink. Once the sky is darker and the moon comes up, things even out a bit."

"A *bit*, sir?"

"Well, of course, anyone dug in behind a bush in darkness has the advantage of anyone moving around. But that can't be helped. I don't expect my men to offer easy targets, but it's our job to accept reasonable risks. We'll be moving on as the moon rises. That gives us the edge if they rode east. It'll be their turn to stand out against the skyline."

Peter Keller said, "Well, that means we have time to coffee you boys."

Susan added, "I've some maple syrup I've been saving, too. If your men have the flour, I'd be proud to rustle up a mess of flapjacks before you ride on."

Matt shook his head and said, "You'd best start packing, ma'am. I'd bury such valuables as I might not need in the next few days, but you'll want spare clothes, bedding, and such. How many riding critters do you folks have?"

Peter Keller looked startled as he answered, "Just the mule, but what are you talking about? We ain't going noplace, mister."

"I'm afraid you are, sir," Matt said. "Your wife and kids will have to ride pillion with three of my men. We can pack a few hundred pounds for you on our ammo mules. We're not carrying you far, just into the next settlement."

"But the Injuns are *gone*, ain't they?"

"They may be. I certainly hope so. If they circle back, I don't mean to have them find you here. You'll be safe in town until we round them up."

"But what about our spread, standing empty and unprotected?"

Matt's voice was bleak as he replied, "They'll loot it and burn it. But they won't be able to scalp it. I'd leave some men here to guard you, if I could, but I can't. Make sure you bundle the children well. It may be cold out on the prairie for them at night."

Matt turned to Windy Mandalian and ignored the muttered protests of the settlers as he asked, "Did you get a line on which way they rode out?"

Windy started to spit, but remembered that there was a lady present, and said, "Due east, direct away from us and moving sudden. I spotted the hoofprints of Red Bishop's army mount. Some jasper's riding it now. They may have picked up a few recruits along the way. With the smoke and drums jawing about war, all sorts of ornery young cusses from other bands may be out looking for trouble."

"That's what they'll find, if they bore straight east. There's a railroad town over that way, isn't there?"

Windy nodded and said, "Yep. I figure they know that, too.

They'll trend north or south after they put some distance between them and us."

As Mr. Taylor rode in, the Kellers were moving back to their soddy to get ready. So they didn't hear as Matt pointed at their backs with his chin and told Taylor, "Those folks just got lucky. Mr. Lo is just over the horizon. American Tears is after easy pickings, like I told you. We ought to nail him within twenty-four hours."

Taylor nodded, but said, "Matt, by now Medicine Wolf is with Gray Elk, and the captain doesn't have thirty able-bodied men, even if we count tough women."

"I know. I mean to get there as quickly as possible. But American Tears is headed the wrong way."

"Jesus Christ, you can take him without my platoon, and the captain really needs us."

Matt shook his head and said, "I need you, too. You have your orders, mister. This is the U.S. Army, not a debating society. Tell your men to tend their mounts and grub themselves, cold rations. We move out just before moonrise."

# eleven

A necklace of moving dots was outlined by the same sunset against the skyline west of Outpost Nine as Warner Conway moved down the line, making sure each of the riflemen manning that side was aware of them. The sun had dropped below the horizon and the sky was a backdrop of brilliant pumpkin near the ground, fading into ruby overhead and purple to the east. Conway turned the corner and moved along the south parapet to where Lieutenant Colonel Bradshaw was talking with Pop Evans, the civilian suttler. Conway joined them as Evans was saying, "They're going to smoke us, sure as hell. The wind is steady from the south."

Conway wet a finger and held it up. There did seem to be a faint south breeze. "The wind will shift to the west as the mountains over there cool off, Pop," he said.

Evans snorted, "Hell, I know that. So do the Cheyenne. That's why I say they'll torch the grass to our south any damned minute now."

Bradshaw shot the captain an inquiring glance. Conway shrugged and said, "They've moved into position a mite late, out on the west flank. They've exposed themselves, too. It could be a diversion."

Bradshaw squinted southward across the rolling swells of purple shaded with tawny orange and said, "I don't see any sign of movement down that way."

Conway nodded and said, "That's what I just said, Colonel. You're not supposed to see Mr. Low when he's making serious plans. Those riders over to the west deliberately picked a rise to string themselves out on. It's a good hour too late for a sunset attack. The naked sun's no longer in our eyes, and it's hard to miss a black outline against a restful orange."

"I can see that," Bradshaw said. "Perhaps it's all a bluff, after all."

Pop Evans said soberly, "They ain't bluffing. My Arapaho, uh . . . housekeeper never come back from Tipi Town. I told her to pick the side she figured to win and she's had all afternoon to study on it. The drumbeats has stopped, too."

"I think I spotted some green paint over among the lodges," Conway said. "Did your girl say if her folks had been invited to the party?"

Evans shrugged and answered, "She didn't have to. This morning she was on our side. This afternoon she went over to the enemy. Yellow Basket don't owe loyalty to no Cheyenne. She knows what her own would do to a squaw they found under a white man's bedstead." He spat and added, "I'd say the main Arapaho band over to the foothills is waiting to see how this turns out, but they sent a delegation of young bucks who ain't had much exercise of late. Torching the grass is a favorite Arapaho trick. That's why I'm betting on it. The green-faced rascals are born firebugs."

Bradshaw stared down at the trampled dust of the fenced and empty horse paddock, directly to the south, and opined, "Even if they set fire to the prairie, that bare earth forms a natural firebreak, doesn't it?"

Evans said, "Well, of course it does. That's the point. They don't want to climb no sod walls all smoldering and crumbling, damn it. They know they can't *burn* us out. They just aim to *smoke* us."

Conway saw that the IG man was confused, so he elaborated, "The tactic he's talking about involves moving in behind a wall of smoke, sir. You're right that the grass fires will smolder out when they reach that fenceline over there. But as you see, a skirmish line breaking out of a cloud of smoke only has a short dash across open ground, in tricky light."

Bradshaw nodded in understanding and said, "All right, we'll have maybe one volley into them before they hit the wall, and then it's butt, stock, and bayonet time. What are you going to do about it, Captain?"

"There's not much I haven't already done, Colonel. I'm open to suggestions."

"All right, if I were in command, I'd have more men manning this side."

"The other three sides can't spare them, sir. In the first place, we haven't seen any smoke. In the second, Pop's right about it being an Arapaho ploy. Medicine Wolf and Gray Elk are Cheyenne, and right now they're probably arguing about who's in command. If the Arapahos get one chief to go along with the notion of a smokescreen, the other's almost certainly bound to disagree about it."

"I hope you're right. They *have* agreed to attack us, haven't they?" Bradshaw asked.

"I'm afraid so, sir. That's one thing any members of the old Dakota Confederacy can agree to without much hesitation, given the odds and what they see as a just cause. But they'd have hit us just before sundown if they had a united command and a settled battle plan. That's what gives us the edge on Mr. Lo. Since Squanto showed the Pilgrims how to plant corn, they've never been able to present a united front. That's why the poor bastards failed to stop us on the beaches. They've been trying and dying for almost three hundred years, and they never learn."

"But meanwhile, we whites have done our share of dying," Bradshaw pointed out. "I'd like to avoid being added to our modest casualty list, Captain. Do you think they can take us, if they do it right, this time?"

Conway said matter-of-factly, "Any position can be taken if the attackers have the numbers and determination. We'll find out if they have, tonight. I was hoping Medicine Wolf would want his own powwow with us, but he's apparently opted for the real thing."

Pop Evans' voice was calm as he cut in, conversationally, "There's the smoke, gents."

They followed his gaze south and Bradshaw breathed, "Oh, Jesus," as he watched a long fencerow of smoke plumes rise violet against the purple sky. As the smoke rose higher, the sun's dying rays gilded the mushroom tops of the plumes, and the sight would have been a pretty one, had they not known what it meant. The columns of smoke were thickening at the bases even as they watched, and Pop Evans said, "Wind's moving it toward us, like I said."

Conway nodded, held up another wet finger, and opined, "Take about three-quarters of an hour before our eyes start to water, right?"

Pop nodded. The men on either side were calling back and forth uneasily, and some shouted, "Fire!"

Conway bellowed, "At ease, damn it! Who yelled that?"

An abashed private stepped away from the bulwark and presented arms. Conway snapped, "Don't you ever yell 'fire' again, soldier! We've enough confusion in this man's army without you shouting what could be taken as an order from an officer or NCO. Carry on."

The nervous nellie moved back into position, and Conway shouted for all to hear, "Don't worry about singed eyelashes, men. Watch for son of bitches moving through the smoke. Zero your weapons on that fenceline. Let the grass burn itself out a bit, and as the flames smolder out, fire for effect into the smoke. Don't volley. I want random ranging and harassing fire until you see your targets. After that, the order is fire at will, and after you hit Will, shoot the son of a bitch behind him!"

The men chuckled at the old joke, and Conway turned back to Bradshaw. "I'm going over to the main gate to make sure Fitzgerald is set up, sir. Pop, here, knows as much about Mr. Lo as any other white man."

But as he started to go, Bradshaw said, "I've been thinking about those Indians we're holding, Captain."

"Sir?"

"That's what this is all about, isn't it? I'll not pretend to be an expert on field tactics, but I am a lawyer, and a good one."

"No offense, sir. But the last thing I need right now is a lawyer!"

"You may be wrong. Those Indians would back off if we were to release those three captives, wouldn't they?"

"Of course, sir. But the U.S. Army does not let renegade Indians go."

"I know. That's the fine print, Captain. I confess I was as hasty as anyone in the first flush of capture, but I've had time to think. Under the rules of Indian policy, a renegade is a treaty Indian who's broken the peace, right?"

"Of course, sir." Conway frowned, wondering what on earth the IG man was getting at. Bradshaw said, "On the other hand, an Indian who's never made peace with us is technically a simple hostile to be pacified by defeat and other persuasion. We don't hang a hostile who's never broken a treaty, right? He's a prisoner of war, not a criminal. Do you see my point?"

Conway nodded, but said, "Technical is right, sir. Those three kids may have been too young to have made their marks and been given a ration number by the BIA, but their folks sure did. They were captured on the warpath and they're from treaty bands, so—"

"I don't think this is the time or place to quibble, Captain," Bradshaw cut in. "As of the moment, no blood's been spilled, and that smoke is drifting closer by the minute. I can see how the War Department might see fit to give those kids the benefit of the doubt, if it means avoiding a very expensive war."

Conway didn't answer.

Bradshaw pressed on, "Isn't it possible to signal for another powwow?"

The captain nodded, then asked, "Are you taking command, here, sir?"

"Of course not. You know I can't relieve the commander of a post without just cause. Look, we've had our differences. I'll admit I have a short fuse, if you'll allow you're a bit casual about the ARs. I'm trying to work with you, not against you, son. Aren't you being a little stiff-necked about those prisoners, considering that you think *I'm* a nitpicker? If I can bend, why can't you? I'll back you up at Regiment."

Conway said, "I wish you'd thought about that technicality when Matt was trying to keep you from holding a drumhead court-martial, Colonel. It's a mite late now."

"You mean the Indians wouldn't be content just to get those kids back?"

"Oh, they'd be delighted, sir. They'd doubtless be only too happy to avoid having to make a frontal assault on a walled-in military garrison, too."

"Then what's the problem?"

"The problem, sir, is that no white man, woman, or child west of the Big Muddy would be safe this summer if the U.S. Army knuckled under to paid-up members of the defeated Dakota Confederacy. Have you any idea of the brag that bunch out there would have on us? We're talking about two full chiefs and at least a couple of important Arapaho. Sure, they'd back off if we let them say they'd rescued three warriors from us. Then Sitting Bull would boil down out of Canada. Crazy Horse would forget he just surrendered. The Sioux would be so pissed off about us being whipped by Cheyenne and Arapaho that they'd be putting on their paint in no time. Oh, and let's not be forgetting the Kiowa and Comanche to the south, or the Blackfoot to the north, either. They've been pretty discouraged of late, but—"

"Damn it, I'm not talking about surrendering the garrison to them, Captain."

"A victory is a victory, Colonel. Red Cloud never would have had the numbers to take Terry and Custer on if he hadn't eliminated Fetterman first."

"I can see that. But won't it look worse for us if they massacre a company instead of just getting those young rascals back?"

Conway shook his head emphatically. "In the first place, they haven't massacred us yet. In the second, if they do, we'll take a lot of them with us. Mr. Lo's no dumber about dying than anyone else, despite his talk. They'll think twice about following a leader who gets people killed a lot. Letting those chiefs have a bloodless victory is unthinkable. It would give them too much medicine. The U.S. Army does not negotiate with a man wearing paint. We'll talk if *they* lay down their arms, but we don't give an inch under duress."

Bradshaw was still muttering about it as Conway walked away. The captain rounded the corner and moved up the east side. He met Ben Cohen coming the other way and said, "Sergeant, I want the reserve squad on this side. The moon will be rising in a little while."

"I understand, sir," Cohen said, and moved to round up the extra help.

Conway found Lieutenant Fitzgerald and his heavy-weapons section bunched up near the gate and their useless Gatling gun. Conway said, "I want you spread out more, Fitzgerald. I've sent for more men, and I'll be commanding here."

"I understand, sir," Fitzgerald replied. "We've been wondering about that smoke down there to the south."

Conway said, "Arapaho, probably acting on their own. If it's not just a ruse, the men down there will stop them. They've exposed some heads to the west. We'll know in a few minutes if I'm right about them making the main assault over here, from the east."

Fitzgerald stared hard at the featureless eastern horizon. The evening stars were winking on above the deep purple prairie. "There hasn't been a sign of movement from that direction, sir," he said finally.

"I know," Conway answered. "The gate is our weakest spot, if they can rush it with an uprooted telegraph pole."

"But, sir, they must know we have a Gatling gun covering it."

"They may suspect or know it's out of order. At least one squaw moved out this afternoon. My fault. I thought she'd stay with her white lover, and it's too late to arrest her now. Even if they don't know the Gatling is out of order, they might not care. They mean to rush the gate before the moon rises."

Ben Cohen came up to them with eight new men, saluted, and announced, "Reserves present, sir."

"Sergeant, I want some light on the subject," Conway told him. "Pick some volunteers to move out a hundred yards and build some bonfires. I want one on either side of the post road, with the others at fifty-foot intervals, north and south, past our corners. Any questions?"

"No, sir, we're on our way. I'll pour some tar on the timbers to keep 'em burning bright at least through moonrise."

"Ben, I asked for volunteers."

"I know, sir. Me and these boys just volunteered. You don't hear anybody saying they won't go, do you?"

Matt Kincaid and his men picked up two more settler families on their way into the railhead. The Indians' trail, as Windy had suggested, swung north well before they saw the winking lights of the little frontier settlement, but Matt detoured to get rid of his now-safe civilians. The town marshal said he'd put the refugees up in his jail for the time being, and suggested rounding up a posse to ride with the soldiers. Matt convinced him, with some difficulty, that armed and willing civilians would more useful guarding the approaches to town. It would have been impolite to point out that the last thing he needed riding with him was a mess of untrained and possibly trigger-happy feather merchants.

He doubled back and fell in with Windy and the outriders on the moonlit trail. Before moving after the Cheyenne again, he called Taylor and all the noncoms together and said, "We're going to need Reb and his bugle more than I like, in the dark. American Tears is a wise-ass who speaks English and sucks around us when he's not out butchering. Do you all think you can handle reversed calls?"

All but the newly promoted Acting Corporal Wilson muttered agreement. Wilson wanted to be sure he understood, so he asked, "Do you mean that if we hear charge we fall back, sir?"

Matt nodded and said, "Right. Left wheel means right wheel. Retreat will mean advance. We'll ride closer interval, of course, but I'm depending on you leaders to use your common sense. When in doubt, don't. If you see an opportunity, grab it. I'll not chew anyone out for acting without orders, unless he makes a mistake. I can't watch every egg in the basket, so each of you has at least eight. For Christ's sake, try not to drop any. Any other questions?"

Taylor said, "Yes. The trail's leading north, directly away from our outpost. I'm formally requesting permission to fall out with my command and ride to their assistance."

"Permission denied. You've had your say in private, and now it's a matter of public record that you don't approve of the way I'm running this show. Is that to be the end of it, mister, or do you want to be relieved of your command? You can ride back and gather up that posse if you want to. Your men stay with me."

Taylor said, "I'll follow your orders, Lieutenant, and we'll say no more about it, for now. But if we ride back to find the post overrun . . ."

"I thought you were going to say no more about it," Matt cut in. Then he nodded to Windy and said, "Move out with the point. But stay within sight and remember you're only a blur in this light."

Windy resisted the impulse to mention that he'd scouted at night before. He knew that many of the enlisted men were thinking about dependents back at Outpost Nine, and this was no time to make Matt look dumb. So the scout just clucked his mount forward as the point riders fell in beside him. Taylor started to say something, but shrugged and rode off to rejoin his own platoon, just visible at pistol range in the moonlight.

Matt gave everyone time to get into position before he said, "Let's move out. Stretch, that guidon isn't doing us much good in the dark. Case the colors and sling the pole on one of the mules for now."

"Yessir. You still want me riding on your right?"

"No. The colors rank me. I rank you. I'm sorry, Stretch, but without the colors you're just a poor private. So load your

Springfield and fall in with your squad leader. I'll let you know when we want to look pretty again."

Dobbs fell back as Matt moved into the vacated fore-to-the-right position and settled down for a moonlight ride. He waited until everyone was dressed down and made sure Taylor was ghosting him properly on his left-rear flank before he spurred his mount into a most uncomfortable but mile-eating trot. He knew the men hated to trot in their ball-busting McClellan saddles; he hated it himself. It was an advantage they had over Mr. Lo. Most Indians avoided discomfort unless they were torturing themselves to make medicine. American Tears and his small war band would prefer either a walk or a comfortable lope as they moved somewhere out ahead. A grass-fed Indian pony loped faster than any army mount could trot, but it couldn't lope more than a mile or so at a time. So the Cheyenne should lope a mile and walk at least two as they pressed on. The army mounts could maintain this nut-busting pace for a good hour, rest ten minutes, and trot on indefinitely. It was only a little slower than a lope, but much faster than a walk, so they had to be gaining on the sons of bitches.

Out on point, Windy picked up the pace as soon as he heard the faster jingle of the brass rifle spiders. The trail was easy enough to follow by moonlight; where the Cheyenne were headed was another matter.

Like all good hunters and trackers, Windy Mandalian knew better than to simply follow a trail with his nose to the ground like a hound. Greenhorns were often astounded by the seemingly uncanny abilities of both white and Indian scouts, who could suddenly point across a featureless expanse and announce that someone they were after was "yonder, up in that there pass."

They didn't do it through a mysterious sixth sense. A man who studied the lay of the land could often guess which way a deer or any other quarry had to be heading, even if he lost eye contact with its trail. Critters were a little easier for Windy. A critter used common sense. It followed the easy path to food and water. It holed up in alder if it had been born a deer, and headed for a dusty draw to wallow in the fly season if its mama had been a buffalo. Indians were a mite more complicated. They hunted, themselves, so they tended to pass up the first sensible place in favor of a second. But sooner or later, every critter, including an Indian, had to be going *some* damned place.

Windy waited until Matt called the first rest before he voiced his suspicions. He rode back to where Matt and his platoon were grazing and watering their mounts in the moonlight, and got off his own to lead it over to the officer. Matt, just to be doing something, was rubbing his bay down with a dry rag as the animal nibbled cool but tasteless straw. Windy said, "They're beelining for the reservation."

Matt said, "I know. I didn't think American Tears was that dumb. He must know we've identified him and can't be far behind. I guess he means to meet us sitting and whittling by the trading post, with his face washed and wearing an innocent expression as we ride in. But it's not going to work this time. I know the Indian agent. He's not as stupid as the last one."

Windy let his own horse graze as he shook his head and said, "American Tears *ain't* that dumb. He's only got a dozen or so with him and, hell, the Indian police could take him on the reservation."

"He might think he's tougher than the BIA's deputized bucks."

"I'm sure he does, but he dasn't fight his own kind with the whole tribe watching and doubtless rooting for one side or t'other. Nope, he's too smart and too yellow to be headed for home."

"All right, where do you think he's headed, then?"

"Only place as makes any sense is back to his mama. I know he seems to be headed the wrong way, but he knows we've cut his trail, and he's nervous about a fair fight. He'll ride north until the moon ball sets. Then he'll make a dash west to the foothills, hoping to make cover afore we pick up his trail again in the daylight."

"Hmm, you could be right," Matt agreed. "But what's to stop him from circling east?"

"Damn it, I just told you. Where in thunder can he lose us to the east? There's nigh eight hundred miles of open grass betwixt here and the Big Muddy. He knows we're bound to gain on him. He has to get some rimrocks and trees around him as he hightails south to rejoin Medicine Wolf."

Matt pondered this and finally opined, "Windy, Medicine Wolf is going to be mad as hell at that fool renegade."

"I know that. So does American Tears. But Medicine

Wolf's only likely to cuss him. He knows we aim to *hang* him! Rejoining his band is his only chance, and it ain't as slim a chance as it might look to a white man. He must know by now that Medicine Wolf is wearing paint. A dozen warriors carrying hair and leading an army brute might catch some hell, but they'll make a welcome addition. I'm sure that's going to be the way American Tears will see it."

Matt smiled bleakly. "Well, *we'd* probably be a welcome addition back at the outpost, too. What are you suggesting, that we break off hot pursuit and try to beat him back there?"

"Shoot, son, you can't take him if he gets anywhere near his chief. It'd be easier to single out a hornet in its nest for branding. But if you think I know my ass from my elbow, I suggest we forget this trail to nowheres important and make our own beeline due west. We can be dug in and waiting in the foothills by sunrise if we start now. American Tears will likely ride on into the dark of the moon afore he makes his own swing west. He'll hit the rough country north of us, then start moving south, looking back over his shoulder, and—"

"I like it," Matt cut in, adding, "Rub your mount down and water it. We've got some riding to do, Windy."

The sky was star-spangled coal tar now, as Ben Cohen's men heaved the last chuck of cordwood on the pile farthest south of the road. The first sergeant said, "Stand clear," and sloshed the contents of a lard bucket over the wood. Dutch Rothausen was having a fit about it, back in the kitchen. They'd taken the last of his firewood, and Dutch claimed you couldn't heat a kitchen range enough to matter with cow chips. But eating one's beans a mite rare beat not eating at all, so what the hell.

Cohen put the bucket noiselessly on the grass, since it was good for nothing after carrying a godawful mixture of axle grease, saddle soap, and pitch, dissolved in turpentine from the paint shop. He straightened up in the dark and said, "All right, Miller, take them back to the gate and try to keep it down to a roar."

Miller asked, "What about you, Sarge? Don't you want us to cover you as you light this stuff?"

"If I wanted you to cover me, I'd *say* I wanted you to cover me. What are you waiting for, a goodbye kiss? Move it, Corporal!"

"Let's go, boys," Miller said, and moved away in the dark.

Cohen watched with grudging approval until they were out of sight. The kid had headed directly for the wall instead of cutting for the gate at an angle. He'd known without being told that the run was safer right under the wall.

Cohen gave them time to get clear as he stood by the woodpile, feeling suddenly very alone and exposed. Somewhere in the night a prairie owl hooted mournfully. If it *was* a prairie owl. Cohen hunkered between the woodpile and the walls of Outpost Nine as he struck a match and touched it to the improvised torch he'd made of oil-soaked rags around a stick. As he torched the first pile, a bullet thudded into the far side.

Cohen muttered, "Up your ass," and started running for the next pile as, off to the east, the Indian's gun muzzles flickered like fireflies. Death hummed like hornets around the burly sergeant as he ran, holding his torch as far from his head as he could. The wood thrummed in his big fist as a bullet hit the torch and showered him with sparks. Then he'd made it to the next pile, dropped behind it, and had a moment's respite before he torched it, took a deep breath, and ran on.

He torched pile after pile as the Cheyenne moved closer, putting round after round through spaces Cohen had just occupied. Up on the wall, army rifles were winking back at the muzzle flashes out on the open prairie, and someone yipped like a kicked dog. Cohen grinned and said, "That'll learn you to mess with Easy!" as the next Indian rifle that flashed at him did so from farther back.

He crossed the road, torching the two larger piles on either side, and risked a glance back as he ran for the next pile. The line of bonfires he'd started was blazing merrily, and he could see the walls clearly now. But the firelight left the upper bulwarks and the men up there in flickering, indistinct light while illuminating the flats between the fires and the base of the sod walls. Anyone trying to lean a climbing pole against them now would have a problem digging all that lead out of his red hide.

Up ahead, unseen by Cohen, a young Cheyenne called Hungry Bird had made his own slick move. Hungry Bird was fourteen and the older men had laughed at him when he put on his paint, but they'd let him come along after telling him to be quiet and stay out of their way. Hungry Bird was too poor to own a gun, but he wouldn't need it if he timed this right. It was a greater coup to strike an enemy unarmed than it was to shoot him at a distance. So as Ben Cohen approached, holding his torch aloft, Hungry Bird crouched by the woodpile, his late grandfather's coup stick in hand.

Cohen torched the last pile but one, then circled out on the Indians' side to throw their aim off with an unexpected move. It worked. At least four bullets spouted dust above the place he should have appeared next, and now he was moving fast and tricky, zigzagging for the last pile.

He'd intended to throw the almost spent torch into the fuel-soaked cordwood, knowing they'd be zeroed in on the pile. As he wound up to throw, Hungry Bird grunted in surprise and pain and staggered to his feet with a Cheyenne bullet in his side. The boy didn't know what had gone wrong, but his enemy was near and there might be time to touch him, however lightly, before the stars went out forever. Cohen drew his Scoff with his free hand as he spotted the Indian coming to meet him. Then Ben saw that he was only a skinny, shot-up kid with a silly, feathered candy cane, and swerved around him to throw the torch. It went end over end into the pile, and as the tinder-dry and tar-soaked wood exploded into a bright blaze, Ben decided it was time to think about getting home to Maggie.

The fool kid was trying to cut him off, waving his coup stick and chanting his death song, and Cohen realized the Indians had ceased fire to avoid hitting him again. He grinned and said, "This is our lucky day, old son." Then he holstered his pistol and slapped the coup stick aside as he bored in and scooped the youth up like a sack of potatoes.

"Put me down!" groaned Hungry Bird as Cohen carried him toward the walls, slung over one shoulder. Of course he was complaining in Cheyenne, and of course Cohen would have done no such thing even if he'd understood. Out in the darkness, the bemused Indians held their fire as they watched. So Ben Cohen made it to the gate, staggered inside, and shouted, "What are you idiots waiting for? Shut the goddamn door!"

A grinning private moved to help as Ben lowered the wounded Cheyenne to the ground. He said, "I see you brung someone home with you, Sarge. I didn't know you liked young boys."

The Indian tried to struggle as his moccasins touched down. Ben cuffed him sensible and turned him over to the grinning private and another as he growled, "Take him over to the kitchen and tell Dutch to patch him up. He ain't hurt bad, so watch him. After Dutch digs the bullet out and puts a plaster on him, take him to the lockup and put him in with the others."

As they led him away, Hungry Bird began to chant his death song again. Ben Cohen snorted in disgust. He'd gotten blood as well as tar on his blues, and Maggie was going to give him pure hell for it.

As he moved toward the nearest ladder, Captain Conway met him, held out a hand, and said, "By God, Ben, I'm putting you in for a medal."

Cohen shook the captain's hand and demurred, "If it's all the same, sir, I'd rather have the diamond that's due me. I've already got some medals. They don't spend too good, come payday."

"I know," Conway sighed. "That's probably why they've given me a cigar box full of the fool things. It doesn't cost them as much to decorate a man as it does to promote him. But you're going to get another medal anyway. You know how many letters I've written them about your temporary rank. What can you tell me about that Indian you captured just now?"

Cohen said, "He's wearing Cheyenne paint, sir. No coup feathers or warrior society marks. I'd say he was a suicide boy. He was only trying to make me look silly. Taking him alive was no big deal."

Conway nodded thoughtfully. "It was damned cool thinking under fire, Ben. That IG officer has some interesting ideas about the status of youngsters who never signed any treaty. You may have given us an edge we hadn't counted on, if your prisoner's from an important clan."

# twelve

The nameless mountain brook purled over a granite outcrop to form a last limpid foothill pond before winding east to die in the thirsty sands of a seasonal wash. The morning air was crisp and cool as Matt Kincaid's command watered their horses and refilled their canteens. Matt walked over to where Windy Mandalian hunkered morosely over a line of hoofprints running up the sandy south bank of the stream. Windy looked up and said, "Well, I was right about where and wrong about when. They had a better lead on us than I thought, and never waited for the dark of the moon to swing west."

Matt said, "We still gained on them by a good ten miles, thanks to your shortcut. But try it another way, Windy. Are you sure American Tears left that sign? We know there are some Arapaho here in these foothills."

Windy picked up a pebble and said, "Steel-shod hoof turned this over. There's a couple of other hoofprints I've met personal afore, Matt. It's them, all right. They're pushing hell outta their mounts, too. See there, where that pony barely made her up the bank? You must have that no-good rascal spooked pretty good. He'd running for his mama like his pony ran on clock-work instead of water and grass. I don't see how they can be an hour ahead of us now. They'll soon be *walking* home, if they don't pay more attention to their ponies."

Mr. Taylor came to join them, in restored good humor now that they seemed headed back toward the others after all. Windy repeated his reading, and Taylor smiled and said, "Good. Let's mount up and tear south after the sons of bitches."

Matt shook his head. "I gave the men fifteen, and they've six or eight to go. We've put them and the horses through the wringer, and they could really do with a full hour's break."

"But Windy says the hostiles are just ahead of us!"

"I know. I heard him. They'll still be just ahead of us at the end of the break. Have you eaten yet, Mr. Taylor?"

"Hell, I'm too keyed up to think of my stomach."

"Well, it's your stomach. I'm going to put some cold rations in mine."

As Matt walked away, Taylor turned back to Windy and said, "Jesus, I can't believe this. We're almost in contact with the enemy and he's still fucking around. This is no time to go by the book, damn it!"

Windy rolled a horse apple over with his finger to see how dry it was, and got to his feet, saying, "I know how you feel, Mr. Taylor. But this does remind me of the old story about the two bulls. They was walking along the fence one day. A young bull full of clover and an old bull full of sense."

"Windy, I'm hardly in the mood for another of your pointless stories."

"This one's got a point, sonny. You see, there was a herd of pretty young cows in the next pasture. So the young bull says, Hey, Pop, let's bust down this fence, run over yonder, and hump one of them cows! So the old bull shakes his horny head and says, I got me a better notion, son. Let's *walk* down to the gate, *walk* over to them cows, and hump 'em *all*!"

Taylor chuckled despite himself and said, "I follow your drift, but I still say we should show a little more enthusiasm around here."

Then he stopped, stared over Windy's shoulder, and muttered, "What the hell?"

Windy followed his gaze along the tawny foothills to the south. A string of cotton balls rose pinkish in the sunrise against the clear azure sky. "Smoke talk," he said. "I make it six or seven miles away. They've moved deeper into the hills."

Windy turned away and, as he'd expected, Matt Kincaid was coming back, chewing on a bar of hard chocolate. Windy called out, "I know. Now you're fixing to ask me what they're saying about us, right?"

Matt said, "I know it's a prearranged code. The question is who's sending and who's receiving."

"As close as it is," Windy said, "the smoke has to be American Tears. I'm not sure they can see it from down near the outpost, but it's barely possible. Anyway, the Cheyenne will have lookouts on rises back from the walls and Tipi Town. I'd say it's a call for help. I told you they'd about drove their ponies into the ground. They've forted up in the high country and sent out the word that we're too close for comfort and have them outnumbered. What do you reckon we ought to do about it, Matt?"

Matt asked, "Is there a choice?"

"Well, we can move in on that smoke and likely take 'em, since we have 'em outnumbered some. But if they've picked a good place to dig in, it'll cost us a lot of time and maybe some casualties. Meanwhile, as we're swapping shots with Mr. Lo, his friends may hit us from ever' which way, with the odds turned inside out."

"I don't like that one, Windy. Try another."

Windy spat and said, "All right, let's say we swing wide, back out across the prairie, and approach the outpost from the northeast. We'll miss any rescue party of Cheyenne and beat 'em back to the walls. That'll put us safe inside, with the garrison at full strength, and American Tears will look like the little boy who cried 'wolf.' They're already likely to be pissed off at him, and—"

"Forget it," Matt cut in. "I didn't ride all over Robin Hood's barn for nothing. We'd be right back where we started. The break is about over. You'll take the point as we move toward that smoke. Taylor, I want you beside me until we have the lay of the land down. They'll probably be dug in on a rise. I'll place you and your men in a position to keep them pinned. Then I'll try to work around behind them to cut off any escape."

Taylor asked, frowning, "Won't that place you and your platoon between the guns of American Tears and anybody coming to his aid?"

"It will if anyone's coming. Meanwhile, we'll be taking pressure off the captain and the others. You'd better get your men ready to move out, mister."

As Taylor moved away, Windy chuckled and said, "We was just talking about how cautious you was, Matt."

"Really? Well, I'm not inclined to take foolish chances, if they can be avoided."

"You ain't, huh? What do you call positioning yourself

between a rock and a hard place, old son? I'd purely hate to be riding with you when you was feeling reckless!"

Medicine Wolf stood on a rise with Gray Elk as they both watched the youth, Hungry Bird, walking toward them from Outpost Nine. The boy wore a bandage across his ribcage and one arm was in a sling. He'd made it to the far rifle range now, and still the soldiers on the walls held their fire. Medicine Wolf said, "This is very odd. You know them better than I do, Gray Elk. What do you think they are doing?"

Gray Elk said, "I don't know. They are always doing something strange. They don't think like people. Maybe the boy can tell us, since they didn't shoot him as he walked away from them, after all."

Hungry Bird came up the slope as a Cheyenne squaw keened wildly and ran down to throw her arms around the son she'd given up forever. She sobbed, "My poor baby, what have they done to you? My face is painted black and I have cut my hair, as you see, but you are not dead."

Hungry Bird muttered the Cheyenne equivalent of "Oh, Ma," and put his good arm around her as they walked up to the two chiefs. Medicine Wolf said, "Go wash those ashes off your face, you silly woman. This is man talk."

Hungry Bird thrilled to the compliment and struck a heroic pose, saying, "Hear me, I was very brave last night. I would have counted coup on that big American, but some idiot shot me."

Medicine Wolf said, "We know what you did, you foolish young man. Now tell us how you got away."

Hungry Bird said, "The trader they allow inside speaks our tongue, so he told me their chief's words."

"I know the man called Evans," said Gray Elk. "He has a good heart, for one of them. He has always spoken straight."

Medicine Wolf grunted and said, "Never mind about the trader Evans. What did they say? Why have they let you go, Hungry Bird? Did you see any of our young men they still hold? Are they still alive?"

"Yes. All three," Hungry Bird replied. "One is wounded, but he says he is feeling better and that they have treated him well. They asked me to tell you that when you take the place, they don't wish to see a squaw named Flora harmed. She is a good person. As to why they let me go, it is hard for me to understand. I don't understand the customs of those people. It had something to do with the treaty they made you older men sign."

"Can't you do any better than that? Our marks on the paper mean nothing, nothing, since it was they who broke the peace."

Hungry Bird frowned in concentration and said, "The trader told me that since I was only a child when our band gave up, I wasn't bound by the treaty. They said Cheyenne who hadn't made their marks were real enemies, not promise-breakers. They said I was an honorable prisoner and that they would take my word. They said if I would agree to fight no more, they could let me go. I did this thing. I made my mark for them. I am not a coward. I am not afraid to die, but it seemed silly to stay there if I didn't have to. I can't fight until my wound heals, anyway. I think they saw this. But if you need me, I will try again."

Gray Elk shook his head and said, "That would be wicked of you, Hungry Bird. They have treated you well and you have given them your word. You can't fight them again until they have given you just cause."

He glanced at Medicine Wolf for confirmation. Medicine Wolf nodded, but said, "There's something very odd about all this. The three boys they now hold never made *their* treaty marks. Yet they fight us rather than give them back to us. You are right, they think and act very crazy."

Hungry Bird brightened and said, "I remember something else now. The trader told me the three young men they hold probably won't hang. He said some of the American war chieftains had spoken for them. He said they knew the prisoners were honorable enemies. But words have been put down on paper and they must be judged. He said the judge-elders would say they could make their marks and then go get their ration numbers from the agent if they promised to fight no more forever."

"It's some kind of trick," growled Medicine Wolf. "If that was all they wanted, why did they make war on us?"

Gray Elk said, "Maybe they think *we* are making war on *them*. They often make such mistakes. What do you think we should do now?"

Before anyone could answer, a mounted Cheyenne rode over to them and called for their attention as he pointed to the barely visible dots of smoke against the northwest sky.

Medicine Wolf said, "That is American Tears. He asks our help. He says he faces many enemies."

Gray Elk grimaced and said, "I think American Tears is crazy, too. What do you suppose he's gotten into now?"

Medicine Wolf shrugged. "I don't know. It looks serious. You stay here and make these soldiers behave. I'll take some men who are not afraid to die and we'll find out what's going on up there."

He saw that Gray Elk was frowning, and realized he'd overstepped the bounds of courtesy between men of the same rank. So he added quickly, "Unless you want to come along, of course."

Mollified, Gray Elk shook his head and said, "I will stay and keep the soldiers pinned down. I would like to wash off my paint and have a talk with them about our young men, but I won't treat with them until you get back. I don't think we'd better attack until you find out what the others are doing up north. I would certainly like to end this nonsense honorably. But of course, if you ride into a real bloodletting, it won't be possible."

Medicine Wolf nodded and strode away, with Hungry Bird tagging along at his heels. The boy said, "I would like to ride with you. If I can't fight, I can hold the ponies while you and the others do."

Medicine Wolf growled, "Go home and behave yourself before your mother starts acting up again. By Matou, sometimes I wonder if you young men are worth all the trouble you put us through."

Far to the north, on the slope of a grassy foothill, another young man was in desperate trouble and he knew it. His name was Many Arrows, and his people were Arapaho of the Turtle Clan. He stood naked, alone, streaked with green stripes and small red dots from hairline to moccasin tops. A belt of braided rawhide circled his waist. From it, four thin rawhide ropes stretched to pegs driven into the earth at all four points of the compass. A staked-out warrior was forbidden by Matou and the other spirits to move from the sacred place where he was meant to die. The boy held a bow as he sang his death song softly. A dozen green-striped arrows stood upright in the sod at his feet. The others had taken his rifle when he'd said his pony could not go on. He supposed this was fair; American

Tears was a great leader. But he was a bit confused about what had happened to him so suddenly. He couldn't remember having volunteered to die like this, but he must have, since even his brother Arapaho had agreed when American Tears announced his brave decision. It had felt good to be praised so, as they stripped him of his worldly vanities and staked him out with the only weapon a brave corpse needed. But now that they'd ridden off and left him here alone, he couldn't help wondering if his pony was really that lame, after all.

The foolish pony was calmly grazing a hundred yards down the slope, favoring its sore leg, but otherwise looking obscenely comfortable. Many Arrows called out, "Hear me, horse, you are no damned good and I am very cross with you!"

The pony paid no attention. It was getting hot and the paint on Many Arrows' body was running. Many Arrows knew dead people weren't supposed to feel hunger or thirst; he supposed he wasn't used to the idea yet. He shrugged and began to chant, "Hear me, spirits, you know me by my secret name, but let the living remember that Many Arrows was not afraid to die. Heya, spirits, send me enemies, many enemies, let them come at me as thick as the stars in the midnight sky. Let them shoot me full of flaming arrows, let them strip the flesh from my bones with knives, and I shall not flinch. Hear me, I am brave. I am ready. Let me go down smiling in their angry faces. Let them work to take my hair. The ones I don't take with me will have earned it!"

The boy's chant stopped with a hiss of indrawn breath as he saw a white man coming over the rise to the north. Many Arrows' bladder betrayed him, and warm liquid ran down one leg as he found himself straining back against the thongs. But then he recovered and bent to pluck an arrow from the sod for his bow. He nocked it and began his soft death chant again as Windy Mandalian sat his mount, bemused, until other riders joined him across the draw. Many Arrows eyed them warily. There were many, and they had guns. He knew they could pepper him safely, from well beyond the reach of his bow. He'd tried to point this out to American Tears, but the damned Cheyenne had insisted the gun he'd had was of more use to the living. How was a man to die with dignity, now? It wasn't fair.

The scout said something to the others and rode forward, not toward the staked-out Arapaho, but toward his injured mount. Many Arrows called out, "Leave my horse alone, you thief! You're suppoed to fight me if you want my horse, damn it!"

Windy dismounted, examined the Indian pony's off-hind leg, and placed his rifle back on its spider before leaving the two horses to graze and get acquainted as he walked up the slope toward the staked-out Arapaho. Many Arrows drew his short-bow and sent an arrow at the white man. His aim was true, but Windy easily sidestepped it, stopped, and called out, "Let's talk first."

Many Arrows plucked another shaft from the earth and rearmed his pathetic weapon before he called back, "You speak our tongue like a man chewing jerky. You are ugly, too. I'll bet nobody but your mother is willing to sleep with you."

"You're not much to look at, either," Windy said. "Why has an Arapaho staked himself out to cover a Cheyenne retreat? Are you dumb as well as ugly?"

"You saw that my horse has a bad leg. What else can a man do when he can't keep up?"

"Well, you might start with washing off that paint and going home. The Arapaho are not at war with anyone this summer."

Many Arrows frowned and said, "You are trying to trick me. You know you are after American Tears, and that I have been riding with him. I will not give up. I have sworn never to give up. I intend to die here. I am ready whenever you are."

Windy said, "Suit yourself. But you sure look silly with that little hunting bow. It's been nice meeting you, but we'll have to be moving on."

"Heya, don't you want to kill me?"

Windy shook his head and said, "No. That would make us as dumb as you. We know you Arapaho just joined American Tears. We know you haven't hurt anybody. Why should we owe a blood debt to your tribe when there's no need to? Go home, son. Your horse isn't hurt too badly to carry you at a walk."

The scout turned away. Many Arrows cursed and launched another shaft at him. It fell short, as Windy had expected it to. The staked-out Indian stared in disbelief as the scout remounted and rode back up to rejoin the soldiers. Windy pointed west, and Many Arrows saw that he was a good tracker. That was, indeed, the way the others had ridden.

Many Arrows watched as the soldiers rode away. He suddenly felt very foolish, now that it was over for the moment.

But the day was young. Who knew what other strange happenings would follow the rising sun? Many Arrows started singing his death chant again. Maybe others would come. If they did, he'd be ready for them.

An hour later, Windy stopped on the crest of a steep hogback. When Matt rode up to join him, he pointed to a granite jumble dominating the next rise and said, "There they be. Like I figured. They call that place Deer Stalker's Rock. It's a holler bowl up top. No water this late after a rain. They're forted fine, and likely hoping help will arrive afore they get really thirsty."

As if to confirm the scout's words, another puff of smoke ballooned up from the depression in the rocks across the way. Mr. Taylor rode up to join them. Matt said, "Well, we've run them to earth. I want you to dig in here, and keep them pinned. Windy and me will circle around and cut off any retreat."

"We could work in closer," Taylor said, "but Matt answered, "No. I said here and I meant here, mister. I'll be on higher ground once I'm behind them. So I'll make any attack that's called for."

"Oh, you agree we haven't time to lay siege?"

"Hell, there's only a dozen or so, and they can go days without fresh water. I'm planning on taking them by noon and getting back to the outfit in time for supper. But let's do it right."

Matt moved back to his own platoon with Windy in tow, as Taylor signaled his squad leaders to join him on the hogback. Matt told Gus Olsen what was up, and Windy took the lead again as they circled in a big hairpin demanded by the grain of the hills.

As they topped the rise behind the Indian's stand, Windy said, "Oh-oh! There goes our boy!"

Matt followed the scout's pointing finger, and saw American Tears, mounted alone on his buckskin and moving at a full gallop down the draw between the rises.

Windy said, "He's thinking of his own hide, aboard the fastest bronc. I figured him for a sqaw-heart."

Matt swung around in his saddle and snapped, "Sergeant

Olsen, dismount First and Second Squads and secure this ridge. You know the plan about the ones up in those rocks. Third Squad, follow me!"

Then, without waiting for a reply, Matt spurred his mount into a slide downslope toward the fugitive American Tears.

Windy Mandalian was riding hard at his elbow, calling out, "It's no use, Matt. He's got too good a lead on us." But Matt rode on, determined. He knew the buckskin was fast, but his own mount was grain-fed and hadn't been as abused as the Cheyenne's famous racer. So it was a contest of endurance against speed.

American Tears rounded a bend and was out of sight for the moment, but he'd ridden like a man throwing his thoughts to the wind, and they'd be back in open country any minute, so Matt wasn't worried.

A few miles farther on, Matt saw that he'd been right. He had American Tears in sight again. The treacherous Cheyenne was moving up a long, grassy slope on a tired mount. They were gaining on him.

Then, without warning, the entire ridge above American Tears bloosomed with mounted Cheyenne, a good fifty warriors in feathers and paint!

Matt slowed to a walk, but kept going as Windy said, "Now is the time for all good men to get the hell *out* of here, old son!"

Matt reined in and sighed, "Yeah, if they'll let us. Hold your positions, men. Corporal, ride back casually and get the others. We'll try and cover for you."

The NCO was already riding back up the draw as Windy spat and said, "Cover my ass, boy. They got the numbers and the high ground. It's pure time to vacate these parts, and *that* gives us a piss-poor chance at best."

Matt said, "Hold on. They're as surprised as we are, and every breath we give our mounts is all to the good. Let's not run for it until we know we have to. What's that fool Indian doing?"

American Tears had slowed to a mocking walk, midway up the slope. He shouted something up to Medicine Wolf and the others. Then he reined in, drove his lance into the sod, and dismounted to stand beside it, arms folded across his chest.

Windy snorted derisively. "Of all the four-flushing stunts. First he leaves a guest brave staked out to cover his retreat, then he lights out, leaving his other kids to face us alone, and now he's standing there pretending to be the champion of the Cheyenne Nation."

"Jesus, do you mean he's inviting a man-to-man duel?"

Windy spat and replied, "Shit, no. He's just showing off and everybody knows it except maybe him. Who in thunder's about to take him up on it?"

Matt swung around, stared up at the all-to-empty skyline behind them, and said, "Let's give it a try. Those others seem to be waiting for an answer, and we might buy some time."

Matt started to spur his mount forward, but Windy said, "Hold it. In the first place, you ain't supposed to advance mounted up, since he's on the ground, and in the second, you're acting foolish."

"Why? Don't you think they understand a fair fight, Windy?"

Windy said, "Oh, Medicine Wolf, up yonder, does. He's as close to honest as most men get. But American Tears ain't about to fight you fair, if you're dumb enough to take him up on his pose. Look at what he's doing now, brandishing his bowie knife like a regular little hero. That's to show how brave he is while still giving himself an out. He's counting on us acting sensible, since damn few white men are about to move into rifle range of fifty hostiles. But just in case one of us turns out to be crazy, he'll be able to drop back with honor, since he ain't packing a pistol."

Matt stared thoughtfully up at the challenger. American Tears' pony had moved off with the Indian's Remington repeater hanging from its saddle pad. American Tears was shuffling around his upright lance, waving the big, gleaming blade in his hand. Matt said, "Windy, loan me your bowie and hang on to my gunbelt for me, will you?"

"Son, you don't know what you're doing!"

But Matt insisted, and the exchange was made. Matt gripped the scout's bowie in his teeth as he dismounted. Then he took it in his fist and said, "Signal for me, Windy. I'm not too good at sign talk."

He started up the slope as, behind him, Windy wigwagged until Medicine Wolf, up on the ridge, replied in kind. Windy called out, "I'm not to follow you, Matt. They say it's you and him, fair and square, but they'll pepper you good if you cheat."

Matt paused and turned to call back, "Are there any rules I should know about?"

"No. You're allowed to do anything but draw a hidden weapon."

"What about that lance he's stuck in the ground?"

"It ain't hid, is it? He'll lance you sure as shit, boy. Get back here and behave yourself, damnit!"

Matt shrugged and started up the slope again, feeling very small and alone on the vast, open expanse of grassy hillside. American Tears had stopped his dance and was eyeing him warily, one hand gripping the knife and the other on the shaft of the upright lance. Matt had made it halfway when Windy called out again to him. Matt turned to see Gus Olsen and First Platoon lined up on the ridge to the north. Even as he watched, Taylor's platoon hove into view, further toward the mountains. So now the tables were turned, and fifty-odd Cheyenne faced over sixty mounted infantrymen. The next move was his.

Matt cupped a hand to his mouth and shouted, "At ease and maintain! Explain it to them, Windy!"

Then he turned around and kept going. He didn't like the idea much. Matt Kincaid did not consider himself a hero. He was a soldier with a job to do, and his job was to keep the peace in these parts. The gesture of American Tears offered the slim hope of an honorable settlement without needless bloodshed, if, of course, the Cheyenne chief was as honorable as Windy thought, and if the saber drill they'd taught him at the Point applied at all in a rough-and-tumble knife fight.

As he moved closer, American Tears yanked his lance from the ground. But he was edging back up the slope toward the other Indians now.

Medicine Wolf frowned down from his paint-daubed stallion and called out, "What are you waiting for, American Tears? The Blue Sleeve wants to fight you. Are you afraid of him?"

American Tears called back, "Heya, his friends are over there with guns, many guns, many. I don't think he means to fight fairly."

Medicine Wolf snorted in disgust. "I see the soldiers. Do you see me riding away? You made the offer, American Tears. You made the offer wearing the paint and feathers of Those Who Cut Fingers. Would you have those people over there laugh at us?"

A young man wearing green stripes with red dots moved up beside the chief and said, "Hear me, I will fight that American down there if American Tears is afraid."

But Medicine Wolf shook his head and said, "No, Arapaho brother. When we found you staked out, I released you from your vows and told you that you had proven you were a man. If your elders will not grant you a coup feather, come back to me and I will see that you are given one. You have already stood as a man in American Tears' place, this day. Now it is time for him to fight his own fight."

He turned from Many Arrows and called out, "What are you waiting for? The Americans are watching as honorable enemies. We are watching, too."

American Tears pleaded, "Hear me, my brothers, I need time to make my medicine. That American is acting crazy, and you know crazy people have medicine."

Not a single Cheyenne answered.

Matt Kincaid stopped a hundred yards downslope and stood quietly, legs braced, the borrowed blade gleaming in his hand as he smiled up at them quizzically. Medicine Wolf nodded in grudging respect and called out in English, "Our man is ready. If you carry a hidden pistol, we will interfere. If you fight fair, the outcome is in the hands of Matou, and the winner walks away with the other's hair. I have spoken."

Then, in Cheyenne, he added, "Fight him, American Tears. Show an old man you called weak how a great Crooked Lancer does it!"

American Tears screamed like a banshee and started down at Matt with the lance in one hand and the knife in the other. But as the big officer dropped into an instinctive knife-fighter's crouch, the Indian wavered, dropped his lance, and ran for his pony. Matt saw that he was after the saddle gun and started after him, forgetting the watching Cheyenne.

American Tears got to his pony and ducked behind it, drawing the Remington to fire over the pony's back at the charging white man. But the shot that echoed across the valley didn't come from American Tears' weapon. The renegade stepped away from his horse with a puzzled smile, and then his legs buckled and American Tears crumpled, dead, to the grass.

Medicine Wolf lowered the muzzle of his own rifle as Matt stood rooted in place, staring warily up at him. The Indian said, "When I call for a fair fight, I mean it to be a fair fight.

I hope you don't think we have many men like that one." Then he waved an arm to indicate Many Arrows. "Would you like to fight this Arapaho, or are you satisfied?"

Matt said, "I don't want to fight anyone I don't have to, Chief."

"Good. I think this boy is too small for you, too. Take your scalp and go. We will keep the peace until you get back to your own friends."

Matt said, "I don't want his scalp, sir."

"Oh? I agree he wasn't worthy, either. After you get back to your own side we can have a proper battle, with much honor to those who come out alive."

Matt pointed to the dead Indian and said, "That one was the only Cheyenne we really wanted, Chief. We know neither you nor any of these men with you took part in American Tears' raids."

That is true. But what about the young men who were with him? Have you killed them all already?"

"No. They're holed up in some rocks to the west. I'm willing to leave it at that, now that we've accounted for the real criminal. I don't think this would be a good day for anyone to die without a good reason, sir. What do you think?"

Medicine Wolf looked at him keenly. "You speak like a man who has seen his share of battle. How shall we call you?"

"I'm Matt Kincaid, Lieutenant, U.S. Mounted Infantry."

"That's a funny name, but no matter, you seem to have a good heart. But hear me, three other young men are being held by your captain. Are you still going to hang them?"

Matt met the Indian's unblinking gaze and answered, "I don't know. They'll have to stand trial. But with American Tears dead, I think the government will be reasonable."

"If it is, it will certainly be a change. But hear me. I am an old soldier, too. I will talk to my people. They may be willing to give the Great White Father another chance. If you offer a truce until we can all get back to find out, I will accept it."

Matt grinned and said, "Chief, you've just made a good deal for all of us, I think."

Later that evening, Captain Conway was alone in the officer's day room with Lieutenant Colonel Bradshaw as he read the IG report. He turned the last page and handed it to Bradshaw, saying, "This was very generous of you, sir."

Bradshaw puffed his cigar and said, "Nonsense, I just reported it as I saw it. I know we've had our differences, but fair is fair, and what the hell, what are a few missing tent pegs compared to keeping an Indian uprising down to a flash in the pan? Do you think the BIA is going to insist on punishing the Cheyenne kids?"

"Not if they know what's good for them," Conway said. "Now that the wire's back up I sent a full report, minimizing a few infractions of the rules and citing Medicine Wolf for aiding in the elimination of American Tears."

"Well, he has left for the reservation, but he did mutter some rather ominous things about the outcome of that trial those three young scamps are facing. I'd have thought you'd simply turn them loose."

Conway smiled. "There's a fine line where reasonableness starts to look like weakness, Colonel. Besides, once a few Indians stand trial and go home acquitted, it should be a simpler matter just to arrest them. We can't afford a war every time some buck steals a settler's horse. It's my hope we'll introduce them to law and order peacefully, once they see we mean to be fair as well as firm."

"I hope you're right. I'll confess I never expected them to be so reasonable in the end. How come you chased old Gray Elk back to the reservation, too? He was the first one to speak up in favor of another peace."

Conway explained, "He was sheltering here illegally, claiming he feared the other Cheyenne. We know he doesn't have to worry about them calling him a sissy now. Fortunately, none of his young men were killed, but we winged a couple and scared the stuffing out of as many more. I just want them the hell away from my own people until tempers cool."

"So, all's well that ends well, eh? I'd better start thinking of how I'm to get back to my own outfit."

Conway smiled and said, "I'm afraid you're stuck here for another night, sir. My wife baked an apple pie as soon as it was safe to light the stoves again. You're going to have to come to my quarters with me and help us eat it."

Outside, Matt Kincaid was acting as OD again, so Windy Mandalian met him near the gate and said, "I'm going over to Tipi Town. Them Arapaho just come over from the hills, and I noticed one of 'em's sort of pretty. Thanks to you, I lost my Cheyenne gal, but what the hell, variety is the spice of life."

He reached in his pocket and took out a shiny brass object as he added, "Oh, you might give this to them heavy-weapons jaspers afore they leave. It looks like that gear they losted from their Gatling gun."

Matt stared down at the gear and marveled, "You crazy son of a bitch! I might have known! What if we'd really needed that Gatling, Windy?"

"Shoot, nobody never needs to fire that loud and long, old son. Wars are bad enough without such infernal devices. They're likely to get rough as hell when ever'body has them fire-hose guns. Ain't it lucky they, ah, mislaid this doohickey? We'd have never settled things so peaceable, had that sassy Fitzgerald peppered the Cheyenne Nation like he'd planned."

"Get out of here, you loony bastard. If anyone asks, you're on an intelligence-gathering mission."

As Windy left, Matt chuckled and pocketed the arming gear. He was still grinning when he met Phoebe Mills on the veranda in front of the guest quarters. She said, "They told me you had night duty again, Matt."

His smile faded as he said, "Yes, we seem to be back to the same old grind, but it could have turned out worse. I, ah, guess you'll be leaving us in the morning, eh?"

She looked away and said, "I'm afraid so. I'm . . . I'm going to miss you, Matt."

"I'll miss you, too. But California and that young man you told me about are waiting for you, and Penderson seems happy with that new guide he hired in town this afternoon."

She said, "I know. I can't believe it all happened so suddenly. I mean, we just met and . . . Do you have a girl, Matt?"

He shrugged and said, "Not steady. Not many women think much of living in a soddy on a junior officer's pay."

"I don't think it would be too much to ask. Maybe you just need to ask the right girl, Matt."

It was his turn to look away as he said, "Maybe I will, someday. I keep putting it off until I get my captain's bars. That's likely to be quite a while, unless the War Department wins the Irish Derby or something."

"Matt, I've been thinking. I don't really have to be in California all that soon. I mean, I could always wait for another wagon party, one that wasn't so crowded. I mean, if I thought there was any reason for me to stay on for a while."

Shaking his head, he answered, "Phoebe, Penderson's already moving west late in the season. If you let them leave without you, you could be stuck here until next spring."

"Would that upset you terribly?"

He didn't answer. Her offer was impossible, of course, but Jesus, it was tempting. She stood there waiting in the moonlight. He knew he had to either kiss her or pour cold water on her, and both ideas were awful.

Then, mercifully, the lookout called, "Rider coming in! Sudden!"

Matt said, "Excuse me, Miss Phoebe, I have to see what's going on."

He legged it over to the gate as it opened and a riderless horse came through. He saw its rider, facedown in the dust outside the gate. Windy had turned back from his walk toward Tipi Town and was bending over the fallen man.

As Matt ran over to them, Windy looked up and said, "You'd best get the captain, old son. He's dead, whoever he was."

Windy drew the arrow from the dead man's back and held it up in the moonlight. "Blackfoot," he said. "Didn't know they were this fur south this summer."

Matt sighed and turned away. Meeting Captain Conway and Ben Cohen as they came out the gate, he said, "Looks like a civilian dispatch rider ran into at least one bad Blackfoot, sir. Shall I order boots and saddles?"

Conway nodded wearily. "Of course, Goddamnit. Here we go again."

SPECIAL PREVIEW

Here are the opening scenes
from

# EASY COMPANY AND THE MEDICINE GUN

the next novel in Jove's exciting
new High Plains adventure series
EASY COMPANY

Available now!

# one

The sun was sure crossing Nebraska faster than they were, thought Elmer "Trash" Jimson, a private recently assigned to the U.S. Army of the West. He turned to his companions and said as much.

"Apollo and his fiery chariot," brayed Private Edward Mulberry III, also a recent addition to that same army.

Jimson waited to hear what Apollo was up to. "So? What does *that* mean?"

Mulberry shrugged, mopping his brow, too whipped to continue. He hadn't expected summer in Nebraska to be so hot. Where were those damned snow-capped mountains he'd heard about?

Roscoe, Ogllala, Brule, Big Spring, one prairie town after another crept by. Slowly.

"Excuse me, but where are you boys headed?" A chubby man with a fringe of whiskers and a bowler hat had leaned across the aisle to address their little group.

James Evinrude, the remaining member of the group, studied the orders. But it was Trash who spoke up:

"Somewhere smack-dab in the middle of the Territory of Wy-*ohm*ing," he declared.

"I think that's about it," confirmed Evinrude. "An Easy Company at a place called Outpost Number Nine."

"What regiment's that?" asked the chubby man. "Sounds like Foreign Legion." He giggled.

Evinrude frowned, studied once more the crumpled and stained paper containing the orders, then told him.

"Aha," said the chubby man. He'd never heard of the regiment, but supposed it was in fact there. "A fine outfit. Er, are you the only ones? An awful lot of Indians out here."

"Naw," said Trash, "but we're the best, and the only ones headed for Easy. There're about forty more towards the back."

The chubby man leaned back in his seat, reassured for the moment.

"Jesus," cried Trash, bringing Chubby bolt upright again, "how much longer we got?"

"No hurry," said Evinrude. "Easy ain't going nowhere, and you're still young."

"I won't be by the time we get there," said Trash. "But hell, why should yóu care? You're *already* old."

True. Hardly ancient but an unlikely recruit, Evinrude had seen action in the Civil War, gone home to Maine in one piece (surely a good omen), and then watched helplessly as, over the next ten-odd years, his entire family fell victim to age, disease, and violence. His son had been the last, skull split by a drunken young logger. Evinrude had killed the logger with his bare hands.

No one wished to prosecute, seeing all the grief he'd already come by, but they had to do something, so they simply told him to leave that part of the country.

He'd heard the army needed men out West, so he'd reenlisted. And since he'd never been more than a private, he didn't mind being that again. He didn't think anyone was after him—that had been an unspoken part of the deal—but now, after five days clackety-clacking two-thirds of the way across the entire continent, he almost wished somebody was. Maybe he should have stuck around, even if it meant hanging. What the hell did he have to live for?

"That town we just passed, Ogllala . . ." Trash's nasal twang pierced Evinrude's thoughts. "Don't that sound familiar?" Who was he talking to? Evinrude wondered.

"That's an Indian tribe," said Mulberry. "A noble tribe. And they spelled it wrong. It should be O-G-L-A-L-A. That's Crazy Horse's tribe, I—"

"Crazy Horse!" squawked Trash, turning a few heads in the coach. "That bloodthirsty maniac?"

"A victim as much as anything," disagreed Mulberry.
"Tell that to them what ain't got their scalps no more."
"I've heard Crazy Horse himself rarely scalps."
"Who you been talking to, his *Mother*?"
Evinrude stared at Mulberry earnestly. "I have yet to understand what a peace-loving man such as you—"
"*Indian*-loving," Trash put in, grinning.
"—what you are planning to do out here," persisted Evinrude. "The main pastime hereabouts seems to be killing Indians."
"There has to be a better way. These redmen are not intrinsically bad."
"Christ," said Jimson, "I'm riding with an old man and a saint. Hope there's no trouble ahead."
Mulberry eyed him, smiled, sighed, and then took out his notebook.
"You gonna *write* them to death?" sneered Trash. "Always writin'."
"Recording impressions."
"Yeah? Record *this* impression." He grabbed his own crotch. "Just see you spell my name right."
"Trash is trash," muttered Mulberry.
"No it ain't. You know how I got—"
"You told us," said Evinrude.
"'Cause there ain't *nobody* I can't trash."
"He's trying to say *thrash*," Mulberry informed anyone who might be listening.
"The hell I am," sputtered Jimson. "*Trash*, like in dee-stroy—'specially some of them ee-feminate cavalry. You seen any yella-stripers around?"
"Just those Blue Legs in the back."
"I said *cav*, not infantry. They got infantry up front, too, in the baggage car. Saw 'em loadin' on. Got a big ol' gun."
Mulberry looked up. "Really? Artillery?"
"Infantry, I said. Damn, don't you never listen? Heavy weapons prob'ly, got a whole baggage—Hey! Maybe *they* got something t' drink, all by their lonely. I'm 'bout to dry up and blow away."
"You know they don't want us drinking right out in public."
"It's the baggage car. That ain't public."
At the next stop the three recruits hopped off the train,

toting their duffels, and ran up to the baggage car. Along the way Jimson started squawking, "Hey, that sign said Julesburg, *Colorado*. I thought we was in Nebraska."

"We was—er, *were*," said Mulberry. "The train takes this little loop into Colorado. Next stop we're back in Nebraska."

They pounded on the baggage car door. "Hey, open up, we're army."

The door slid open to reveal a second lieutenant.

"Whoops," said Jimson. "Guess I didn't see you . . . sir."

The train started to move.

"Oh, for God's sake," said the lieutenant, in a high voice.

Jimson grinned, then he and the others started to trot alongside the moving train.

"Get them in here," said the lieutenant to a couple of burly teamsters, one black and one white, who yanked the recruits airborne as easily as if they were feathers, and dumped them in the car.

Jimson, unruffled, leaped to his feet, which he cautiously spread to combat the sway, yelled, "Private Jimson reporting, *sir*," and then threw up a snappy salute.

The lieutenant, eyes dulling, returned the salute desultorily and then threw up his hands as he saw Evinrude and Mulberry preparing to match Jimson. "Christ!" he swore. A trio of parade-ground nitwits. "I'm Lieutenant Clark," he went on, "and I don't know what you think you're doing up here, but—"

Clark told them the proper way to and from the rear of the train while Jimson looked around for booze. He thought he spied a bottle, half hidden, but how could he explain about his sudden thirst? Easy. Mulberry would do it.

"Jimson came because he thought there might be something to drink up here, sir—"

The lieutenant's eyes got even duller. "There is. What'd he do, smell it. Too damn much, in fact, but I don't know anything about it. It's unmilitary, General Grant notwithstanding."

"But I—" continued Mulberry, "Private Mulberry, sir—I came up to look at that gun you're hauling. A Gatling, sir, unless I'm mistaken."

The lieutenant brightened. "Indeed it is, and you men keep that booze hidden for a while." He strolled toward the rear of the car, thin shoulders squared, head erect on a slender neck, pride of ownership manifest. Gunner Foreman and Gunner's

Mate Willoughby winked at each other. Mulberry followed the lieutenant, trailed by Jimson and Evinrude.

"This is the newest model," Clark said. "The 1877 Gatling. It's similar to the '74, but each year has brought a number of improvements. This is the standard musket-length model, ten thirty-two inch barrels, forty-nine inches overall."

"What kind of ammo does it take?" asked Evinrude, eyeing the piece.

"Standard," answered Mulberry.

"Yes, standard," repeated Lieutenant Clark, glaring at Mulberry, "the .45-70 issue cartridge."

"Fires pretty fast, huh?" offered Jimson.

"In the latest tests at Annapolis," Clark said, "the guns were fitted with ammo drums containing four hundred cartridges. In slightly more than ten minutes, ten of those drums were emptied. That's about four hundred a minute. Theoretically, its rate of fire is a good deal faster than that, but—" a smile—"it's physically impossible to push it to its limits. Cranking it, changing magazines, all that sort of thing, wastes time."

"Sure wish we had those things in the War," said Evinrude wistfully.

"Actually, you did—er, *we* did. Toward the end, there were some. Butler—*Beast* Butler—he had some. And Lincoln was always ready for a new invention, a new weapon. But they'd already tried some revolving guns, revolving-chamber rifles, and they'd been busts, and that kind of soured everybody. Also, they used an *awful* lot of ammo. This Gatling's much improved. The early models couldn't change elevation, couldn't traverse, but this one can. And the early ones were also apt to be used like artillery. Quite ineffective. Then there were, and *are*, the logistics. You have to plan a whole new way of fighting. You don't just pick it up and run to the next place; it weighs too much. The gun alone weighs two hundred pounds. Its carriage weighs 326, and the limber—" he pointed to the other two-wheeler—"that carries the ammo caisson weighs 287, *without* the ammo."

"What do you haul it with, elephants?" Jimson seemed to be trying for Clark's shitlist.

"Some privates like yourself, most often," said the lieutenant drily. "We chain them to the gun and whip them along the trail."

"Are there many of these guns out here?" asked Evinrude.

"Quite a few, actually. The army bought eight of the '74 model, forty-four of the '75 model, eighteen '76ers, and eleven of this model. A large number, I should imagine, are out West here. I know they had some up around Little Big Horn. General Terry had three, General Gibbon two. General Custer had a chance to take the three from the Twentieth Infantry—Terry's outfit—but he left them behind. He was probably right. They were these big kind, hard to haul over difficult ground, and they probably couldn't have kept up with the cav. Later, when Terry tried to haul them over some rough ground, they went so slowly they finally got lost. But Terry's still got them. And General Howard's got them—he's up there somewhere, chasing the Nez Perce I think. *This* one, this one's headed for Fort Keogh and General Miles."

Mulberry was scratching his head. "Begging your pardon, sir, but one might conjecture that they'd be better off with camel guns."

Clark gave Mulberry a long stare. Finally he said, "*Or* a bulldog."

Mulberry frowned. Score one for Clark.

"What in the world's a camel gun?" asked Jimson.

"It's a short Gatling," said Mulberry, with Clark's nodded permission. "An eighteen-inch barrel, ten of them, weighs a lot less, can be fitted on a lightweight cavalry cart, or a tripod. But never a camel, as far as I know. There was a picture of one mounted on a camel, but that was just for advertising. But the bulldog?" He looked to the lieutenant.

"Lighter yet," said Clark. "Just five barrels. Weighed about ninety pounds. The camel gun weighs in at one hundred thirty-five. This gun here is the full-size model. But it'll go on a tripod, too."

"Oh, yeah?" sneered Jimson. "With who liftin' . . . sir?"

The lieutenant smiled unpleasantly. "I don't think you're long for this army, trooper."

*"Trooper?"* yelped Jimson. Didn't this looey know *cav* were called troopers? "Well, sir, now that I know what yer luggin' around, I kin see why your squad looks like a bunch of wrasslers."

"Don't mind him, sir," said Evinrude. "He's just stupid."

"And now," said Lieutenant Clark, "I think I'll go join a

few of my fellow officers. I don't need to tell you not to overdo the drinking."

"You can depend on us, sir," said Corporal Foreman, the gunner.

Clark's eyes narrowed. But without any further word, he left.

Jimson whistled. "You been with him long?"

"Hardly," grinned Foreman. "We're still alive, ain't we? Naw, he's never seen any combat. What he knows he's gotten from books." Hearing that, Jimson eyed Mulberry. The gunner went on, "He's really just along to learn how to fight and to sign papers, and get us where we're going."

"What are you writin' *now*?" cried Jimson.

"Notes on the gun," explained Mulberry.

"*Always* writin'. Readin' and writin'," complained Trash. "How come you're so interested in this gun, you such a peace-lovin' person?"

"I'm fascinated by guns, that's all. I went to school at a military academy. Not by choice, I might add."

"Can't wait to get them hostiles lined up in your sights, right?"

Mulberry didn't bother answering.

And the group fell to drinking from bottles plucked out of clever hiding places.

Gunner Foreman and Gunner's Mate Willoughby were both squat, brawny young men. They weren't old, but the way they patiently tolerated Jimson made them seem older. Perhaps the fact that either could have broken Jimson in two accounted for it. A sure confidence.

They tried not to drink much, just enough to loosen them up. The two teamsters—white, raw-boned Cummings and black, musclebound Jefferson—drank more. Mulberry and Evinrude hardly drank at all. Jimson drank as much as all the rest combined.

The gun crew talked about the fighting they'd seen, filling the recruits in on the finer points of Indian warfare. Of course, they hadn't seen that much action themselves, but they waxed eloquent nonetheless.

"This'll be Cheyenne country we'll soon be coming into," said Willoughby. He was sandy-haired, with a slow grin. "Hang onto your scalps."

Jimson grinned, stared at Jefferson, and said, "Injuns would have a hard time gettin' hold of *your* scalp."

Jefferson ran a hand over his stubbly, close-cropped scalp. "Sure as hell would. That's if he even got close enough."

"Fast on your feet, huh? Wonder if there's anything special 'bout a nigger scalp—"

Jefferson's ebony features clouded. He began to rise.

"To an Injun, I mean," Jimson added hastily.

"What's yo' name, *boy*?" drawled Jefferson, ominously.

"Jimson. I already *told* the looey."

"*Trash* Jimson," elaborated Evinrude helpfully, earning himself a glare from Trash.

"Trash?" said Jefferson. "*Trash.*"

"Yeah, 'cause of how I got the rep of trashin' anybody that stands in my way."

Not true, thought Mulberry, who was tired of hearing that explanation. Trash, in a drunken moment, had told him the truth. His family, poor to start with, had headed South after the War and, with apparently hereditary stupidity, had ended up even poorer. Had ended up white trash. And the name Trash had stuck. But Mulberry didn't offer this revelation to the immediate gathering, despite his irritation. Trash had threatened his life if he ever let it out, and Mulberry was not a very physical gent.

Mulberry distracted himself by staring down the car at the Gatling, the magnificent gun. He muttered, "Medicine gun."

The talk had abated at just that moment, and all heard him. "What's that?" asked Foreman. "Medicine gun? What's a medicine gun?"

"The Gatling. That's what the Indians call it."

"How do *you* know?"

"'Cause he read it," said Jimson. "That's how he knows everything. You oughta hear him talk about 'loose women,' 'soiled ladies.'"

"Why 'medicine'?" pursued Foreman.

"Because medicine doesn't mean the same thing to an Indian as it does to us. Medicine, to an Indian, is somewhere between magic and luck—"

"So?" interjected Jimson, laughing. "That's what it means to white men, too, don't it?"

"Anyone with a killing machine like this," Mulberry went on, "an Indian has to think he's got powerful medicine. They'd probably make it sacred if it weren't busy killing them. As a matter of fact, I'm surprised they don't call it an owl gun, or something like that. Owl, to them, means death and destruction."

"Jeez," said Jimson, "does General Sheridan know about you? Indians wouldn't have a chance with you giving him advice."

"Medicine gun, huh?" murmured Foreman. "Guess they'd probably like to get hold of one."

"Probably," agreed Mulberry. "And as for *you*," he said, looking up at Jefferson and deciding to impress them all, "there's a story about a hostile who was going to scalp a colored man, and the colored man's short, kinky hair puzzled him so much he decided the colored man must have some special medicine, so he hauled him off and nursed him back to health."

"You hear *that*, boy?" Jefferson roared at Jimson. He bent over, showing Trash his head. "This here burr-head is powerful medicine." And he roared with laughter.

Jimson didn't care for coloreds. "Let's get this here door open," he said. "It's *hot* in here. And I want to see some of this Cheyenne country."

They exchanged looks. Why not? The door was slid open.

Flat, rolling prairie, not an Indian in sight.

The men spent a few minutes looking out at nothing, swaying as the train rocked. Finally Jimson said, "Well, bust my britches if this ain't the boringest trip I ever took. Not even one of Mulberry's noble Cheyenne."

They all eyed Mulberry, who replied defensively, "I never said the Cheyenne were noble."

"Who *did* you say, then?"

Mulberry was trying to think of an inoffensive Eastern tribe, and Foreman was muttering, "Troublemaker, ain't he?" when Jimson went galloping off in still another direction. "Hey! Gunner!"

Foreman groaned. "*Corporal* to you, *private*."

"Yeah, you. Show us how the gun works. Fire off some rounds."

"In here?"

"Out the door, dummy."

"In about two seconds, *you're* going out that door."

"Gee, I'm sorry," oozed Trash. "So come on, Corporal, do it."

Foreman was about to refuse adamantly when he saw Mulberry come alive. And the corporal might have had a bit too much to drink. "The lieutenant—"

"He's getting sloshed with them officers, you know that."

"Clark? *Sloshed?* Right, we'll give it a try." He grinned foolishly. "Prob'ly scare the bejesus outta them soldiers in back."

"Good. They're likely as bored as us. Come on."

The seven of them wrestled the Gatling forward and around until it was pointing out over the passing plains.

Willoughby opened a box and loaded several twenty-round magazines and shoved one into the gun's hopper. It was top-loading, the rounds fed by gravity.

"Take a look out the door, Will," Foreman said.

Willoughby looked out and then yelled, "Let 'er rip!" Foreman took a deep breath and started cranking.

An earsplitting roar filled the car as twenty .45-caliber slugs shot off across the prairie.

Then there was silence, save for some muffled noise from farther back along the train, and a few peremptory squawks, also from farther back.

Jimson's mouth was open, Mulberry was writing, Evinrude croaked, "Jesus wept," and the gun crew were all grinning.

Jimson grabbed another magazine and replaced the empty. "Let me try it," he said, "'fore the lieutenant gets here screamin'."

"Naw."

"Come on. What could happen?"

"What could happen?" asked Mulberry, with a faraway look. "I remember reading about the early models. After firing a while, they got real hot and expanded and they were impossible to crank. But they had a screw that adjusted the space between the barrels and the breech. The only thing was, to turn this screw you had to stand out in front of the gun." He grinned. "They had a few casualties before they put a crank-lock on it."

Jimson stared at Mulberry, then demanded of the gun crew, "You got a lock on this?"

"Yeah, we have one," Foreman said, though he wished they didn't. "But you ain't plannin' to stand in front of it, are you?" And he wondered what was keeping Lieutenant Clark.

"Hell, no," said Jimson, taking that as an invitation, and Foreman had to scramble to get out of his way. Foreman sort of staggered to the side. What the hell, he thought boozily, my ass already is in a sling.

"Wait'll I take a look—" began Willoughby, but before he could do it, Jimson started cranking and the deafening roar started up again.

Just then, some cattle came into sight. They'd been grazing by the track and were now stumbling away as the train passed. They began to stumble even more, going to their knees. Blood spurted from the neck wound of one. Then, suddenly, there was a mounted cowboy, a puzzled look on his face. And he went down. And the gun went silent, even though Jimson kept cranking away.

"You killed him!" screamed Willoughby.

"Killed who?"

"That cowboy. Didn't you see him? And all those *cows* you shot?"

"Cows? Cowboy? No I didn't see. Who the hell can see when this thing's going off? An' what the hell was he doing out there anyway? This is *Cheyenne* country. You said so yourself."

"Maybe I was wrong."

They looked back. Cattle were running, but there was no sign of cowboy or horse, except, way off in the distance, someone was riding hell-bent after the train.

"Lemme have them magazines!" Trash shouted. "Either those are Cheyenne out there, or we're in big trouble."

They all caught on fast, and soon the Gatling was spraying more death out onto the plains, assuming there was anything out there to die.

The door at the rear end of the car slammed open and Lieutenant Clark entered with gun drawn and, as predicted, screaming. "What the hell's going on?!"

"Cheyenne," said Jimson.

"Road agents," said Mulberry.

"Cheyenne?" repeated Clark, flabbergasted. "Road agents?"

"Train robbers. Sorry. Got confused."

"Yeah," said Jimson. "First we thought they was Cheyenne, since this is Cheyenne country, an' they kinda rose up outta the grass after the engine passed. But then we saw they was owlhoots. Probably wanted the Gatling. We got the gun going and left them in the grass."

Clark was still pop-eyed. But now his eyes began to narrow.

"Now just a minute. What are *you* doing behind that gun?"
"I was closest, they was right there, I started cranking."
Clark was staring down the baggage car at where the Gatling used to be. "Why was the—"
"One of the robbers is trying to catch us, sir—" interrupted Mulberry, almost apologetically. "I think."
The lieutenant frowned, jumped to the open side door, and looked back.
There in the distance, but closing fast, were a horse and rider. The man was firing his gun into the air.
Clark reacted quickly. He drew his gun and threw a shot toward the rider. Then he leaped to the door at the rear of the car, exclaiming, "No telling how many there are!" He opened the door and disappeared. They heard him shouting, "Train robbers, coming up in back," as he moved through the train.
The gun crew and recruits positioned themselves carefully so they could all see out the side door.
There was about a twenty-second delay. The rider got closer, still waving his gun, which, by then, had to be empty. Then there was a thunderous fusillade from the rear of the train, and the rider went down in a tangle of man and horse. Both lay still, accompanied by cheers, until they were lost in the distance.
Everyone in the baggage car had paled, even Jefferson. They took a long while to collect their thoughts, most of which probably concerned Jimson.
Mulberry murmured to Foreman, "Troublemaker, did you say?"
And Jimson said, "I think this calls for a drink."
Since they couldn't kill Jimson, they drank with him.
By the time the lieutenant returned, they were nearly unconscious. Clark had been thinking the matter over—the time sequence, getting the Gatling in position . . . What was it doing pointing out the door in the first place? Yes, he had some hard questions to ask. But he decided he'd better wait until they were conscious and sober. Judging from the bottles strewn about, he guessed that might take a while.

Racing Elk moved his band steadily northward. They'd stayed east of Denver and Greeley and were now east of the Denver Pacific Railroad on the trail north to Cheyenne.
Racing Elk had spent the previous year carousing, killing

and pillaging on the southern plains. Good hunting and good experience.

His band, the Oglala Sioux part of it, had been the *akicita* of their tribe early the previous summer. The *akicita* societies performed, primarily, as police, or soldiers, within the tribe. They kept order. They were a kind of embryonic Civil Government, or State. Inevitably such authority carried with it the

## THE WEST WAS NEVER WILDER...

**Especially for the men of Easy Company. Their job was to police the High Plains tribes, keep the peace...and stay alive. No one ever said it would be easy.**

**Now a band of blood-lusting Cheyenne "suicide boys" are using Outpost Nine for target practice. A lost wagon train is in trouble, and scouts are picked off for scalps. When the death toll rises, it's up to Lt. Matt Kincaid to stop the bloodshed–without igniting a full-scale uprising.**

**With a nit-picking Army Inspector cramping the Company's style, and raw, unruly recruits to forge into fighting machines, Kincaid tries to end the killing, and finds himself knife-to-knife with the Cheyenne leader, a firebrand named "American Tears"...**

## EASY COMPANY

**ROUGH-RIDING ADVENTURE ON THE HIGH PLAINS!**

**DON'T MISS OTHERS IN THE SERIES!**

0 71152 00195 05761

ISBN 0-515-05761-4

PRINTED IN U.S.A.